Gavilan Mesa

EA Mayes

Book Cover by Book Designers.

ONE

Minoa paused with boot tips in mid-air to peer across the Rio Grande valley to the Manzano Mountains, slumbering on the eastern horizon. 'Grande' was a joke. Barely a trickle in October in a good year, and this year fell in the middle of a worst-in-a-millennium drought. Dried tumbleweeds cuddled the base of the rocky ridge top she stood on. A hollyhock sky glowed above. She teetered there, muscles buzzing from hours of walking, dried sweat parching her face, inhaling air so arid it abraded her lungs. She had to admit it felt good to get back in shape, even if her mind spent half the day screaming for a quiet carrel in a research library.

She cocked back her mashed goat roper hat and panned a full circle. Rangeland every which way. To the southwest a couple tiny figures moved. Weird. She never saw another soul when she was out walking Gavilan Mesa. Maybe surveyors? No cattle out here to steal and no water or oil to drill for.

The sun looked bloated to bursting and the soles of her feet felt like old leather. Could she finally get out of here? She took a vote. A majority of one voted yes. So she started striding back toward the gate, boot heels scalloping the dirt between silvery bunch grass and prickly pear cactus, scanning the ground as she walked, ever alert for rattlers. That's why she noticed those mounds, dirt humps, long and low, cheatgrass on top. Not much to see but they didn't look natural. She paused sensing a pulse of excitement, phone halfway out of her pocket. After days walking Gavilan she'd found nothing to report on the archaeological survey. A find, even a small one, would make her feel less useless. But had Ron insinuated that she wasn't supposed to find anything?

A check of GIS for aerial identified sites at these coordinates turned up zip. Luckily there was a touch of coverage out here with nothing between her and the cell company's twirling orbiting satellites but glare and a hue of Albuquerque smog. She squinted at a western horizon so far away it blended into sky, considering. Was she going to do her job, temp status be damned, or try to read between the lines creasing Ron's weathered face? With a sigh she pulled stakes and twine out of her backpack and marked a perimeter. Then she snapped photos from different angles.

The mounds didn't align in a rectangular shape. Could she be wasting time photographing somebody's illegal dumping site? Maybe they were refuse heaps left by Spanish colonial sheep herders at a summer grazing camp? Or hasty frontier burials?

Small chance these dirt humps sticking out of a tract of land only cattle hooves had touched for hundreds of years could have archaeological importance. Still, at least she'd have something to report in her Friday wrap-up. Pocketing her phone, she kept walking.

The long-suffering truck sat just outside a stock gate, crusted with dirt. She tossed her backpack onto the bench seat, hoisted herself in, cranked the gear shifter and started down the rutted track. Down, down along the border of a fenced parcel of grazing land, then right across rabbit weed plains toward a flat-backed butte curving above the horizon. The track flattened into a graded road and the interstate appeared in the distance, scratched into the mesa side, a couple of toy semi-trucks inching across.

Nearing the frontage road she spotted red lights pulsing between machines in a cluster of parked road construction equipment. She slowed as she drove closer, fixing her eyes on the shapes. The humps and flashes resolved into graders, compactors, bulldozers and dump trucks with a gaggle of patrol cars behind, lights on top gyrating. What was Albuquerque police doing out here on the far West Mesa at the Paseo de Pradera construction site? She pulled up even with the earth movers and flagged an officer standing near a patrol car parked sideways to block the road.

"Officer, what's going on here?"

"Police operation. Stand back."

"Police? Could you tell me when I can get through?"

"If I was you I'd head back the way you come. Civil disturbance here and this road could be closed for a while."

"But there is no other way out and ..."

He'd already walked away. She pulled off the dirt road onto scruffy desert, parked the truck, pocketed her phone and stepped out. Officers milled between the frontage road and the machines. Off to the side stood a group of construction workers in baseball caps, sipping coffee out of thermoses.

The cops paid no attention as she circled around the orange and green equipment, massive road graders, bulldozers, excavators, drum rollers and a paver parked on a dirt lot scraped out of rangeland stretching from one horizon to another. Reaching the far side she spied figures amidst the machinery. She edged closer, then stopped and stared. A gray-haired woman stood leaning into a bulldozer. What was she doing out here? Moving down the row she spotted a tall guy with a blond ponytail beside a monstrous backhoe. Now she noticed a bike chain locked to his ankle. The other end hooked to an O ring below the cabin. Through gaps between the parked machines she glimpsed officers on the other side grouping into a formation, some holding riot shields. Continuing down the line she came to a couple more people chained to machinery. On the back side of the lot, beside the shovel of a gigantic bulldozer, she spied Carter, ski goggles on her forehead below a pileup of brown curls. A dented football helmet hung from one hand. Minoa hurried over.

"Pssst! Carter, what's going on?"

Carter's head swiveled around. Her leg stayed chained to a latch.

"Hey, Minoa. Civil disobedience action. Our protests of Gavilan and the Paseo de Pradera highway are going nowhere. Too much money changing hands for the politicians to care that nobody wants this development. We have to get aggressive."

"Aren't you still on supervised release for that protest at the city council meeting? If you're arrested again, you won't get bail."

"The DA dropped the charges. We were exercising our first amendment rights and it was a public meeting anyway."

"They'll figure out how to cut those chains pretty quick and haul you off to jail."

"Nope. You can't cut these chains with a bolt cutter. They'll have to get a hydraulic cutter or a blowtorch."

"Carter, it's not a good idea to make APD mad. They're known for excessive force."

"True. But if they use those batons, the mainstream press might prick their ears."

"You'll get great press coverage if somebody is shot dead."

Carter flashed her a sarcastic frown as sounds of raised voices filled the alleyways between parked machines. She adjusted the goggles over her eyes and pulled on the football helmet, white with a red horse insignia.

"Quick, take my phone and film what the cops do. Maybe they won't arrest you."

"Arrest me? What are you talking about? I can't get arrested. I need this job."

"Min, what's more important? Your underpaid contractor gig or the viability of a regional ecosystem?"

Minoa grumbled as she slipped Carter's phone into a pocket and ran to the back of the bulldozer. While Carter adjusted the helmet's chin strap an officer appeared in the gap between the bulldozer and a road grader the size of a mobile home. He strode over and pointed his baton at Carter's face. His cranberry cheeks moved as if he were pushing a gumball around the inside of his mouth.

"You're trespassing. You're ordered to vacate immediately."

"Water for the people!" Carter called out. "Not for the bankers!"

Others joined in, maybe seven or eight voices, repeating, "Water for the people!"

Carted yelled, "This is a citizen protest against misuse of our taxes."

"Hands behind your back. Now!"

The cop lifted the baton as if preparing to swing it down.

"*Fuera* British Bank of Commerce and Credit!" A chorus of voices screamed over and over, "*Fuera* BBCC!"

Minoa took steps toward him lifting her hands in a 'don't shoot' posture.

"You... you can't do that."

The corners of his lips dug into his cheeks as he sliced the baton through the air to slam onto the helmet with a crack. Carter doubled forward.

"Stop that!"

Minoa waved her arms back and forth. He was raising his arm for another blow as Carter straightened.

She locked eyes with him yelling, "*Fuera* foreign banks."

He whipped the baton back and spun it down at the same time as Minoa leaped forward bringing her arms up to meet his forearm. The baton flew through the air to clatter down a side panel of the grader's cabin. Minoa jumped back wrapping a hand around each wrist, grimacing, suppressing a moan. The cop's face went haywire, his cheeks pumping in and out like balloons that wouldn't fill.

"Don't move!" he screamed. "You're both under arrest."

Carter reached a hand to Minoa's shoulder and whispered. "Run. I'll distract him."

Minoa calculated for a second, then spun around and sprinted into the desert. When she paused to look back, panting hard, she saw Carter crawling up the side of the dozer with the cop pulling on her leg from below. She focussed her phone camera on one protester after another. An officer had backed the fellow with a blond ponytail against a road grader and was laying into him with the baton, short staccato chops that made the guy jerk like a marionette. The gray-haired woman yelled at a cop pinning her against a six-foot tire. Farther down the line a young woman shrieked as an officer wrenched her arms around to cuff her behind her back. Minoa panned back and forth to capture the scene, then texted the video to Ireni. She had started a message explaining where to send it when she saw two officers walking her way. Reaching her they took a straddle stance with arms crossed over their chests. One reared back his head and peered at her through eye slits, the other rested a hand on the weapon in his belt.

"You're obstructing justice, lady," said the first.

"Interfering with a police operation," said the other.

"I work here. I work for the New Mexico State Office of Archaeological Studies. We're surveying this land."

The two officers exchanged glances.

"Government employee?" said the first guy. "You got an ID?"

Minoa fished her badge out from under her shirt.

"Let her go," said the other.

"You can't film a police operation without a press pass," said the first. He snatched the phone out of her hand. "Consider yourself lucky if we let you go without a charge."

"I already sent that video to the news media and the governor. So you can give me back my phone."

"Judge will decide that. You move on now."

The two of them smirked and walked away. She stifled the urge to yell something pointless like 'that's my property.' Okay, it was a refurbished model but it had cost her a half-day's worth of contractor monotony and it still functioned if she recharged the battery a lot. She turned her back, pulled Carter's phone out of her pocket and started another text to Ireni: Send that video right away to the Albuquerque Journal, KUNM, KOB, the New Mexican, the governor and anybody else you can think of. Tell them APD is attacking a peaceful protest at the construction site of the Paseo de Pradera. Contact me on Carter's phone. I'll explain later. Ireni responded with a thumbs up.

Circling through saltbush she made her way back to the truck. Cops were pacing in front of the machinery. No protesters visible. If Carter was right about the bolt cutter, and if some bored journalist got wind of this and decided it was worth a drive outside town on the chance some APD brute would draw blood on camera or, god forbid, shoot somebody, maybe Carter's latest environmental protest would be worth another arrest. A couple police vans were speeding up the road from the highway trailing dust bubbles. She slid onto the truck's worn seat. Glancing at the rearview she saw an officer looking her way, raising an arm, spreading lips wide to yell. She took off bushwhacking into the desert, slaloming around cactus, cutting a wide semicircle. Below the cluster of patrol cars she rocked back onto the gravel road and hightailed it out of there.

TWO

She made the trip north to Santa Fe sipping a gigantic ice tea from a taco drive-through in Old Town Albuquerque, scrolling posts on her phone when she could spare a glance to see if any journalists were covering the protest. Not a word. Another of Carter's pointless environmental actions. Doomed idealism, she told herself, noticing her brittle defensiveness. She heard Carter's voice arguing back: *Commit to something, Min, or get bitter while you get old*. She squeezed the bridge of her nose till it hurt and fixed her gaze on the highway..

South of Santa Fe at Caja del Rio Road she took the exit and soon arrived at the state archaeology office. The yellowish stucco building baked in the bread warmer temperature of an Indian summer going strong. Through a window she glimpsed Ron, his eyes hidden inside the furrows of a sun-fried complexion. Splashing ice tea onto the linoleum floor, she headed down the hallway to his office, knocked on the partly open door with an elbow and stepped inside.

"Hey there. Got that survey finished?"

He spoke without raising his eyes from a computer screen.

"Hi Ron. Almost. There's a protest against the Paseo de Pradera highway at the site where they park the road construction equipment. People chained themselves to earth movers and APD is angry."

He looked up, cranking his eyebrows into deep brow furrows.

"Ow. Not a good look."

"They shut the entry road down. I had to go cross-country to get out."

"Ow again. Let's hope they don't shut it for long. The sooner we finish there the better."

He poised the fingertips of his two hands together, peering over the top in an unfocused gaze out the window.

"And the cops stole my phone."

He turned back to look at her, letting his hands drift apart.

"Not one of ours, was it?"

She shook her head.

"Can't help you with that then. Try APD's citizen complaint line."

"What do I call with?"

"Haha. Good point. Probably best not to call police from an office phone. Just in case."

"Got it."

An awkward silence carpeted the room as he squinted at something on his computer screen, clacking keys. She glanced out the window at gamma grass scrub stretching far out to swan dive into the Rio Grande valley. When he leaned back in his office chair, the fingertips rejoined and began a rippling sequence, touching thumb to thumb, index to index, middle, ring, pinky, over and over. She stared, trying to figure out what he was thinking, wondering if she should ask about upcoming projects. After a moment he sat up straight and posed elbows on the desktop.

"Okay, I admit Gavilan is politically problematic. But it's not our problem."

"Our problem ...?"

"Look, between you and me I may even agree with the protesters. Clearly there's no water out there and twenty thousand suburban lawns will need water. There's nothing up for grabs in the Rio Grande so they'll have to steal it from the small farmers in the South Valley. Excuse me, I meant to say reallocate. But our job, our only job, is to produce an archaeological field survey for the environmental impact statement the developer can then submit to get their master plan approved, complying with the letter, if not the intent, of the law. It's a foregone conclusion what the Albuquerque City Council will decide. The damn development is going to get approved no matter what we do, so we may as well make some spare change to put into the projects with archaeological significance. It's a moral trade-off like everything in the real world. Just finish this unpleasant little chore and then, well, we may have some more interesting projects coming up."

"More projects? That's great. Oh, I almost forgot. I spotted some dirt mounds."

His palms tumbled to the desk.

"What? Probably just some pre-war sheep herder's hut. Didn't show on GIS, did it?"

"No. Although the mounds didn't define a rectangular shape. More like a couple of 'Z's."

"'Z', huh? Maybe Zorro knew the Duke of Alburquerque." He snorted a guffaw. "Any rubble around? Other signs?"

"I just notated the coordinates and staked it before I left."

A deep breath as his expression relaxed.

"Okay, sounds like a minor obstacle. I'll send the GPR tech out, do a subterranean radar assessment just to cover our butts. Should only delay us a day or so."

The desk phone rang out. After punching a button he picked up the receiver.

"Mr. Montoya, yes sir."

Ron threaded a binder clip onto a pen and twirled it around.

"I've got the tech right here in the office with me. She assured me she'll be done in a couple of days."

He squinted a frown.

"No, no finds at all except for some mounds. Nothing to worry about. We'll use ground-penetrating radar. Be done in a jiffy. No need to dig."

He exhaled loudly and jabbed at his watch for her benefit.

"Yes sir, no delays. I guarantee it. Happy to serve." He hung up. "I'll have that site analyzed. Couldn't have just walked on by? All I ask is you get this guy off my ass. Damn corrupt politicos."

He focused on some papers on his desk so she stepped out of the office and walked back down the hallway to the entrance. Outside the glare bouncing off cement forced tears as she headed for the parking lot. At the truck she dumped out the remaining tea and climbed in. She sat there staring out the dust-mottled windshield at an afternoon resigning itself to coming night, coming winter. It was Friday. She had a week of contractor day gigs under her belt and would pick up a few more before the Gavilan survey was done. And Ron said he had more work coming up, although Ron thought in terms of archaeological periods, not monthly bill cycles. Still, she wasn't completely broke. She should be happy like every other poor working fool in America. She torqued her face into a clown smile, then dropped the curtain down hard as she threw the truck into gear and drove off.

THREE

The truck rumbled to a stop on the dirt drive separating Minoa's guesthouse from Brent Harrison's pueblo revival mega-home, spitting up veils of white dust. She stared. Somebody had parked in her spot. A sparkly blue European sports car. It looked like a sedan that had wandered into the path of a steamroller before getting a custom paint job. Still, it must have cost as much as a couple of Harrison's luxury vehicles so she'd just park over on the side of the guesthouse by the pile of tossed lumber and say 'no problem at all, sir.'

She stumbled to the guesthouse door, pretended to unlock it in case anybody was peering out from the big house. As she figured it, why bother to throw the deadbolt on a glorified shed in full view of a mansion with a first class security system? She pulled it shut behind her, dropped her backpack on her door-on-cement-blocks desk and paused to think. Big mistake. Avoiding excess thinking was her favorite hobby these days.

Better not to think about how she'd ended up working on the wrong side of what Carter called the Water Wars or renting some multimillionaire's maid's quarters in a town she'd left forever at age eighteen. The territory of memories between eighteen and thirty-six was posted 'no trespassing.'

For now, she'd need to keep tabs on Carter's arrest process so she could time her drive back to Albuquerque to pay a bail bondsman and get her out of jail, although she doubted even pushing the old pickup back down the interstate at a tire-shimmying speed would save Carter from a night in jail. And that word 'pay' produced a cattle prod of anxiety. Maybe Ireni could afford this one. She had a real job, right?

But Ireni had paid most of the fee last time after Carter and the other water defenders disrupted an Albuquerque City Council meeting dressed as La Llorona pouring pitchers of water on the councilors' heads. The press clips had been comical. The entertainment value was almost worth a rough arrest and a criminal charge but what had it accomplished? According to Ron the development was going through no matter how many creative protests activists launched. And even though the DA dropped the charges, they'd never see the bondsman's fee again.

She located a bottle of Brandy & Benedictine under the sink in the kitchenette, a single countertop, a couple cabinets and a camper-style fridge. With a tumbler of the amber liquor she sat down in one of her equipale chairs, a leather cubby on a base of cedar strips, propped her feet on the windowsill and stared out the window. Up the hill to the side of Harrison's house she spied two Latino guys in cowboy hats and western shirts shoveling something into the prairie dog burrows. What were Brent's day workers up to now? Surely they weren't feeding the charismatic little rodents?

Suddenly his front door swung open and out walked Findley Malbore—one of Harrison's millionaire buddies; she'd privately named him 'the shrimp'—followed by some string bean woman with flyaway brown hair. Brent stood on the threshold smiling and waving. Malbore and the woman smiled and waved back. Life was good for the one-percenters. No idea who the woman was. Malbore's girlfriend was blonde, unless he'd ordered a replacement.

Malbore and the woman drove off in the sapphire sports car and Brent disappeared. Minoa sent a text to Valeria, found out she was with little Leah in the rec room behind the main house. She sighed through a smile of satisfaction. At least she'd done one good deed. When Valeria got arrested during an ICE raid at the body shop where her brother worked, Minoa had helped bail her out of immigration detention and arranged a nanny job with Brent.

'So there, Carter. I'm not just an apolitical individualist with zero social conscience.'

In her imagination Carter responded with a hesitant thumbs up. Ireni would half-frown, hesitant in the other direction. She'd better let her know Carter was in jail again. She punched her number into Carter's phone.

"Hello?" A voice as clear as an icy rivulet. "Carter, what's up?"

"It's Minoa, remember? I've got Carter's phone. APD stole mine and Carter's being booked right now. You saw the video. Were you able to send it out?"

"The governor's office has a copy in their citizen comment inbox. I'll check the local news to see if they cover it, but they're biased in favor of Gavilan development so I doubt they will. Maybe the college interns at KUNM will take an interest."

"We'll have to drive to 'Querque' tomorrow to bail her out."

"I paid most of the fee for her last bond."

"No friendly reimbursement yet?"

"She's too busy getting herself arrested again."

"I'm a little short so she may have to buy her own way out this time."

"Don't you still have work with Ron?"

"A few more days, then it's back to the breadline."

"You're not really starving, are you?"

"Just kidding, Reni. Ron has been paying me enough for a burger and fries every hour I'm out at Gavilan."

"Good things are coming your way, Min. I can feel it."

"Glad you can. Some dancing later might help counter my pessimism."

"I have to work late. How's Valeria doing with your landlord's daughter?"

"I'll check on her."

As she clicked off, Brent's front door flew open and his live-in girlfriend, Crystal, charged out. She tried to slam the door but Brent appeared on the threshold raising both palms to stop it. Spinning around, she ran toward the row of luxury SUVs parked along the front of the house. He caught up and grabbed her arm. She twirled around to face him. Both of their mouths stretched one way and another but Minoa couldn't hear anything through the glass. Crystal flung her arm free, lurching backward as she pulled a phone out of her pocket. As Brent approached she backed up, filming him. He swatted at the phone but she moved it in time.

She ran to a black Range Rover, jerked open the door, slid into the driver's seat. Held up the phone to film him again. He strode over and locked hands on the door handle leading to a tug of war that whacked the car door back and forth. She floored the accelerator, spraying dirt off the wheels as she sped down the circular drive, dragging him along for a few paces until he slid to the ground. Jumping up he stood there glaring at the retreating car, hands in fists.

After a moment he looked her way. She snapped her eyes shut and feigned sleep. Kept them squeezed shut as she counted in whispered Spanish but, just as she reached *veintidós*, a knock rattled the door. She took a few steps over, tugged it partway open and peered out. Brent smiled as if expecting her to invite him in. Dust speckled his chinchilla pelt of hair and frosted one side of his shirt. Within the open buttons of his shirt she spied a bullhead tattoo.

"Hey, your friend Valeria is great with Leah."

Minoa nodded, mind lurching among possibilities. Was this demented? Chatting after he'd tussled with Crystal? Or had they been playacting a dispute and weren't angry? Maybe they juiced their relationship with games like this?

"So, I finally get full custody of Leah and Crystal picks this moment to lose her mind."

No idea what to say. Oh yeah, would this be a good moment for her request?

"Really? Uh, I was wondering if I could have a few more days to pay the rent?"

"No worries. Listen, your friend is doing a great job with Leah. I appreciate you finding me a nanny on short notice. I'm having a party to celebrate the custody decision tomorrow night. You're invited. Bring a friend if you want."

"Great, thanks."

"By the way, they're exterminating the prairie dogs so stay away from the substance you see around their burrows."

"What?" She edged the door wider. "Why are you having them killed?"

"I don't want Leah to step in a hole and twist her ankle. Anyway, they attract coyotes."

He turned and walked back toward the big house. As soon as he disappeared inside, she headed around the main house to a remodeled six-car garage behind it. She could hear screaming before she peered through double French doors. Inside two table-size flat screens checkered the walls; pool, ping-pong and foosball tables filled space between leather sectionals. Little Leah writhed on the floor, flinging arms, kicking legs, face squeezed around a mouth stretched wide, fringes of hair flying side to side.

She opened the door, running smack into deafening screams. Valeria, creamy round face and serious brows under a wave of thick black hair, glanced over at her, then returned to the child with a stream of calming words that weren't penetrating the tantrum. She reached down arms but Leah swatted her away, scooting across the tile floor.

Valeria straightened, made a 'who knows' gesture at Minoa. When Leah noticed Valeria had backed off, her screams transformed into wails and she rolled over onto her belly and convulsed a string of sobs, pounding her fists. Valeria squatted beside her patting her back, humming a tune. Finally she scooped her up and carried her over to a couch where she sat cradling the child on her lap. Minoa sat beside her. Leah quieted as Valeria stroked locks of wavy nut-brown hair off her forehead. Valeria looked at Minoa, speaking in a low voice.

"She's been like this since Brent told her that her mom isn't coming to pick her up. He made it sound like she's abandoning her daughter. What mother would do that?"

"Brent and Mercedes have been in a custody battle for years. When I moved in he was on a regime of supervised visits. I guess he took revenge by suing for sole custody. He's having a party to celebrate the custody decision. He even invited us."

Leah slipped off Valeria's lap and wandered over to a toy chest. She pulled out a robot puppy and began using a controller to move it around. Valeria flashed Minoa a glance.

"He invited me? I don't think so."

"I mean, he said bring friends, or a friend. What do I care? He can afford me bringing a busload of people."

"I'm the nanny, Minoa. I'm sure he didn't mean me."

"Maybe you're right. Sorry. But this job is just while you're sorting out your immigration case. Then you can go back to UNM and finish your degree."

"I wish I was so sure. Of course I'm grateful for your help. When I was in that detention center I thought I'd be deported without seeing anyone again."

Minoa patted her shoulder.

"It was awful but try to relax. The important thing is you're out on bail."

"Which is a miracle since I didn't appear for my first court hearing."

"So we used a rich guy's name to get you out. Now you have time to work on a defense."

"I don't have a defense. We're just delaying. I'm not going to get legal status."

"Keep the faith. Maybe Brent will sponsor you. By the way, Brent and Crystal had a screaming fight out in front. She may have walked out."

Valeria stood, moved behind the bar and took a sip from a water bottle. Spoke with her eyes focused on Leah.

"What was she mad about?"

"Who knows? I may have misunderstood. Brent acted like it was nothing."

"So now it will be Brent and Leah and me in the house."

"Maybe he'll pay you more."

"Even if he does, it will take a long time to save enough for a lawyer."

Minoa joined her leaning against the bar.

"Try not to sweat the details. The important thing is you're out of detention and you're not going back."

Leah waved the controller up and down. The puppy lurched, chirping a recorded series of yips.

"Uh, if I lose this job would it be a violation of the conditions of my bond?"

"I'm not sure. Just keep the job until you get a lawyer to prepare your case. Then you can decide on your next move."

Valeria shifted snacks around a plate like tiles on a slide puzzle.

"Are you alright?"

She looked up.

"My brother has no idea where I am."

"Can't you call him?"

"I tried but a recording says it's a non-working number."

"Maybe one of his friends?"

"It's best for him. ICE is tracking people through cell phone connections and they have my phone."

"Isn't that phone yours?"

"Brent got me this one. He gave me a car to drive too."

"That's great."

The smile surfaced, then sank as if weighted with stones.

"When is my mom coming?"

Leah turned to them, hands dangling. Valeria hurried over.

"I'm not sure, Leah. But we can play now and have fun. Let me show you how to make the puppy somersault."

She stood behind the child, arms circling her, hands on the controller. Shot Minoa a pained glance and then focused on the toy. The robot puppy leaped up, turned in midair and flopped down on its paws.

Leah shrieked, "Let me do it!"

Minoa waved and headed for the door.

FOUR

She told herself an early night would be good for her. But an antsy feeling sandpapering her nerve endings was winning out. After turning side to side until the top sheet knotted itself, she stood up out of bed, walked across a frigid tile floor to the door and slid out into the night. The chill of an October evening on Santa Fe's high altitude plateau cut like razor blades on her bare legs. Up above, stars dangled like glowing fruit on a blackened tree of countless branches. There was Cassiopeia, called jaguar cub by the Huaorani. She tried to recall the Huaorani word but her command of the language had deteriorated over the years since she finished her fieldwork. She spotted Orion and Scorpio, rhinestone sprinkles against an ebony sky varnished by city lights. The night sky in southeastern Ecuador had been even darker, like a pit full of Christmas lights.

She thought back to all those nights spent with the Huaorani, trying to understand enough of what people said to catch the meaning of their endless stories, jotting notes when something made sense. What good had it done to spend years of her life there studying cultural practices fading under the onslaught of missionaries and oil exploration? And then to find no teaching jobs back home, no museum or foundation gigs, no jobs at all till she landed back in her hometown and started pouring drinks at a casino. Replaced now by Ron's contractor assignments for the state archaeology office. Another joke. She knew next to nothing about archaeology. Anthropology had been her passion and now that it was gone from her life she felt lost, unsure which direction to head next or what to aim for.

A light came on in the upper floor of Brent's house and Valeria's silhouette passed across the window. Valeria saved from detention and employed in a multimillionaire's house. A flush of pride warmed her for a moment.

Then sage bushes along the drive rustled igniting a flicker of anxiety. She jumped back inside, pulling the door partly shut. A coyote trotted up the drive, paused to stare her way and loped off. Soon frenzied yelping broke out on the hilltop at the back of the property. She stepped back outside, craned her head, pursed her lips. Let loose a howl midway between coyote girl and crazy gringa. For a moment she felt kinship with the four-leggeds up on the hilltop singing pack unity and moon worship. Then the howling died out and desert emptiness reconquered.

She shut the door and fell back into bed, drifting to sleep almost as soon as her head hit the pillow. Some time later she woke, sat up in darkness. Had someone knocked? She stumbled to the door, flung it open. Cassiopeia, Scorpio, Orion had whirled. The windows on Brent's house gaped shadow in the intervals between yellowish cones of ornamental floodlights. Squinting down the dirt drive she could only make out black shadow pools merging into night. She slumped into a wrought iron chair on her tiny porch, trying to think.

Pieces of a dream flashed by, coalesced. Something had moved in the darkness, a pack of coyotes. They were lunging at some prey on the ground, baring teeth and growling, grabbing a mouthful, snapping at each other as they competed. Then she'd seen it: a family of prairie dogs in their midst. The poor little things stared up at her with button eyes, pleading as the coyotes tore them to shreds. Horrible.

A full-body shudder almost knocked her off the chair. Why, why, why these endless nightmares? And now she was dreaming of the poor murdered prairie dogs? She wasn't responsible for their extermination so why should she suffer? Yet that sad little family staring at her as coyotes destroyed them provoked a stabbing pain deep in her gut.

Three prairie dogs, a dad, mom and child. She shook her head. Ridiculous. Prairie dogs didn't live in nuclear families. So the dream must be referring to her own childhood family of three people. Until her mom left. Stop. She wasn't going down that memory lane. Maybe her unconscious was dramatizing Brent's responsibility for killing the little creatures. But why the reference to a family, a couple with one child? Was the reference to Brent, Crystal and little Leah? But Crystal wasn't

Leah's mom, so the sacrificed family of three would be Brent, Leah and her mother Mercedes. Oh, why try to figure out these nightmares?

She wrapped arms around her rib cage, tucked her chin, squinted up at an infinitude of stars boring through the night sky like diamond drill bits. The edge of the chair freezer-burned the bare flesh of her thighs. Another night, another nightmare. She whistled out a breath. Some things didn't change no matter where you went.

FIVE

"Hey Min, there's a dead body out here."

Minoa considered as she brushed her bushy hair hard, trying to make it lay smooth. Carter's voice, so it had to be an exaggeration. She walked over to the door of the guesthouse, opened it, scanned the dirt parking area at the center of Brent's estate, a swathe of bare hills dotted with piñon and juniper sloping up to the fringe of the Sangre de Cristos. Her eyes came to rest on a golden-furred bread loaf near Carter's feet.

"That's the dead body?"

"It's a dead prairie dog and it's lying on the drive beside your truck." Ireni stood near Carter staring down. "Did you hit it?"

Carter blared a nasty squint at her.

"This innocent creature is a victim of chemical poisoning. Bhopal for New Mexico rodents."

"Oh yeah, I forgot." Ireni shrugged. "Pest control."

"'Pest control' is a euphemism for murder."

Minoa approached the carcass, stared down at fans of dried blood below a pert rodent nose, round brown eyes stuck wide open.

"I had a nightmare about this."

"Explain."

Ireni curt, demanding logic.

"I dreamed these little guys were dying a horrific death. Coyotes were tearing them to pieces."

"Coyotes are predators, just like capitalists," Carter cut in. "Capitalists think they can kill anything they want without repercussions."

"Brent's not an ecologist and he owns this place. What am I supposed to do?"

"Where's the prairie dog town? I'm going to take photos for evidence."

Minoa pointed at the mounds up the hill from Brent's fake adobe mansion. Carter strode away. Ireni moved to Minoa's side as they watched her rangy form thinning against the wheat toast background of high plains foothills.

"You shouldn't have told her."

"Better to let her erupt before we go inside."

"About that party. I was thinking I could wait in your house and after we could go to a movie?"

Ireni, blond hair straggling off her shoulders, turned melting iceberg eyes to Minoa.

"We need to make an appearance. Brent's not only my landlord, he inadvertently got Valeria out of the ICE detention center on bail. And now he's her employer. We have to be friendly."

"Emphasis on inadvertently."

Minoa grabbed a bagged bottle from a stool by the door and yelled as they walked to the door of the big house.

"We're going in, Carter."

A black Porsche sped up the drive past a row of high end vehicles and squeezed into the space next to the front door, forcing Minoa and Ireni to jump sideways. Two doors flapped open and out stepped Findley Malbore in a cream jacket, accompanied this time by a spindly blonde in asymmetrical spandex split up to the hip. For a moment Minoa's amber eyes locked with his colorless ones.

"Hi."

Her reflexive wave truncated half-way up. He started to extend the hand with the keys in it, then reconsidered, turned and levered the blonde to the door with an arm around her midsection. As they stepped inside Ireni nudged her.

"Not the type to kiss babies, is he?"

"That's Findley Malbore. He has business dealings with Brent. He seems to think I'm the valet."

"What am I going to say to people like him? I think I should just wait for you."

"Courage, Reni."

Carter trotted up as they reached the door.

"I was going to stuff myself on this dude's food but now I feel sick. He's holocausting a keystone species."

Minoa patted Carter's back.

"Look, killing those little cuties sucks but give your appetite five. You've got to stay nourished for the coming revolution."

"Who was that oligarch who drove up with his trophy girlfriend?"

"You know that round house up the mountain that looks like a spaceship? That's Malbore's place. Brent said he has a tennis court suspended over the canyon on cables."

"Bad serves polluting national forest land. Humph."

Carter turned, hands on hips, to stare up at the Sangre de Cristos, all teal velvet crossed by a ribbon of gold. Minoa and Ireni exchanged glances. Then Minoa grabbed an arm of each and propelled them over the threshold.

"C'mon. It's just Santa Fe style conspicuous consumption. We got this."

The three women moved through a two story entry into a living area the size of a railway waiting room where scattered groups chatted. A young man in a black vest and bow tie moved through the crowd handing out fluted cups of champagne off a tray. A vast picture window showcased Santa Fe Baldy against an evening sky that silvered chamisa in the foreground and burnished the pine forest's collar of turning aspens.

"Give me a minute. I'm gonna hide my fifteen dollar bottle of wine in the kitchen so nobody knows who brought it."

"They'll know, Min."

Heading into the home's interior Minoa found a kitchen the size of a conference room lined by granite countertops dotted with high end appliances. A woman in a maid's uniform with a little peaked cap pinned over a black bun stood at an island taking foil covers off tins of catered food items. A tall red-haired woman stood at the end, squeezing her face into a birdlike expression that deepened the forehead lines and made her buck teeth more prominent. She bobbed her head in repeated nods as she spoke.

"Do you have any tongs? For the Caesar salad? Seeeee-zar."

"*Como*?"

"Tongs, I need tongs."

She extended her hand, snapped fingers and thumb together like a biting mouth. The maid stared at her.

"*Tenacillas, por favor.*"

Minoa smiled. The woman smiled back, avoiding looking at the red-haired woman.

"*Si, claro.*"

She fetched tongs from a drawer. The red-haired woman frowned at Minoa, then headed out with the salad. Minoa placed the wine behind a forest of liquor bottles on a side table and asked in Spanish for the bathroom. She wound down hallways to a bathroom lined by floor-to-ceiling mirrors.

When she was opening the door to leave, she heard whispers, a sound of smooching? She pulled the door shut, waited, then cracked it open as high heels tick-tocked down the Mexican tile hallway. Peeking out she glimpsed a tight short shift, the coral hue of Indian paintbrush blossoms, sway around a corner. As she pushed the door wider, she heard heavier footsteps thudding down the hall and jerked the door back. Through the crack she spied an ice blue linen sports shirt turning the same corner.

She made her way back to the party and located her friends in another gigantic room. Carter was exiting a buffet line with a heaped plate and a silly grin.

"You were right. Got to keep up my strength for the struggle."

Ireni stood staring.

"OMG, Carter. Did you know forty-eight million people become ill from food contamination every year? Buffets are the most dangerous place to eat. Think of all the microorganisms exhaled onto that food, not to mention all the hands that touched it."

"You think pesticides and genetic modification don't kill a lot more?"

Minoa sliced a hand between them.

"I assume you two never tried *chicha*. Women chew up yucca and spit it into a bowl to speed the fermentation process. It looks like skim milk gone bad."

"I can not believe you tried that."

"I guzzled it every chance I got."

"Hey, Rainstorm." Carter waved a piled-up fork at Ireni. "You better feed your brain or those genius boys at the lab will crowd you out."

"Hah! They're scared of me."

"I suppose I should eat something to recoup my wine investment."

"Can you ladies recommend something here that won't burn the palate of a fair-complexioned Southern gentleman?"

The three of them spun around. There stood a blond fellow of middle height dressed in a navy blazer, bolo tie, jeans, and cowboy boots.

"Hi Eldon," said Minoa.

"Aren't you going to introduce me to your lovely friends? Eldon Bohnefeld the Third." He swept a hand over his clothing. "I dress to blend in with the natives but I hail from Athens, Georgia."

"Try the chile rellenos." Carter held up a batter-coated chile pepper on her fork. "It's mild enough for a baby."

"Without ranch dressing I don't think I better risk it." He peered at Carter's plate, then turned to Minoa and Ireni. "Do you two know something she doesn't?"

"I prefer to create a buzz before I ruin it with nourishment."

Eldon appraised Minoa.

"I never imagined you'd have southern sensibilities."

"She lived in the Southern Hemisphere," said Ireni, "not the American south."

"I worked in the Amazon headwaters, an ethnographic project."

Eldon's pale brows rose.

"Oh, really? You must have encountered boas on a daily basis."

"Plenty. But the Fer-de-Lance gave me most of my panic attacks. It loves human dwellings and is a renowned grouch. The bite causes massive tissue destruction and internal bleeding. Then there's the eyelash pit viper. It hangs out of trees spying for something to bite. Ditto with grouchiness and severe tissue damage. I could go on about the jumping viper."

"Don't tell me—it jumps?"

"Exactly."

"Impressive. You know your snakes."

"It's self-defense."

Eldon patted his belly.

"The worst thing I have to defend myself against these days is chile-burn in the lower tract."

Carter interrupted her chewing.

"I grew up in McLean, Virginia but since I came to New Mexico I eat green chile every day. Super good for the microbiome. And it kills parasites."

"Did you have the long slithery kind or the squirming buggy kind?"

"She never discusses her intestinal fauna with strangers," said Minoa.

"A well-founded defense of your friend's Fourth Amendment right to bodily privacy. I concede the point."

Eldon glanced over at Findley Malbore and his girlfriend sipping champagne from stemmed glasses before a picture window.

"Now, if you ladies will kindly excuse me, I hope we can continue this stimulating conversation before the evening wanes."

He walked away.

Minoa leaned toward her friends and whispered, "Eldon's a wackadoo."

"I think he likes you."

Carter gave her a devious smile.

"*Por dios.*"

Minoa shoved her.

"Don't think you can get out of this by switching languages."

"I just did."

"Speaking of men, what happened to that mysterious Hopi guy, the one who could flip rattlers while painting works of art?" said Carter.

"Yeah, the native artist who saved you from a giant rattlesnake." Ireni fluttered a hand over her chest. "So romantic."

"Lewis? I haven't seen him."

"Why don't you call him up?"

"I'm supposed to be putting my own quail in a row, remember?"

On the other side of the room she saw Eldon strike up a conversation with Findley Malbore.

"Who is the wackadoo?"

Carter looked over her shoulder.

"Brent's lawyer."

Ireni's voice pulled them back.

"BTW, Solaris is showing at Jean Cocteau."

"Showtimes?"

"I think we can make the late show."

"I told Valeria we'd take turns visiting her."

"Right."

After a moment Brent strode into the room and paused, scanning faces. He wore an ice blue linen shirt. Minoa scanned the crowd for an Indian paintbrush shift but saw no one. Brent frowned when he spotted Eldon and Malbore but instantly smoothed his face, turning to a man nearby in a Burberry blazer with a business haircut. A woman lounged beside him in an emerald dress with flounced hemline.

"Dan, Chloe, how are the kids?"

Brent patted the man on the shoulder.

"They're doing well, Brent. Congratulations on the custody decision."

"Thanks. It's a huge relief. Now that Leah will be here every weekend, maybe we can enroll the kids in ski school together?"

"We prefer Taos." The woman kicked one foot in a high heel made of scaly leather. "We have a house up there. The snow quality is magnificent."

"I've been thinking about getting a place up there for weekends."

"You'll love it. It's authentic New Mexico, so picturesque."

Brent's gaze jerked. The woman in the Indian paintbrush dress strolled into the room sipping from a champagne glass. She was all lines and dots: straight fine hair and aquiline nose contrasting a splash of freckles and a lacquered bow of a mouth.

Minoa recognized her as the 'string bean' woman who had walked out of the house with Findley Malbore the day before.

"See that woman." Carter huffed a whisper. "She's the lobbyist for that water-sucking sprawl monster you're surveying out at Gavilan Mesa."

"Really? She's a lobbyist? BTW that's not all she is."

Minoa arched her eyebrows but Carter went on as if.

"Right. She's married to Barney Trujillo, the Albuquerque city council member. He voted to approve the development plan for Gavilan Mesa that his wife gets paid to promote. Convenient. Now it's full speed ahead for BBCC's long-distance despoliation of our state."

"Don't get any ideas about protesting, Carter. This is a private party and we're guests."

"But this is a perfect opportunity to put all these leeches on notice that we're not going to just sit there and take more of their environmentally disastrous—"

"Carter. If you misbehave I will never let you off leash again."

"Don't worry," said Ireni. "She knows who got her out of jail. She'll play nice."

Carter glared at them, then swung her head to stare as a paunchy fellow with spiked hair in a regulation suit and tie joined the lobbyist, highball in hand.

"That's Trujillo, the city council member."

Ireni turned to Carter with a perplexed expression.

"Isn't there a law or ethics guideline that prohibits lawmakers' spouses from lobbying for projects in their district?"

"Not in New Mexico," Carter mumbled, cramming a forkful of oozing enchiladas into her mouth.

At that moment a loud female voice rang out from the entry.

"Where is he?"

Heads turned toward the foyer as a woman strode into the room dressed like a tropical beauty queen: tight jeans over yellow high heels, a skimpy yellow halter top under a stonewash jacket, hair poofed and eyebrows dramatic. She spotted Brent and paced over, not forgetting to sway her hips. Brent scowled.

"Mercedes, what in the hell are you doing here?"

Mercedes jammed an index finger toward his chest like a jackhammer.

"How dare you steal my daughter?"

"The trial is over and you lost. So get out and stop disturbing my guests."

"You say this is over, you *traidor*? You'll see you can't do this to me no matter how filthy rich you are!"

"Waiters!"

Brent glanced around clicking his fingers in the air. One sheepish fellow with a belly jiggling beneath his black vest came out of the kitchen while another wiry guy in the same outfit approached from a different direction.

"Escort this woman out of here. She wasn't invited."

The two young men exchanged clueless glances, then turned nervous expressions to Brent.

"Sir?"

"Take this woman out now."

"But ...?"

They shrugged, set down their trays and reached arms out toward Mercedes. She spun around slapping them away.

"Touch me, you *imbéciles*, and you and your *malditas* families will regret it for the rest of your days."

"Eldon, call the police!"

Eldon took steps toward Brent curving wide to stay out of her reach.

"Brent, I don't think that's a good idea. Mercedes, why don't we resolve this amicably?"

"I said call the police."

Without another word Eldon turned and trotted out of the room. Mercedes faced off again with Brent.

"You've gone too far this time, you *sinvergüenza*. I know enough to bury you and I'm going to do it."

"I know things about you too, Mercedes. Don't forget that."

She shot him a venomous look and then stormed out of the room. The front door slammed. Brent scattered smiles to all his guests.

"Well, folks, you can see why I had to sue for custody. I couldn't leave my daughter in the hands of that maniac. I apologize for the disturbance. Please enjoy your drinks and appetizers."

He strode out following in Eldon's steps. Minoa turned to her friends.

"This evening is getting interesting."

"I'd rather watch a good movie. *Solaris* late show begins in–"

Carter cut in.

"You find Russian sci-fi more amusing than the antics of our entitled elite?"

At that moment a cascade of loud knocks sounded from the entry. They heard the front door open and voices rising in volume. Minoa sidled over to a doorway leading to the entry and looked out. Two Santa Fe County sheriffs stood outside the front door, greenish-gray uniforms outlined by floodlights against a charcoal sky.

"You got here quickly." Brent strode toward the doorway where Eldon stood. "She should still be nearby. She committed trespassing, threatened me and assaulted my waiters."

The officers exchanged questioning glances and then one handed Brent a paper.

"Brent Harrison, you're hereby served with a protection order."

"What ... what are you talking about? Arrest my ex-wife immediately." Brent thrust the paper at Eldon. "What the hell is this?"

Eldon skimmed the document.

"It's a temporary order of protection ordering you to desist from all communication, whether in person, telephonic, written or digital, with Crystal Roybal, and maintain a distance of one hundred yards from her, her home, her place of work and her vehicle at all times on pain of immediate arrest. Her vehicle? Wait a minute. That's not boilerplate." He looked up at Brent. "What do you know about her vehicle?"

"I know I paid for it."

"You're to appear in court next Monday at ten AM."

He handed the document back to Brent.

"What does she think she's doing? I should get a protection order against her. She takes everything she can carry and runs off without a word of explanation. I'll file charges for robbery and breach of trust."

"Brent, need I remind you breach of trust is a violation of the duties of members of a management board of a financial institution as defined in the Stock Corporation Act, not a lover who ditches you."

He took Brent by the arm and led him down the hallway.

Brent called over his shoulder, "Arrest Mercedes Harrison. That's what I called you for."

Eldon continued pulling him away, calling out, "Thank you, officers."

Carter peered around Minoa.

"What's all that about?"

"Looks like he has plenty of trouble with women. His ex-live-in girlfriend, Crystal, took out a protection order against him."

"Incredible."

As they rejoined Ireni, Carter said, "She'll never get a permanent protection order against a rich dude. That lawyer of his will put on an OJ-level defense."

"Carter, judges in New Mexico have to face re-election."

"As if anybody votes in local elections."

Minoa and Ireni flicked eyebrows at each other.

SIX

Brent reappeared in a doorway, face washed clean of emotion, and called out, "Please join me in the dining room for toasts and tasting."

"Do we have to?" said Ireni.

"We'll sneak out when everyone is distracted by the expensive liquor," Minoa said.

The party crowd moved into another hall with a dining table long enough for a board meeting and a ceiling high enough for a church. Brent stood at the head of the table before a Byzantine city of bottles of exotic shapes and shades surrounded by glasses ranging from stemmed goblets to monogrammed tumblers. The wiry waiter approached and began opening bottles. The chubby one moved through the crowd with more champagne cups. Brent held up his glass and a crop of others followed.

"I'd like to start with a toast. To my beautiful daughter Leah!"

"Cheers! Here here!"

"Let's start the tasting with a few unusual brandies," Brent called out. "We have *Slivovitza*, a plum brandy from Serbia, and *Kappa Pisco*, a Chilean offering made of muscat grapes. And my favorite, KWV 10 Year, a South African brandy aged for ten years."

"My professional advice is to stay far away from that table. It's going to get worse before it gets better."

They craned their necks seeking the source of the voice. Found Eldon standing behind them. Carter trained a scowl on him.

"Do you manage all Brent's affairs?"

"Not the romantic ones."

"What about the prairie dogs?" Carter said. "Could you influence him to stop poisoning them? He's breaking the law because black ferrets are endangered and they depend on prairie dog burrows to survive."

"I could try the legal angle. But it would be more effective if little Leah tells him how cute they are."

"We'll get to the whiskies in a moment," Brent went on. "But first, who will volunteer to try my exotic offerings?"

"Let me hide behind you until the whiskey comes out."

Eldon crouched behind Minoa. She frowned at him over her shoulder. In the back of the room she noticed Findley Malbore staring at Brent, ignoring his girlfriend's chatter. One of Brent's assistants pulled the stoppers out of bottles and placed them before him. When a few people milled to the side giving Minoa a clear view of the table, she gasped. One bottle contained a snake curled up inside filling it from bottom to top.

"Here we have a Vietnamese snake wine. It's rice wine distilled with a baby cobra and is reputed to cure baldness and impotence. Step forward if you need help with either of those."

Amidst laughter, Brent poured himself a shot and downed it.

"He can't see me, can he?"

Eldon snuggled behind Minoa.

"Eldon, would you please stop?"

"And here we have a traditionally brewed mezcal from the state of Jalisco, Mexico. Workers hand gather the larvae of a maguey moth for each bottle."

Brent held up the bottle against the light, revealing a fat whitish worm at the bottom.

"I vote for Solaris," said Carter.

"Me too," said Ireni.

"I agree," said Minoa. "Why don't we just say goodbye to Valeria first?"

"For contrast, here is a double-distilled one-hundred percent scorpion mezcal."

Brent turned the bottle to catch the light. At the bottom sat a dark shape with a curled tail.

"By the way, the venom is not poisonous when ingested. You can even eat the scorpion for an extra burst of protein."

He poured a glass of the butterscotch liquid, raised it to pursed lips and downed it in one long draught. Set it on the table with a cough.

"That has a bite to it. Robust, high proof, invigorating. Gentlemen with *hoo-eh-voze* step forward."

"What is he talking about?"

Ireni leaned toward Minoa's ear.

"I think he meant *huevos*, balls for you monolinguals. Let's go."

"Don't leave me."

Eldon crouch-walked alongside Minoa. She glared at him as Brent's voice rang out.

"This is better than a shot of testosterone. All real *hombres* should try it."

"I'll have some."

Barney Trujillo, the lobbyist's husband, moved to the table, picked up a glass and took a tenuous sip. Brent watched him and laughed.

"Like I said, this stuff requires balls."

He poured another, held it out to Barney in a taunting toast and then guzzled it. Barney wet his lips, sputtered, glanced around the room.

"Looks like you're the only one willing to drink turpentine, Harrison. Maybe you should think twice before you get into things that aren't good for you."

He sent Brent a mean squint but Brent laughed.

"Good doesn't come close to it, Trujillo. The word is exquisite."

Brent sniffed the glass and smiled. He and Trujillo locked eyes looking like bulls ready to charge. After a tense moment,

Trujillo set his glass down too hard, sloshing liquor onto the tablecloth, turned and padded over to the picture window. Brent poured more mezcal into his tumbler, held it out as if toasting and drained it.

When he set the glass down, he wiped his mouth with the back of his hand. Everyone in the room sucked thin desert air and stared. Threads of blood trickled out of both nostrils. Eldon ducked around Minoa and hurried to his side.

"Brent, you've got a nosebleed."

Brent grabbed a handful of cocktail napkins, held them to his nose. When he pulled them away, burgundy rivulets shot out of both nostrils, running over his mouth, down his chin.

"Maybe you should lie down for a minute."

Brent looked at him like a puzzled child, then groaned and doubled over.

"Brent, are you okay?" Eldon patted him on the back. "Maybe you should lay off the poison potions."

Brent twisted his torso back and forth as if trying to straighten up. Guests in the room exchanged questioning glances.

"I can't believe it," Carter said. "A rich dude is finally paying a price for indulging in pointless luxury commodities."

Ireni frowned at her.

"Carter, the man is in pain."

Brent forced himself upright and gaped at his guests.

"OMG he's going to throw up," said Carter.

An enraged expression passed across his face. He tried to smile but one side of his mouth sagged. Rearing back his head he tipped forward to pour a torrent of blood onto his glacial linen shirt. Then he folded and slumped to the floor. Cries and exclamations rang out. The red-haired woman from the kitchen rushed into the room and dropped to her knees at his side.

"What happened?" she screamed.

"Don't touch him!"

Carter was speed-walking toward him. Minoa grabbed her arm but she shook free and continued. Minoa turned back to Ireni.

"She's not going to give him CPR, is she?"

"Let's hope not. He could have Ebola."

Carter lifted up the red-haired woman by her arms and forced her back a few feet. Then she put a finger on the side of his neck and felt for a pulse. Eldon stood watching, pulling one hand, then the other, as if removing gloves over and over.

"Ebola? Not a chance. Plague is more likely. Prairie dogs can carry plague-infected fleas."

Ireni flashed her a horrified expression.

"Carter was walking all over those prairie dog burrows. And you live here. You probably infected me. We're all going to die!" She punched at her phone. "I'm calling 911."

Next to Brent's face, blood puddled on the Saltillo tiles. As people formed a gawking circle around him, a stain appeared on the seat of his pants. Soon blood pooled next to his buttocks. People stiffened, whispering in small groups. Carter used some napkins to lift Brent's head and Eldon stuck a cushion beneath it. Then they both stood beside him. After an agonizing wait the sound of a siren approached. It diminished as the ambulance drove past the estate. Eldon ran over to peer out the picture window. The siren increased again and Eldon ran out of the room. After a moment the siren shut off and EMT's dashed into the room followed by Eldon.

They took one look at Brent on the ground in a lake of blood and called out, "Was he injured? A knife wound?"

"Probable poisoning," said Carter, pointing to the liquor bottles. "One of those."

"Any recent travel to Africa?"

"No, none."

Eldon's voice cracked.

The EMT's suited up in masks, gloves and coveralls before situating Brent on a gurney and wheeling him out. Guests shuffled out leaving a wide berth around the congealing lake of blood. Eldon and the red-haired woman disappeared into the kitchen. Suddenly Minoa remembered Valeria.

The three friends hurried around to the rec room behind the house and recounted what had happened. Valeria slid onto a couch, burying her face in her hands. Everyone gathered around patting her back and muttering reassurances. Leah looked on with terrified eyes so Minoa hunkered down beside her and tried to engage her in a floor puzzle of a New Mexico map decorated with symbols like chile peppers and oil derricks to indicate regional industries. Finally, Valeria dried her eyes and said she would take care of Leah and wait to hear about Brent.

SEVEN

Minoa woke to the sound of tires crunching graveled dirt. She rolled around in bed, yawning and stretching, until the memory of last night's events hit. Jumping up she jogged to the window. A police car sat in front of Brent's house. An officer was wrapping yellow crime scene tape around the entry. She tugged on jeans and a tee and hurried over.

"What's going on?"

"This is a crime scene." The officer didn't look up. "You can't go in."

An unmarked car sped up the drive, spitting pebbles as it slid to a stop. Out stepped a man in a fitted shirt and striped tie with a flip of black hair in the shape of a frozen wave. She walked over.

"Detective Martinez?"

His brown eyes bugged.

"Do I know you?"

"I live here. In that guesthouse."

"But didn't you ...?"

"Uh, must have been someone else."

His abundant eyebrows arched as he scanned her face, then slid back into place. Luckily his memory for faces was imperfect. No use reminding him she'd invaded one of his crime scenes in the Ortiz Mountains. He turned and walked toward Brent's front door. She tagged along.

"Why are you treating this like a crime scene? Did Brent Harrison die? If he did it was food poisoning, or rather liquor poisoning."

He paused.

"How do you know Brent Harrison was poisoned?"

She scanned the grounds of Brent's estate. Mica-crusted dirt, twisted juniper trees and scattered clumps of yellowed bunchgrass. The land appeared accustomed to loss and death. She turned back to Martinez.

"I was there. I saw him become ill."

"You were a guest at the party? Or were you working there?"

"A guest."

He squinted at her.

"You'll be asked to make a statement."

"But why are you investigating? Do you investigate food poisoning deaths?"

"Who said this was food poisoning?"

"You mean he had a pre-existing condition?"

He glared his baby-browns at her.

"Stand back."

As he walked toward the house, something clicked inside her abdomen like a ticking timer. Her thoughts whirled to a dead stop depositing, in front of her mind's eye, an image of the immigration court where a judge had decided to release Valeria on bail. That stern judge with the shrinking hairline. That government attorney in crisp white shirt and blue suit offering Valeria two months to leave the country voluntarily to avoid deportation. That reluctant granting of bail after Minoa assured the judge Valeria had employment with the well-known financier Brent Harrison.

Then, as they walked out of the courtroom, Valeria's temporary attorney warning, "Make sure she avoids contact with the law. Even a ticket for jaywalking could violate her release conditions."

The cramp in her belly exploded sending shock waves out her extremities. She ran after Martinez and when he kept walking, she jumped in front to block his steps.

"Wait!"

He gave her an impatient once-over.

"What are you doing?"

"I can give you a list of people I saw at the party who were there when Harrison became ill and I can tell you what he drank. Come over to my house and I'll jot it down."

"Right now I have to–"

"It will only take a second. It will save time with the investigation. Come over to my place and I'll jot it down for you."

She jogged halfway to the guesthouse and glanced back. He hadn't budged.

"Over here."

Finally he turned around and dragged his shiny lace-ups across the hardened dirt parking area. At the guesthouse, she flung open the door and bounded to the desk for her phone. Texted so fast her thumbs were a blur. Would Valeria pick up the message right away? Would she act quickly? No time to think.

When he appeared in the doorway she slammed down the phone behind a pile of books and pretended to rummage for a pen, then tapped it against her temple as if thinking. He glanced around the room, frowning at the disorder. She scratched a few lines on a notepad, ripped out the page and carried it over to him.

“Here are the names of people I recognized at the party. If I think of any more, I’ll notify police. And I wrote down the liquors I saw him consume: a Vietnamese snake wine, a tequila with a worm in it and a bottle of scorpion mezcal. He had some champagne before that.”

“Scorpion mezcal? Snake wine? What was he thinking?”

“He described them as gourmet liquors. Nobody else wanted to touch them. Except Barney Trujillo. He took a sip but I don’t think he drank much.”

“Okay. We’ll be in touch.”

He folded the paper, put it in his pocket and turned to leave.

“Should I go to police headquarters to make a statement or will you contact me?”

He huffed in exasperation.

"Someone will contact you."

He walked back to Brent's house and went inside. She grabbed her keys off the stool by the door and sauntered to the truck, throwing an appeasing grin at the officer guarding Brent's doorway. He frowned, the rest of him stiff as a post, watching her roll out the driveway at a pedestrian pace. Where the dirt strip met the street, she turned right rather than the usual left and took off as fast as the truck's clunky transmission would allow.

After speeding for about a quarter mile past southwestern style luxury homes, she slowed where the road curved to pass over an arroyo. No one in sight. She pulled onto the shoulder and cut the engine. Her breathing slowed as the engine cooled and October sunshine tap-danced on the mottled blue hood of the truck.

Her adrenaline-fueled plan to rescue Valeria began to lose definition like an old black-and-white photo left in the sun. What if Martinez saw Valeria hurrying out the back door with Leah? He wouldn't suspect her of anything because of that, would he? Just leaving the house didn't suggest guilt, did it? And guilt of what? Brent died of food poisoning so what difference did it make? Valeria wasn't doing anything wrong, just avoiding unnecessary contact with police.

As her eyes followed the wide sandy riverbed down past an island of salt cedar bordered by gray river rocks, sandy channels on either side hardened into flow patterns from the last flash flood, she forbade her mind to conjure an image of Valeria grabbed by an officer as she slunk out the back door of the mansion. This set-up had seemed so perfect, a multimillionaire's home for Valeria to chill in while looking for a way to solve her immigration problem. Sure, when they first got the call that Valeria was in detention, Ireni had suggested caution but that's what Ireni always did. When they found out she'd missed a court date and was facing deportation, Carter pushed for radical action. So Minoa came up with that plan to get her a job as Brent's nanny and see if a judge would buy it. Now she'd wafted Valeria out of Brent's house with no idea what to do next. Impulsive decisions were her specialty.

She stared down the arroyo, a glittery bed of crushed quartz with low banks sculpted by decades of occasional overflow. Watery eyes made the landscape undulate. As she pondered, staring, it was like watching time lapse photography: seasons of drought cut by rare cloudbursts molding this arroyo into another arroyo, one she'd walked down, waited by.

She'd made a flash decision to get the hell out of a foster home, escape the stupid house rules. intrusive social workers, sappy therapists. After climbing out her second-floor window and shinnying down a rain gutter, she ran to an arroyo and labored upstream to where a road crossed over. She'd stood by the side, anger dribbling down to the ground as a hot wind flapped her thin clothing, little slaps against naked skin, waiting for someone to drive by and offer her a ride. The lonely country of crumbly mesas and withered sage had pressed in on her, squeezing out her courage like drops of perspiration evaporating off her skin. But she'd gone ahead, climbed into the car that pulled over, taken that ride that led down one road and another to the next ride and the next.

She shook her head, refocusing on the riverbed she could see out the window. Damn memories. Being back in her hometown was like those paintings art experts discovered painted on top of a lost work of art. When cracks appeared bits of the earlier image poked through, not enough to make sense of the past but enough to confuse the way things looked now.

Downstream, around a bushy juniper at the bend, Valeria appeared tugging little Leah by the hand. Minoa watched them struggle through the sand. When they reached the truck and climbed in, she cranked the ignition without a word and sped away on the back route so she wouldn't pass Brent's entry drive.

EIGHT

Minoa and Valeria talked while Leah climbed on some equipment at a school playground near downtown.

"What am I going to do now?"

Leah laughed as she jiggled down a bumpy slide made of conveyor rollers.

"Look, we bought you time by getting you out of there. For some crazy reason they're investigating Brent's death, but soon they'll figure out it was caused by contaminated scorpion booze. Then you can find another job or come up with some other plan."

"But I have to notify the immigration court if I change addresses."

"Why don't we set you up in a new situation and then you can report it?"

"What about Leah?"

"We take her to her mom. It's better for her than being put into state custody. Trust me, I've been a ward of the state. It's not fun."

"Where is her mom?"

"Uh, good question. Her name is Mercedes Harrison, unless she's using her maiden name. I'll check county property records."

After a few minutes noodling on her phone, Minoa called, "C'mon Leah, let's go see your mom."

***

Mercedes, dressed in a leather skirt and lacy top, hurtled out the door of an upscale condo in a complex nestled into juniper-flecked hills north of downtown. A sign in the yard, and another on the door, said 'Estate Sale.' Leah, Valeria and Minoa were standing on the sidewalk. As soon as Leah saw her mother, she sprinted to her and clasped arms around her waist. Mercedes smothered the top of her head with kisses, then shot a suspicious frown at Minoa and Valeria.

"Why are you here? What's going on?"

"We brought Leah over because police showed up at Brent's house."

"Police?"

Her eyes bugged out. Pulling Leah by the hand she walked over to the condo and deposited her inside the open door. Came speed-walking back, muttering.

"Tell me what happened."

She gave Valeria an accusatory once-over as Minoa spoke.

"I figured it's better that she's with you than in Social Services custody."

Mercedes stiffened, then folded at the waist with a deep groan. She straightened clutching her belly.

"I knew this would happen. He abused her. That *canalla*. Did they arrest him? Was there ... penetration?"

"Mercedes, that's not it. Brent is dead. He died last night."

She slammed her glossy lips together, dropped her arms and scanned Minoa and Valeria.

"How do you know that?"

"I'm his ... I mean, I was his tenant. I saw him collapse last night and this morning a police detective came to the house saying he died during the night."

Mercedes squinted at Minoa.

"How do you know he was a real detective?"

"Why wouldn't he be real?"

"Don't be stupid. Brent has the resources to fake his death. You see him become ill, or pretend to be ill. Then some man comes and tells you he died. Meanwhile Brent has a plastic surgeon remodel some poor *mequetrefe's* face and then has him killed and puts the corpse in his place."

"Why ... why would Brent do that?"

Valeria slapped a hand over her heart and squeezed out, "Brent killed people?"

"The man is capable of anything. Don't underestimate him. He found a way out of paying child support and now that he stole custody of my daughter, he's faked his death and he'll escape to Switzerland or Argentina or Dubai or some island in Polynesia. I'm sure it was always his plan to steal Leah and disappear. *Gracias a Dios* you saved her."

She crossed herself.

"Look, Mercedes, I'm pretty sure that was a real detective and Brent really died. We brought Leah to you partly because Valeria needed to get out of there. Just don't tell anyone we were here, okay?"

Mercedes glanced at Valeria.

"Was she his latest girlfriend?"

Valeria backed up a step and Minoa positioned herself to protect.

"She was Leah's nanny."

"Does she know about the others?"

"The others?"

From behind Minoa heard Valeria's suctioned breath as she watched Mercedes peer around her shoulder to launch a sneer at Valeria.

"Don't think you're getting a dime out of Brent's will. Leah is his heir."

Minoa took another step sideways to block her view of Valeria.

"Please leave Valeria out of this. She was Brent's employee, that's all. She had nothing to do with what happened."

Mercedes huffed and glanced back at Leah, standing in the doorway staring at them.

"Alright. You did the right thing bringing Leah here. She didn't see him die or pretend to die, did she?"

"She didn't see a thing. She doesn't know what happened."

"The *Virgencita* saved us. I thought she had forgotten me, so far from home, so long away. I couldn't believe she let Brent win that evil custody case. But now he's gone and since people think he's dead, he can never come back."

"He's dead. Honestly. We saw him loaded into an ambulance. One of his specialty liquors was poisonous."

"Like his soul. A fitting end, if it killed him. At least he'll be declared dead and Leah will inherit her rightful fortune. Unless he moved all his money offshore. Oh my god! What if it's all in Panama under shell companies?"

Leah was waving at Valeria. Valeria waved back. Mercedes turned around and started walking back to where Leah waited.

"Valeria took great care of Leah. You won't mention we were here, right?"

She glanced back without pausing.

"What? Oh, *gracias*. I'm going to call my lawyer."

She ripped the 'Estate Sale' sign off the door, took Leah by the hand and disappeared inside. Minoa and Valeria climbed back into the truck.

"She seems a little crazy," Minoa said, turning to look at Valeria, who stared straight ahead.

"She doesn't like me."

"Look, she's consumed with hatred. Or maybe she knows something about Brent we don't. Anyway, it's not our problem. Leah is with her mother and you can stay out of sight at your friend's house until the police figure out Brent died of an accidental poisoning."

"Are you sure it was a good idea to avoid the police? Eldon will probably tell them I was the nanny."

"He doesn't know who you are or where to find you. This is the best of your alternatives."

"I sure hope this doesn't mess up my immigration case."

"We're making sure it doesn't."

Minoa headed toward the highway that circled around town to the rural area on the south side where Valeria's friend lived.

NINE

She reread Ron's text: Mounds suspicious. APD investigating. Job on hold.

She launched a few curses out the window of the guesthouse into the sunshine thumping Brent's house and property as if nobody had just died there. Then rifled about on her door-on-cement-blocks desk. She found Eldon's card on a pile of unread mail.

Texted: Hey Eldon, Just wondered if rent can be a bit late given all the hubbub?

She glanced out the window toward the prairie dog town. No little heads popped up, so she couldn't play her pastime amusement of trying to predict out of which hole a little jack-in-the-box sentry would emerge next. Sickening to think they all might be dead now. Maybe Brent would run into them in the hereafter.

The answer popped up on her screen: Meet me at Plaza de Toros for a late lunch? I'll explain then.

She pondered what he might want to explain while staring blankly out the window. Something moved out there. She squinted. A doughy fellow in baggy clothes, corn silk hair sticking out of a baseball cap, was scuffing around near the prairie dog town. He reached down and picked up a rock. Couldn't be a crime scene investigator, could it? Maybe some retired neighbor with dementia? She grabbed her cell and headed out.

"Do you have business here?" she called out as she approached.

He looked up. Plastic-rimmed glasses rested on puffy cheeks.

"Just collecting my property. No need to worry."

"Your property? This is Brent Harrison's land."

He dropped the rock he was holding into a bag.

"I was carrying out a surveillance job here. It's over so I'm collecting my equipment."

"What are you talking about? You just put a rock in that bag."

"Rock camera."

"Are you with the police?"

"No. I used to work for the PD's office years ago. Now I'm independent."

"I don't understand."

"I'm a PI. I gather evidence for divorce cases, child support, custody, harassment. Occasional criminal work."

"So were you surveilling Brent for the custody case or for the protection order?"

He drew a zipper across his mouth, then continued shuffling along, gaze trained down. She watched as he puttered around the perimeter of Brent's house putting more 'rocks' into his bag. Suddenly he fell to the ground. She ran over.

"Are you alright?"

"Goddamned rodents."

He pushed his bulk up to a sitting position as he extricated his foot from a prairie dog hole, leaving the shoe stuck toe down. She pulled the loafer out, then remembering the poison shook it out before handing it to him. As she turned it right side up a dime glinted silver within the slot on the instep.

"Careful, these burrows are full of poison."

"I'll be okay."

He slid the loafer onto a bare foot and struggled to his feet. Limped back along the front of the house heading toward the property entrance. She watched him for a moment and then ran to catch up.

"Did you find out anything damning?"

"About Harrison? That's confidential. Irrelevant now though."

He hobbled down the drive and climbed into an aging Volvo wagon parked outside the gate.

She watched him drive away, wondering who hired a PI to watch Brent. What would those rock cameras have captured anyway? Seemed like a waste of money. Still, she scanned every rock she passed on her way back to her house, wondering if he missed one of his cameras.

TEN

She paused on a carpeted step waiting for her eyes to adjust. The light level at the Plaza de Toros Restaurant was a moonless night, wait staff floating around like wraiths. Out of the darkness appeared an arm moving back and forth, pale hand on top waving. She tiptoed over and slid into a circular booth. The arm waved again and Eldon ordered Mexican beer and green chile potato skins for them both.

"I don't drink beer before, let's say, eight pm."

She situated herself at the opposite end of the booth.

"It's just to quash the chile burn. This dish reminds me of home. When you're from the South everything has to be greasy or sugary or both, like chocolate-covered bacon."

"I'm not hungry."

"No problem. I'm just being sociable. Why don't you tell me about your Margaret Mead expeditions?"

"Margaret Mead went to the South Pacific. I went to South America."

"Even more exciting. Did you ride around on lamas or shoot monkeys with blow darts?"

"I'm not accurate with a blowgun and adults don't ride lamas."

A waiter deposited two mugs of beer on the table. Eldon took a sip.

"You're Indiana Jones and I'm a boring civil attorney. But I assure you I can be compelling in an abstract sense."

Under the light of a red-shaded lamp, his pale face glowed pink.

"The law is fascinating, I'm sure. Not to ask for free legal advice, but the Albuquerque police seized my phone for no good reason. Do you have any idea how I could get it back?"

"Sounds like a minor example of civil asset forfeiture. Did they believe the phone was used in the commission of a crime?"

"The only crime was their abuse of protesters that I filmed."

"Even more reason for their touchiness. Many police employ a liberal interpretation of the practice. Judges can rule it a violation of the fourth amendment right to freedom from unreasonable searches and seizures, but they rarely do. It makes billions for police and local government and does nothing to fight crime. Still, I doubt you'll see that phone again."

"I figured it was hopeless so I replaced it, but the only thing I could afford was this antique." She pulled out a phone and shook it; the screen flickered. "Could you let me know when I have to move out?"

"Move out? What's your hurry?"

"I assume Brent's estate will be sold?"

"In this market that could take years. Meanwhile, I need a presence on the property. Why don't you keep an eye on things in exchange for your rent?"

"You mean pay nothing?"

"Your rent is far less than a millisecond market fluctuation in Brent's investments. It's insignificant—not that you're insignificant. No, ma'am, you're highly significant."

She took a sip of beer and squinted at the other patrons. Boxy shapes milled around in the dim light, lawyers and politicians in blazers.

"Did you know Brent was under surveillance?"

He sat up straight, set both palms on the table.

"By the feds?"

"I spotted a guy picking up surveillance cameras from the estate."

He relaxed back with a smile.

"Oh that. Mercedes had Brent watched to try to defeat his custody bid. It didn't work, obviously."

"But what did she hope to catch him doing?"

"As Brent's legal counsel I'm not in a position to comment."

The waiter served two plates of toasted potato skins topped with melted cheese and diced green chile. Minoa took a sip of beer.

"*Bon appetit*," he said, picking up a gooey potato half.

"Did you represent Brent in the custody case?"

He chewed, suppressing a choke. Pounded on his chest with a fist.

"Whoa, that burns a trail of fire down the esophagus. The custody case? A *tour de force* if I do say so myself, and an unexpected venture into family law. Surprisingly, I had a knack for it. But I will never see my bonus for winning that one. It was a gentleman's agreement and Brent had the effrontery to die before he paid me."

"Why did you help Brent take custody away from Mercedes?"

"An attorney is a hired gun, as they say here in the West. Besides, the boss man offered a sizable reward."

"So you consider it ethical to take a child away from her mother simply because the father is angry at her?"

"What's legal and what's ethical are distant cousins. Or perhaps my moral fiber has frayed due to spending the prime of my life helping rich people avoid paying taxes."

"Did that include underpaying child support?"

Eldon squinted at her as he patted his mouth with a napkin.

"You've been talking to Mercedes."

"What about Crystal? Why did she hate Brent?"

"Similar complaints, minus the child, but delivered with more hysteria and less ruthlessness."

"Are you accusing Brent's ex's of overreaction?"

"Not at all. I only meant to distinguish the two of them. Unlike the impetuous Crystal, Mercedes is a formidable adversary. She should have gone into law."

"Do you know why Brent and Mercedes ended up hating each other?"

"The breakup occurred before my appearance on the scene. Brent found strong-willed women irresistible until they came within his sphere of influence, at which point he demanded compliance. One can hardly imagine Mercedes bending to his will."

"Ever since I moved onto the estate, he's been cursing her like ... like some poor woman accused of witchcraft and scheduled for burning at the stake."

"She was one of the few people in his sphere who stood up to him. Ergo, from Brent's point of view she deserved punishment."

"Did you stand up to him?"

"No comment. My firmness or my subservience in my dealings with Brent is covered by attorney-client privilege."

"Do you think the police are investigating his death just because so many people hated him?"

"People? Or ex-girlfriends?"

"No idea. But it's obvious that scorpion mezcal was poisonous. So why are police calling it murder?"

"As a civil attorney I'm not qualified to speculate on the way the Santa Fe Police Department applies the criminal code. Between you and me, all those varmint tinctures looked capable of causing group hemorrhaging. That's why I hid behind your extremely aesthetic backside."

"Don't be crude."

"A southern gentleman is never crude. Why don't we talk about something more interesting? Tell me about yourself, your idyllic childhood growing up in the 'city different.'"

"I don't see the relevance."

"It would be if you agree to see Solarized with me this evening."

"It's Solaris, not Solarized."

"Well, what about it?"

"Uh..."

Her phone buzzed.

"Hello?"

She listened, took the phone away from her ear and stared at it.

"Are you alright?"

He held his fork in mid-air, a strip of potato skin dangling down. She put the phone on speaker and propped it against a salt shaker. Her hand shook so hard she knocked both over and struggled to prop up the phone again.

"Wha-what did you say?"

The voice crashed along like a stretch of rapids on a river.

"They arrested me, Minoa. The police put me in jail. What should I do? Please help me."

Minoa looked at Eldon, her mouth moving though no sound came out. She looked back at the phone.

"Who is that?"

His voice sounded far away. She kept staring at the cell phone.

"Minoa, I'm sorry. I didn't know what to do. I thought they wanted help with their investigation. But then they accused me of murdering Brent. I don't understand. I don't know what to do." A cascade of sobs.

Minoa blinked over and over, trying to clear her mind, trying to think, failing. Her mind felt calcified. Far below, the cavern of her torso loomed empty, heartbeat faint. Felt herself shrinking down to nothing, falling. Grabbed a rockhold at the last minute. Took control of her mouth. Spoke in a monotone.

"Tell them you want a lawyer and don't say anything else." She glanced at Eldon. "I'll get a lawyer down there quick."

His fair brows arched.

"Is that Brent's nanny?"

"It's my friend, Valeria. She needs a lawyer right away."

"I'm an expert in tax and business law. The only time I've seen the inside of a criminal courtroom is on cop and robber shows."

"She has no money to hire a lawyer."

"They'll give her a public defender but it will take a few days."

Little hiccuped sobs popped out of the phone speaker. Eldon watched Minoa staring at the phone screen. Then he stabbed the potato skin down onto the plate and twisted the fork back and forth.

"Okay, okay. I can tell her not to say anything as well as anybody."

She turned to look at him as if waking.

"How could this happen? I don't understand."

"There are several possible explanations. They're under pressure to make an arrest and an immigrant is less likely to sue later for false arrest. Or they found circumstantial evidence connecting your friend to the contaminated liquor. Or did she perchance poison her employer?"

"Of course not. This is ridiculous."

"There's a reason they portray Lady Justice as blind."

"Let's go."

ELEVEN

As each sliding metal door slid open, the preceding door clanked shut. Minoa and Eldon walked down halls of linoleum and cement blocks until an officer in a glass enclosed cubicle waved them to a tiny room with a table and three plastic chairs. They sat down and waited, not speaking a word. She bit her lip over and over hoping to draw blood, but before she tasted anything Valeria scuffed in wearing a faded orange jumpsuit and slip-on sneakers. Minoa leaped up and threw her arms around her. Valeria remained as limp and flat-eyed as a dead fish. She crumpled into a chair.

"How are you holding up?"

She shook her head, gaze flicking to Eldon. He gave a curt professional nod.

"Eldon got me in as his paralegal. They'll assign you a public defender soon. Then you can request bond."

"Don't get her hopes up," Eldon whispered out the side of his mouth. Out loud he said, "The public defenders in this town are unusually good, almost as good as private counsel."

Minoa flashed him a frown.

"Eldon said he stopped you from signing anything. That's good."

Valeria's eyes flooded.

"But they must have recorded everything. They said they were on my side. I thought I was just helping their investigation. I got so confused. Oh Minoa, I don't even know for sure what I said."

"Valeria, take a few deep breaths and then go through it step by step, telling us everything you remember."

"They came to my friend's house and said they needed information about Brent's death. I told them I didn't know anything, that I had been in the rec room behind the house all evening. They said they needed to take my statement. I repeated that I hadn't seen anything. But they stood there with guns on their belts telling me I had to go with them so I went."

Minoa flashed a question mark at Eldon.

"Investigative detention, I suppose," he said. "Did you ask if they were detaining you?"

"What good would that have done? They had guns. I know this is America and people supposedly have rights here, but where I come from when armed men come to your door, there's no point in asking questions."

"What happened next?"

"They drove me to a police station and took me to a room with no windows. They gave me coffee and one officer was kind to me and I thought they just wanted help with the investigation. So I told them everything I could remember, how Brent had been out, that deliveries came to the house all afternoon and the caterers brought food. I helped Dolores in the kitchen and then I set out food containers and liquor bottles on tables. And Brent asked me to translate for the workers in the yard. And that red-haired woman came into the kitchen before the party started and gave some orders."

"There's nothing incriminating in that."

"But this other officer said they knew I had poisoned him, that they had fingerprints and witnesses. Minoa, I couldn't believe it. They accused me of putting poison in one of Brent's liquor bottles. Why would I do that? I don't have any poison. I wouldn't hurt anyone."

She dropped her head onto folded arms on the table as muffled sobs rippled through her body. Minoa shot an inquiring look at Eldon.

"Why do the police think someone put poison into that scorpion mezcal? Maybe it was just toxic. I mean, when you dump poisonous insects into a drink for human consumption there must be risks."

He shrugged. After a moment Valeria sat up wiping her eyes.

"The first officer acted like he was on my side. He said there was probably a good reason why I was angry at Brent, that if I told them then everyone would understand and things would go easy for me."

Minoa turned to Eldon. "They were trying to coerce a confession. Is that legal?"

"Unfortunately it is. You didn't admit to killing Brent, did you?"

"No. But it went on so long and I was terrified and confused and I thought if I showed I was trying to help, it would be obvious I'm not guilty. And I thought if they understood how difficult my situation was ... Oh Minoa, will I be sent to the penitentiary? Or will they execute me?"

The lower lids of her swollen eyes trembled. Minoa looked at Eldon.

"This is ridiculous. They can't make a murder accusation out of a few fingerprints on a bottle. Besides, she had every motivation to keep Brent alive to assure continuation of her immigration bond."

"Their case is weak, but then people have sat on death row for years before DNA evidence exonerated them."

Valeria's eyes stretched wider. Minoa glared at him, then turned to Valeria with a forced smile.

"Did you notice anyone else handling the alcohol?"

"I don't think so, but I was trying to keep Leah occupied with coloring books and toys while I worked. I didn't pay attention to anything else."

"How about the housekeeper?"

"Maybe those hired waiters did."

"Sure they did. The case against you is ludicrous. This is just for a little while, Valie. Stay strong. The confusion will be cleared up soon. Do you want me to contact your brother?"

"Remember? His number isn't working."

"I could go to his workplace."

"If he's still there."

"What's it called?"

"C & A Body Shop on South Second Street in Albuquerque."

"I'll find him."

"I'll never see him again," she sniffled, "and that's best for him."

Minoa stood up, walked around the table and wrapped her arms around her.

"Valeria, please fight this depression. You're not going to be in here long. They made a mistake, that's all."

Valeria looked up at her. Her splayed gaze turned diamond point.

"What if they didn't make a mistake?"

"What are you talking about? You didn't poison Brent. You just have an impulsive friend who got you a short-term job at his house at the worst possible moment. And then stupidly encouraged you to hide out."

Minoa slapped herself on the forehead.

"Transient global amnesia, Minoa. I could have deliberately poisoned Brent and forgotten about it."

Minoa flashed Eldon a look.

"She's a psychology major."

He nodded. Valeria clamped her mouth shut and looked down at the table. Minoa returned to her chair, grabbed Valeria's hands over the table, squeezed hard.

"Is there anything else you remember about your time at Brent's?"

"Every day I took Leah to school and picked her up after. In between I did chores around the house. Crystal and Brent would have dinner with Leah and then leave. I put her to bed and ... that's all. Even if they let me out of jail, *la migra* will pick me up when I get out, won't they?"

"I ... I don't know. I'm going to talk to an immigration lawyer to find out. Meanwhile, we keep working to get you out of here fast. Do you know the housekeeper's name and how to contact her?"

"It's Dolores. Brent thought her last name was Sanchez, but that was a fake name. He paid her in cash. She's illegal."

Minoa nailed Eldon with a look. "Brent, the multimillionaire, hiring undocumented people to avoid paying social security on his domestic employees?"

"He didn't follow my advice on everything."

"She mentioned Cabeza de Cabra Condos." Valeria fixed her eyes on Minoa. "I have to ask a favor."

"What is it?"

"Could you go into Brent's house and get something out of the computer room on the second floor?"

"What do you need?"

"It's a stack of printed sheets with information and forms for applying for refugee status in Canada. I was going to help Berto apply since it's become so dangerous here. I filled out the forms with his full name and address and birth date and everything. I don't want the police to find it."

"Okay, I have your keys. I'll manage it and I'll try to find him. Just keep the faith, okay?"

"I'll try."

As Minoa and Eldon waited for the sliding metal door to open, after Valeria had been led away in handcuffs, he bumped her with an elbow.

"With that guilty look they may conclude I'm trying to smuggle out a detainee."

"If it weren't for me she wouldn't be in this situation."

"The ways of our judicial system are impossible for mere mortals to fathom."

"Regardless, she's getting out of this even if I have to arrange a jailbreak."

"I didn't hear that."

Outside the visitors' entrance, they headed to their cars.

"You may require some anonymous pro bono legal advice if you're planning a prison escape?" he called out.

"Sorry, I've got things to do."

TWELVE

Driving up Highway 14 from the county detention center, the sinking sun glinted off razor-wire encircling the New Mexico State Penitentiary. Minoa fixed her eyes on the centerline and kept them there until she hit Cerrillos Road. She started scanning for the sign for Cabeza de Cabra Condos. At Camino Carlos Rey she turned into the complex.

A group of middle school boys inspected her as she parked. She flashed them a school administrator frown and headed for a sign that said 'Office' propped over a door in the middle of a *cafe con leche* stucco facade. The building was the first of a series of two-story apartment blocks striping the property. When she opened the office door a teenage girl on platform heels barged out pushing a stroller. The girl drew a few catcalls from the boys. Inside, behind a desk heaped with papers, cigarette packs, styrofoam cups, sat a woman with bulbous body parts—eyelids, double chins, ear lobes, forearms all looked like some maniac had attacked her with an air blowgun. Minoa explained she was hoping to hire a woman who had worked for a friend, but only had her first name. The woman behind the desk said they could not give out information about tenants.

"This will be a great economic opportunity. I'm sure Dolores would be grateful for your help making contact."

She feigned a patrician tone. The woman stuck a cigarette between peppermint lips and puffed, maintaining eye contact. Minoa shrugged and walked out.

Back outside she asked the tough boys if they knew a woman named Dolores. They knew a couple: one had an aunt in Durango named Dolores, another said his dad's girlfriend had that name although she preferred Dolly. She thanked them and headed back toward the car. On the way she noticed a steel door open on the side of the main building and peered inside. It was the laundry room. On one wall she spied a bulletin board. Fishing a piece of paper out of the trash she wrote a note on it and tacked it up.

Exiting the laundry room she noticed the boys had moved closer. As she walked to the parking area, one yelled that he had thought of another Dolores. He shouted out an obscene phrase in Spanish connecting *dolores,* or pains, to the damage an enormous member could cause. The other boys doubled over laughing. Accelerating her pace, she glanced over her shoulder to keep an eye on them. At the truck she jumped in and gunned it out of the parking lot.

***

After parking in front of the guesthouse, she stepped out into a bubble sealed under a blown glass sky. From the hushed grounds of Brent's estate up to the piñon-dotted foothills nudging the mountains, not a soul moved. Yellow crime scene tape dangled loose from one side of Brent's front door.

She grabbed Valeria's keys from the stool inside her door, scanning for a security key or code as she walked over to the big house and let herself in, locking the door behind her. At a keypad in a wall box she typed in the code printed on a card on the keyring and paused listening. Had anyone even turned on the security system after Brent died and Valeria fled? Glasses and cocktail napkins littered surfaces in the living areas as if the partygoers had dropped everything and run for their lives. Beside the long table still carrying a few liquor bottles, blood flaked off the floor tiles. In the kitchen dishes and utensils cluttered the counter.

Upstairs she continued down a hallway, peeking into each open paneled door. She found a bedroom with the T-shirt and sweatpants she had loaned Valeria on a chair. She scooped them up. Drawers were pulled out, hangers scattered across the floor. Valeria had few possessions at Brent's house. They couldn't have found anything suspicious here. Across the hall she saw a room with several desktop computers and a printer on a table. Beside the printer she spotted a stack of document trays. In one she found some printouts describing the process for requesting refugee status in Canada with a filled-out application. She folded the papers and tucked them into her pocket.

Farther down the hall she spied Brent's room, neat as only a maid could manage. She stepped in, pausing under the kryptonite stare of a silver-haired gentleman in a full-length portrait. His portly form in a gray three-piece suit and bow tie overlay a faint image of a bull. The face recalled Brent's even countenance and fleshy nose. On another wall a huge picture window framed the Sangre De Cristos, teal-blue sisters girded by a belt of gold and tipped by snow.

She stepped around the room peering at the bed backed by a massive mahogany slab, a walk-in closet packed with suits and shirts and trousers and ties. A huge TV screen hung on one wall, a digital photo album atop a dresser flashed photos every few seconds: Leah running after a soccer ball, Leah in pink ski suit on tiny skis, Brent with his arm around his mom prim in a Jacque-Kennedy-style suit, Brent and Crystal on the peak of some mountain, arms around each other, smiling. In an open top drawer she spotted a container of gold jeweled cufflinks and tie clips. Beside it a pair of plastic handcuffs.

The next room contained a huge desk positioned before the same mountain view. She told herself not to go in, that it was probably unethical and certainly against police procedures to prowl through the office of a dead man, murdered man in their opinion. But curiosity won out. She walked around the desk scanning documents scattered across the glass top. There were spreadsheets, reports and countless sheets topped with the word 'analysis': Technical Analysis, Market Data Analysis, Trend Analysis, Comparative Analysis. A couple of books served as paperweights: *How to Lie with Numbers, Capital Returns Through Regional Investing.*

On a corner of the desk she noticed a stack of bound reports. On top sat the *Gavilan Mesa Development Master Plan*. She picked it up. It weighed several pounds. Why did he have the Gavilan Mesa development plan? He must have been planning to invest in the project. How was he sure the Albuquerque City Council would approve it, or did he have insider information?

Below it sat the *Peabody Mesa Annual Report*. Peabody Mesa rang a bell. Lewis, her Hopi friend–no, better to call him an acquaintance, had told her about a dispute the Hopi had with Peabody over a Black Mesa coal mine that drained huge amounts of water out of the aquifer the Hopi depended on for drinking water. She heard Carter's voice screaming inside her head: a man who slaughters prairie dogs wouldn't care about investing in a mine that destroys people's water source. Or stealing water rights from traditional users to construct a massive desert housing project that steals water from traditional users, Carter would add.

She set the report aside revealing the next bound volume on the stack, a Mictlan Energy Company prospectus: *Hydraulic Fracturing in the Greater Chaco Region*. Mictlan Energy; she'd never heard of that enterprise but fracking near Chaco Canyon sounded like a bad idea. She dropped the booklets back onto the stack to stifle Carter's internalized yells and moved to another corner of the desk.

On top of this pile sat a bound document entitled *IMF Staff Country Reports: Mexico: Detailed Assessment of International Money Laundering Strategies Employed by Criminal Organizations*. Money laundering strategies? A palms-width of article print-outs sat below. She spread them out and scanned a few headlines: *Bank of China replaces HSBC as Cartel Money Laundering Haven*, *Sinaloa Cartel Uses Restaurants and Retail to Launder Cash*, *Cash Smuggling Over Southwestern Border Subject of Regional Law Enforcement Effort*.

Not that she knew one damn thing about managing large amounts of money, but was research into money laundering considered due diligence? She snapped a couple photos, then returned everything to its original place. Retraced her steps, relocking the front door.

Back at the guesthouse she brewed a cup of double-strength mate and sat down at her desk. Flipped through Valeria's refugee application for Berto. How was she going to tell him that his sister was in jail again, this time on a murder charge? Glanced at the photos she'd snapped. Why Brent's interest in methods Mexican cartels use to clean up their dirty money? Carter would say that dirty money flowed throughout the economy and supported banks like BBCC. Maybe it even tainted Brent Harrison's investment empire.

Her phone pinged. A text from Carter.

Get ur haunches down 2 Angelo's tonite. SB there for u to meet.

Carter and Ireni didn't yet know Valeria was in jail, she remembered, much less that Minoa had helped her flee police contact, which hadn't worked out too well. Might even have made police suspect her more. Might even have gotten her arrested.

Her head sank, her fists knotted. Felt a flush of guilt and desperation rush from her belly to the top of her head. Another of her bad decisions but now somebody else was paying for it. She grabbed her phone, typed with spider fingers. Texted Ireni with the news. Hesitated. She'd tell Carter when she saw her at the bar. And she'd fix it, she'd damn well fix it.

THIRTEEN

Minoa snagged Carter's shirttail as her friend took off without a word, beer in hand, worming her way into a packed crowd in Angelo's Bar.

"Carter, wait. We need to talk."

With over-amped anarcho-punk throbbing, she didn't seem to hear. Uranium Death March was the name of the band Minoa recalled from a handwritten poster outside the front door. Scribbled below was the infamous 'No Credit Cards,' local dialect for tourists not honored here.

Minoa tripped over floorboards worn into troughs, jerking Carter's shirt so hard both of them lost their footing and slipped sideways, prevented from falling to the floor by squeezed bodies.

"Minoa, what the hell?"

They groped back to standing, grabbing the clothing of a few people who squirmed around to frown.

"Valeria's in jail."

Carter's face congealed in shock. She leaned close. After a moment's interchange at two inches, inaudible at two feet, she turned around shaking her head and continued snaking her way through. They pushed past a vintage wooden bar backed by black-and-white photos of the bar's WWII era namesake, continued to a back room, past the bathrooms, down a sort of tunnel into another soundscape, this one swinging to norteño-inflected rock.

Still in a choo-choo train they oozed around the dance floor to a table near the back wall. Carter dropped into a chair, Minoa did the same. Across the table sat a woman with mounds of curly burgundy hair, enormous pink starburst sunglasses and black lipstick. Carter yelled over the music.

"They arrested our friend, Valeria, for Harrison's murder."

The blackened lips stretched longways.

"No way! Why are they trying to pin this on her?"

"They figure it's easy to scapegoat a disempowered undocumented immigrant. Make people think immigration is the problem, not capitalists controlling our resources."

Carter slammed a fist into the table, then turned to Minoa.

"What's the basis for the allegation?"

"They found her fingerprints on the poisoned bottle. It's ridiculous."

The other woman leaned way back in her chair, then rocked forward landing her elbows on the table.

"I wonder how this will affect the whole scam."

"Scam? What scam?"

Carter gestured to the other woman.

"Matahari writes a stack called 'The Inside Dirt' about New Mexico politics. She found out Harrison was planning to purchase the Gavilan Mesa tract from those BBCC toads at Big Sky Holding Company."

"BBCC toads? Big Sky?"

"Big Sky Holding is the local face of BBCC so people here don't realize a British bank owns a huge chunk of New Mexico land. That's the message we've been publicizing, that an international bank is behind the Gavilan development. Once they grab water rights and sell a bunch of energy-wasting ticky-tacky houses, they'll disappear with the profits and leave us with an environmental wasteland, right Matahari?

The other woman shrugged..

"Maybe. I mean, Big Sky is orchestrating the plan to turn Gavilan Mesa into a suburban mini-city. But my source says Harrison and a silent partner were in negotiations to purchase the entire property through a shell company called High Desert Capital. It's possible High Desert would go ahead with the development project. Why else would they spend so much money on a piece of open desert? But now that Harrison is dead, that deal could fall through. I even wonder if a competing bidder had Harrison whacked."

"Who says he was whacked?" Carter gestured with her beer bottle. "The dude drank contaminated liquor. It's simple."

"Nothing is simple at Gavilan."

Minoa looked back and forth at Carter and the other woman, screwing up her face in disbelief.

"I've spent days walking around Gavilan Mesa. There's no water out there. In fact, there's not much of anything except some over-grazed scrubland. Why is it such a big deal?"

Matahari took off her sunglasses and squinted at Minoa.

"Are you kidding? We're talking 158,000 acres of prime land on the westside of Albuquerque. A historic stolen land grant. A casualty of the 2008 crash. And what investors are salivating over as Albuquerque's biggest real estate development in history."

"Land grant? 2008? Please explain."

Minoa leaned forward over the table to hear through booming music. Matahari's tensed lids glittered with sparkly eyeshadow.

"After the Pueblo Revolt of 1690 and the Spanish reconquest, Diego de Vargas, governor of New Spain, gave a huge land grant west of what is now Albuquerque to a group of settlers. The grant survived the US takeover after the Mexican-American war and was owned collectively till the 1960's. Then heirs of the original land grant families incorporated under a company that would supposedly represent their interests and make them money off the land."

"And the company went under in 2008?"

"No. Before that the managing company engineered the sale of the entire tract at a questionable price. Maybe they were bribed. Who knows? Anyway, opponents of the sale objected so they made a deal to pacify them. The buyers promised to make annual donations into a scholarship fund for the heirs' kids. But when 2008 rolled around the buyers defaulted on their loan. BBCC repossessed and the scholarship fund went poof. A British bank—"

"—known for money laundering and banking sex traffickers!" Carter cut in.

"Right. That bank was left holding a big empty space in the middle of a distant desert."

Minoa flashed both palms in a 'why not' gesture.

"So a British bank ended up with a tract of land that was originally stolen by Mexicans from the Indians. Wouldn't it be better if New Mexican interests buy it?"

"Harrison and his partner weren't buying the land as a public service. They planned to make millions, either off a multimillion dollar housing development or some other scam."

Carter waved a hand.

"Nobody needs all that extra housing. And even if it was needed, sprawl is the worst way to add capacity. A carbon nightmare."

"It's a water nightmare too. The city is offering the developers huge water allotments and the Paseo de la Pradera, that highway-to-nowhere, in exchange for a promise of jobs. But there won't be any new jobs."

"Why not?"

"BBCC doesn't want to administer a massive land development project in New Mexico. They just want to unload Gavilan

Mesa without taking a loss. All the concessions, like the water allocation and road, make the land more attractive so it commands a better price. That way BBCC doesn't end up in the red when they sell. They might even come out of this with a pretty profit on their books. And the new buyer will have no incentive to honor agreements made by the previous owner."

"The city could force them to."

"Fat chance," said Carter.

"I don't think they'll end up building anything." Matahari shrugged her shoulders. "Albuquerque is losing population. The real estate market is soft. That's what I can't figure out: why would they even want to buy Gavilan Mesa?"

"Isn't she brilliant?" gushed Carter. "No one else is reporting all this."

"You think this secret purchase of Gavilan might have something to do with Harrison's death?" Minoa said. "Maybe the land grant heirs were so furious over the sale of the land that they poisoned him."

"That makes no sense. They lost control when the land was first sold. Another sale now wouldn't change that."

"Then maybe environmental opponents of the Gavilan development decided that killing Brent was the best way to halt the project."

"Now you're accusing the Save Gavilan Mesa group of regicide?"

Carter's brown eyes bugged out.

"I don't mean your group in particular. But the police have arrested Valeria for his murder. She had no motive. The murder, if it was murder, stopped the Gavilan sale. So an opponent to the deal, a fierce opponent, would have a motive, right?"

"I suppose, unless the silent partner will go through with the purchase anyway."

Carter leaned in.

"That lawyer of Brent's who's after your hide, you could pump him to get the identity of the silent partner."

Minoa flashed her a frown.

"I don't need to pump Eldon, as you put it. The silent partner is Findley Malbore."

"Are you sure?"

"Reasonably. Brent mentioned he and Findley were working on a deal."

"How well do you know that guy?"

"Not at all. He moves in elite circles."

Matahari dropped a fist to the table.

"I'll investigate the dude."

She stood, walked onto the dance floor and began swinging her arms up and down as if climbing a sizzling dynamite fuse.

"What's she planning to do?"

"Matahari loves undercover investigations. And she's a dope hacker. She'll come up with something awesome."

"Does she always dress like that?"

"She's into disguises. And by the way, her real name is Nellie."

"Nellie?"

"Nellie Martinez. Her stack is super radical. She's part of our new activist group."

"You formed a new group because everyone from the old group is in jail?"

"Very funny. We all committed to bring in at least one new member."

"Don't tell me."

"This is your chance to do something significant with your life, Minoa."

"I have crippling claustrophobia whenever steel bars are involved."

"Okay, okay. The movement has room for cowards. You can inform from the inside."

"Inside of what?"

"The Brent Harrison financial empire."

"It's about to become the Leah Harrison Trust Fund."

"Well, you can get cozy with Eldon and collect info on Malbore's dealings. I saw Eldon talking to that dude at the party. Maybe he's going to be legal counsel for Malbore. You'll find a way, Min baby. Don't let those over-educated smarts go to waste."

Carter shook a finger at Minoa's head. Minoa pushed it away.

"I may be a confused aged-out Bohemian, but I don't usually fake interest in men to steal financial secrets."

"The struggle comes before sentimental attachments."

"Does the struggle require spying and dishonesty?"

"It requires a total commitment."

"First priority is springing Valeria from the Santa Fe County Detention Center."

"Like you said, somebody else had a motive for killing Brent. We just have to follow the money and we'll figure out who. You know, do the work for the police since they're too dirty to bother."

"Carter, not all police are bad."

"Tell that to Fred Hampton. C'mon, get those old bones moving."

Carter leaped onto the dance floor and started vigorous elbow and knee movements. After a few more sips of beer, Minoa joined in.

FOURTEEN

They stepped out of Angelo's into a freeze-dried after-midnight. Walking through wedges of blue shadow cut by chinks of light from establishments still open, Carter weaved a bit. When they got to their cars, Minoa insisted on driving her home.

"Let's head south," said Carter after they started. "There's something I want to show you."

"This late?"

"Don't tell me you're getting too old for nightlife?"

"You know what to say to manipulate me."

Carter directed her onto the highway south toward Albuquerque, then dozed. Within a cavern whittled out of darkness by headlights, the highway's dotted white line pulsed. Carter's breaths puffed rhythmically, her wild filly nature temporarily stilled. Though miles sped by, nothing seemed to move until the illuminated cave dissolved in the lights of Albuquerque.

Carter lifted her head as Minoa approached the cloverleaf at the intersection with I-40 and told her to head west.

"This better be worth it," Minoa grumbled.

But when they passed Coors Boulevard, the Coca-Cola plant and the giant RV lot outside the city line, Minoa balked.

"Carter, what the hell?"

"Trust me."

She guided Minoa to turn onto the graveled road that led to Gavilan Mesa. They pulled up beside the highway construction equipment. Carter stepped out. Minoa rolled down the window.

"Carter, get back in right now."

Carter raised her arms to the sky.

"Minoa, Minoa, Minoa. When are you going to stop playing it safe and start standing up for something?"

She stumbled toward the equipment, pulling a wrench out of her shoulder bag. Leaving the truck and headlights on Minoa hurried after.

"Carter!"

When she caught up, Carter was unscrewing a giant nut from the arm of a road grader.

"Carter, this is crazy. They're giving long prison sentences to monkey wrenchers these days."

"So what are you going to do, Minoa? Just give in while the planet burns and the capitalists rape what's left of functioning ecosystems? Or do you figure you'll anthropology your escape from New Mexico and go study some culture far away where you can stay uninvolved and unaffected until climate change produces mass extinctions?"

Minoa picked up the giant nut from the ground and started screwing it back on with her hands.

"You're drunk. I'm tempted to drive off and leave you here until you sober up."

"I will have taken apart the whole place by then, Minoa. Don't you feel compelled to save me from myself?"

"Don't count on it."

Minoa glanced in the direction of the truck and froze. A pair of headlights had turned off the interstate frontage road heading up the gravel entry road.

"Get in the truck quick! Somebody's coming!"

"Maybe one of the gang is coming to help."

"Now. It could be police. How are we going to explain being out here after midnight?"

Carter zigzagged toward the truck.

"You work here. Tell them that's why we're here."

"At this hour? C'mon."

Minoa hurried Carter onto the passenger-side of the seat, then climbed in, cut the headlights and peeled out heading up the road toward the Gavilan gate.

"Do you think they can see us?"

"But this is private land. Why would they come out here after midnight?"

Without answering, she sped blind along the road she had taken every morning and evening for days, relying on muscle memory. Where the road jogged left she skidded out of the turn, then spun wheels trailing a barbed-wire fence. Looking back she saw the car speeding up the road toward them. Worse, a searchlight on the roof of the car flipped on, sweeping across the desert.

"*Puchica madre.*"

"Is there a back way out?"

"Not unless this truck can fly and swim."

"What could they charge us with? They didn't see anything."

"They'll think of something."

She pushed the truck faster, squinting left to discern lines of barbed wire strung from thin metal posts. Light flashed in the rearview mirror as the patrol car turned the corner starting up the same track they were following. With headlights, the police car traveled faster. There was no way out now, she thought, imagining Ron's face when he found out she had been arrested in the middle of the night on the border of the Gavilan tract, and she had to face him one last time in that office looking out on a desert as empty as her subsequent life would be. That would signify the end of her last chance, minor as it was, to use the precious degree she'd labored at for more than a decade.

"Can't you drive any faster?"

Minoa clamped her mouth, slammed the accelerator to the rusting floorboard, scanning darkness for the spur that led to the Gavilan gate. She perceived a break in the fence and fishtailed in. Raced down a few hundred yards, hit the brake pedal, sliding across pebbly dirt to a stop. She threw open the door, jumped out and ran to the metal stock gate. Down at the end of the entry road, the patrol car, searchlight rotating above, barreled past. By pure luck the searchlight didn't spin her way to catch the break in the fence or rake across the truck. She squatted by the padlock on the gate, fingers quaking, spinning the dial, muttering "*Hijo de la gran* ...," hands so palsied she couldn't set the dial to numbers she couldn't see. At that moment the patrol car, now a blurred point of light farther up the boundary fence, stopped, turned around, started back.

The lock fell open. Sprinting back to the truck she jumped in, drove through, closed the gate, relocked the padlock. Then cut left instead of following the track. The truck bucked up a slope topped, as she recalled, by rock ledges. The cops had turned the corner onto the Gavilan spur road and approached fast.

"Stop where you are and throw out all weapons," roared the loudspeaker.

She sped blindly up the slope not caring if she was heading toward an abyss. The cops stopped at the gate just as the truck tipped over rocks at the crest. Twenty yards down the back side of the hill she cut the engine, leaped out and ran back up the hill, crouching so her head just peeked over the top. Below, dust swirled in a trembling light bubble around the patrol car. She watched a figure move in and out of the light. Heard voices blunt-edged like mallets.

"Padlock is locked. What the hell are we supposed to do?"

The other voice faded in and out. "... -vate property. Maybe... owner... risk my... and... hotshot... a complaint..."

A car door slammed shut. Then quiet, except for a muffled rumbling that might have been the patrol car's engine or it might have been blood pumping past her eardrums. Finally the car turned around crunching gravel and trundled back down the road. She squatted on the hilltop watching the taillights bump across blackness until pinpricks merged into the glow of the distant interstate. Stood up.

Walking down the hill to the truck she spied a broken span in the barbed wire fence. Moving closer she saw the wires had been cut in the middle and rolled back. She'd never noticed it before. Had cattle rustlers done this when the land grant was still used for grazing? Or did people now use Gavilan Mesa as an unofficial dump? What difference did it make? The place would soon be surveyed and marked into lots, trenched for sewer and electricity and checkered with identical framed units on lawns of Kentucky bluegrass. No matter what Carter said or did. When she got back to the truck Carter's head was tipped back, mouth wide open, long breaths fluttering in and out. Minoa gunned the truck down the hill and picked her way back to the interstate.

FIFTEEN

“... first-degree murder, a capital felony punishable by up to life imprisonment without parole.”

Valeria’s head swung around to scan the gallery. Her pageboy hung in clumps, her cheery smile fractured. Reporters outnumbered spectators in the courtroom. Looked like the local news media viewed the alleged murder of a multimillionaire by his undocumented nanny as prime headline fodder.

Catching Minoa’s eyes Valeria injected a transfusion of terror and agony into her soul before a deputy forced her to turn back to the judge. The public defender sat beside her, bald head as shiny as the polished wood defense table. At the other table sat two District Attorneys, combined ages about the same as Valeria’s lawyer. The judge, a fierce-faced suburban dad, did the arraignment without glancing at the paperwork.

Valeria threw one more visual SOS to Minoa before being led out a door in the back of the courtroom. Minoa staggered into the hallway, collapsed against the wainscotting, choking on emotion. Footsteps across the marble floor roused her.

The PD was walking down the hall. She staggered over and stepped in front of him.

"Look." She put up a hand like a stop sign. "I'm Valeria's friend and I want to know what's going on with her case."

"I can only reveal case information to blood relations or spouse."

"Assuming she has any of those, they're too terrified to come forward so you're going to have to speak to me."

His eyelids puffed. He handed her a card.

"You can call my office to make an appointment."

He continued walking, scuffed Oxfords slapping the floor. She took a few long steps, positioned herself in front of him again. They both stared. He motioned at a door.

"Alright, we can talk in there."

Once inside the client conference room he shut the door, folded into a chair, squinted at her from the far side of a bony sternum.

"What is it you'd like to know?"

She glanced at his card.

"Here's the first thing I'd like to know, Mr. Biegler: does she have a choice as to which Public Defender she gets?"

He leaned back his head, bald but for a ring of steely survivors, and roared, revealing a mouthful of browning teeth. By the time the head came back down the expression was clamped tight and calculating, the defense attorney poised to begin arguments before an unpredictable jury.

"Listen Ms.?"

"Diamond."

"Ms. Diamond, I've defended hundreds of people accused of homicide and, given the fact that the majority were indubitably guilty, my record is incomparable. Do you remember the scissors murder a few years ago? I defended the guy and, between you and me, it was pretty clear he ran into the house of an old woman who screamed at him for urinating in her yard and stabbed her seventy-one times with a pair of sewing scissors. He was a homeless vet, crazy sonofabitch, but I got him a six-year sentence on a reduced manslaughter charge by introducing graphic testimony by a recognized PTSD expert on the experiences of service members in Iraq. Guy runs a non-profit advocating for vets with war-induced mental health issues. Luckily he testified for free as we wouldn't have been able to pay his fee. The guy will be out in four-and-a-half. I may be able to get a similar deal for your friend."

"Deal?" She smothered a scream. "She doesn't need a deal. She's innocent!"

He gave her a world-weary look.

"Maybe she is. Nevertheless she's facing a first-degree murder charge."

"But how can they possibly think she did it? She just started working for him as a nanny. It makes no sense."

"The discovery process is revving up but here's what we know so far. That bottle of scorpion mezcal that killed her investor boss was saturated with rat poison and had her fingerprints all over it."

"Rat poison?"

"Opened sack of that rat-killer was found in the garage and is now in state's evidence, along with a pair of her panties."

"Her panties?"

"Yes, her panties that are being analyzed for residues of her boss' semen. She mentioned a sexual encounter to the cops. But don't get your hopes up they're going to write this off as one of those abuse victim self-defense cases. The DA sees 'unwanted sex' as an excellent motive for premeditated murder. And everybody knows poison is a woman's murder weapon of choice."

She tried to breathe and failed. A fog of panic engulfed her senses as her toe seemed to touch a void at the edge of a promontory.

"It's bad, but maybe not as bad as it looks. The DA will make a decent offer because your friend is an attractive young woman and juries hesitate to give harsh sentences to cute females, unless they kill their kids. The feminists will be all over the case once it's revealed there was a rape. In any case, the rape narrative serves us and the perpetrator is not around to contest our version. If necessary we can put her on the stand to testify about the brutality and obscenity of Harrison's assault on her."

"Even if he raped her that doesn't mean she poisoned him. Brent Harrison was a rich and powerful man who must have had enemies. If they look into his affairs, they'll find loads of possible suspects."

"Any suggestions?"

"Well, he was contemplating the purchase of a large tract of land that many people don't want developed."

Biegler's Marx Brothers eyebrows twitched as if he was suppressing a chuckle.

"So some historic preservation aficionado found out and sent him poisoned liquor?"

"He invested all over New Mexico. What about Peabody Energy? A lot of people in the four corners region hate them."

The eyebrows arched higher. Minoa raced on.

"Or some company called Mictlan. They're fracking near Chaco Canyon. I bet New Mexicans are outraged."

"Postulating environmentalist assassins will not help your friend. If you find anything more concrete, let me know."

He stood. Minoa struggled to speak.

"Wait. Valeria has immigration problems. She's out on bail after being detained by ICE."

"Most people south of Airport Road have similar problems."

"So even if she gets released, she may be deported."

"She'd probably rather be sent home on a jetliner than sit around here in jail. Maybe I can use that in the negotiation process."

He picked up his briefcase.

"I think something terrible happened to her in El Salvador. That's why she fled."

"Are you suggesting mental impairment?"

"Maybe PTSD?"

"If that can be substantiated, keep in mind the deal I got in the scissors murder case."

He walked to the door. She gathered herself, shot up out of her chair.

"Stop talking about negotiations and mitigating factors. She didn't do it and you have to get her off."

A touch of sympathy mellowed his wizened stare.

"I'm simply trying to convey to you, Ms. Desmond, that while the maximum sentence for first-degree murder is life without parole, I can try to bargain it down to manslaughter which carries a six-year max. That's a little less frightening, isn't it?"

"It's Diamond, Mr. Bugler. Why don't you focus on defending her innocence instead of selling her out from the get-go? I'll be in touch, you can count on that."

She swirled past him, jerked open the door of the conference room and hurtled down the hall and stairs. Outside, confronting the razor-edged sunshine, she squeezed her eyes shut to ward off a burning sensation as if acid were squeezing out of her tear ducts. Within the spinning hurricane of emotion she felt herself slipping down down down into a dark hole. What was already terrible had just gotten worse. Rape as Valeria's motive to murder Brent? For a millisecond she wondered if it could be true, if Valeria had felt so enraged by Brent's assault yet gagged by her circumstances that she filtered poison into his booze as an act of revenge. Maybe she'd only wanted to make him sick. Maybe. Stop, she screamed at her thoughts. Valeria didn't poison Brent. She mustn't let this ridiculous allegation undermine her faith in her friend. She wavered there for a moment as the sounds of traffic and everyday busyness filtered in, calming her mind, then took a few steps toward the parking garage and paused.

SIXTEEN

In front of the courthouse, Brent's mom sat on a bench beside a woman with strawberry hair who dwarfed her. Mrs. Harrison sat stiffly, hands stacked atop a box purse, staring straight ahead. Minoa walked over.

"I'm very sorry for your loss, Mrs. Harrison. I was there when your son became ill."

Mrs. Harrison frowned at her.

"You don't remember me? I'm Minoa. I was Brent's tenant."

"Of course. How do you do?" She fixed a blank look on the street, repositioning the purse on her lap.

"Are you waiting for a cab?"

She threw Minoa a furious grimace.

"I can't even pay for a taxi to go home after they charged my only son's killer. Until the distribution of the estate I'm utterly fundless."

She returned to squinting into the distance, tensing crow's feet. The other woman gave Minoa a hostile look.

"We're waiting for the seniors' van."

"I can drive you home. It's no problem at all."

Mrs. Harrison lifted her chin, sniffled.

"That will be fine."

"Just give me a minute to go get the truck."

"Truck?"

"It's rustic but it will do the job."

"Oh."

She made it sound like a question. A few minutes later Minoa pulled into the drop-off lane in front of the courthouse. The sight of Minoa's vintage blue truck with the painted yellow wheel rims made Mrs. Harrison gasp. But the other woman stood and Mrs. Harrison followed suit. Then the large woman wrapped an arm under her seat and another around her back, picked her up and carried her over to plop her onto the seat. She slid in after, maneuvering Mrs. Harrison sideways with hip pushes to make room on the seat for all three of them.

As they traveled to a south side address, Brent's mother stared straight ahead, petunia-splashed cheeks jiggling with road vibrations. They pulled up in front of a modest stucco crammed in behind the rodeo grounds.

"You will join me for a cup of coffee?"

"Sure."

Inside, Minoa sat across from Mrs. Harrison at a dining table while the other woman banged pots in the kitchen. When she came out carrying two cups, porcelain glazed with Orioles flitting among branches, she set Minoa's cup down so hard coffee sloshed into the saucer. She was a large woman with large arms and large features. Her nose was round like a ball at the tip with freckles across the bridge. She flopped into another chair and scrolled through her phone under the table.

"Although I was a tenant on Brent's estate, I got to know him a bit. You must have been proud of him."

Mrs. Harrison spasmed, smoothed her embossed blouse, then peered at Minoa from under half-lowered lids.

"He was always a good boy. But he made terrible decisions about women. They took advantage of his generosity."

"Are you referring to his ex-wife?"

"All of them. Mercedes is a drug-trafficker's harlot. That Crystal is a common thief. And now that Mexican woman that he took under his roof has murdered him. Why was he so kind to people who didn't deserve it?"

"The police have made a mistake. And she's not Mexican."

"I always figured Mercedes would try something. She's a maniac."

"Had she threatened to kill Brent in the past?"

"She threatened all kinds of things. She was a gold digger, a fortune hunter with no scruples. She expected him to provide her with the lifestyle of some El Chapo hussy. I warned Brent before he married her, but he stopped taking my advice years ago."

Mrs. Harrison huffed and sipped.

"Do you think Brent had enemies in the financial or business community?"

"Any man who's successful makes enemies. A baker's dozen of Wall Street traders would have loved to slit his father's throat, but Gerald was too smart for them. Poor Brent never matched his father's genius."

Minoa took a sip of coffee and glanced at the other woman, who stared back.

"Do you know of any other people who would benefit from his death?"

"Brent had friends among the influential set in this frontier outpost. All I can say is that I hope he had the wits to structure his will to keep that cartel temptress from taking control."

"Was Leah his only heir?"

Mrs. Harrison glared at her.

"I'm his mother and Brent was dutiful about family obligations. I'm sure the majority will go to me. I'll take care of little Leah and prevent her mother from stealing the fortune."

The other woman made a clicking noise that Mrs. Harrison seemed not to hear.

"So no one else profits from his tragic death?"

"That slimy lawyer will extort more than his due."

"Eldon Bohnefeld? You don't trust him?"

Brent's mother aimed her pond blue eyes at Minoa, matte within papery skin and mascara-tipped gray lashes. They must have been sapphire when she was young.

"My dear, we're from New York City. We know flimflammers and finaglers of every stripe. That lawyer is no innocent provincial solicitor." She set down her cup. "More coffee please, Caitlin."

Caitlin scowled but pushed to standing and fetched a coffee pot from the kitchen.

"It's kind of you to help Brent's mother, Miss?"

Caitlin cocked a sandy eyebrow at her.

"My name is not Miss."

"Miss Romero has worked for me since soon after I moved to Santa Fe."

Mrs. Harrison stretched her lips into a brief fake smile.

"Great. When did you move to Santa Fe?"

"Brent convinced me to sell my Park Avenue apartment not long after Gerald died and move out to this ... this desert. In retrospect a mistake. Unless you're interested in bidding on cowboy paintings, there is absolutely nothing to do here."

"Will you stay here or return to New York?"

"Apart from my duties as a grandmother there's little to hold me here. I think I'll travel. Caitlin must apply for a passport."

Minoa glanced at Caitlin.

"Where to?"

"Europe, of course."

Caitlin held her gaze while Mrs. Harrison continued.

"The rest of the world is so ... unstable."

Minoa expressed her condolences again and escaped to the truck. After turning a corner she paused, thinking over Mrs.

Harrison's comments. Brent's mom hated everyone in Brent's world. She even seemed to have a low opinion of her son. The only person she appeared to trust was her helper, Caitlin Romero.

Grabbing her phone she started a search to check Caitlin's criminal record. A bit of clicking led her to three Caitlin Romeros with case files. She picked the one in her early thirties with a Santa Fe address and read her history.

If this was Nurse Romero, she had a few petty larceny convictions along with one credit card fraud, but that was pretty standard for a state where a quarter of the population lived below poverty and received food stamps. Then there was an embezzlement charge resolved with restitution and community service, suggesting she'd stolen money from a kind-hearted employer who agreed to a rehabilitative plea deal that allowed her to pay back the money, do some community service and avoid jail.

The big one was a charge for armed robbery a couple years ago, dropped to simple assault in the plea with only probation as a sentence. She must have cooperated with the DA's office and testified against co-defendants to get that sweet of a deal. Or did it go further than that? Did she agree to serve as a confidential informant to avoid jail time? And would that suggest the authorities were investigating Brent?

No, placing an informant in his mother's house didn't sound like an efficient way to spy on Brent. More likely Caitlin Romero was someone with a rough past keeping her eyes open for the next opportunity. Had this local woman with a Home Health Aide certificate reached the point where she would poison her employer's son to access a fortune she might have a shot at embezzling?

Despite boasting of big city smarts, Brent's mother seemed unaware of her employee's record. She was even contemplating taking her along on the Grand Tour of Europe like the penniless companion of some dowager duchess from an E. M. Forster novel. Might she have chosen Caitlin Romero precisely because of her criminal record so she could help with the more distasteful parts of offing her son? Mrs. Harrison presented as an entitled snob but surely she wouldn't murder her own son. Still, it was puzzling how, after the death of a husband who was a successful Wall St. trader, she ended up impoverished in Santa Fe while her son lived like a sultan.

Minoa threw the truck into gear. Neither Mrs. Harrison nor her nurse made likely murderers. If Brent was murdered, no one had a better motive than Mercedes. Brent had deprived her of custody and she could have poisoned him for the inheritance money that would go to her daughter. When the PI's surveillance recordings hadn't defeated Brent's custody bid, she'd resorted to drastic measures. That theory made more sense than Brent's mom hiring a female ex-con to poison her son. She'd talk to that PI to find out what he did and didn't learn about Brent. But first there were some unpleasant errands to run for Valeria.

SEVENTEEN

Razor wire glittered atop the yard fence. A few car hulks remained inside the body shop yard, a yellow bug with a smashed roof, a twisted Silverado on cement blocks, a couple others bashed and battered. Minoa walked over to the office and peered through the dusty glass of the front door. A placard hanging behind the glass said *C & A Body Shop; Cuentas claras, Amistades largas*. On the back wall a calendar hung askew. The desktop at the back of the office showed a checkerboard pattern formed by dust drifting around vanished stacks of papers. In front some chairs lined the wall, upholstered in colorful vinyl with fuzzy white padding peeking out of cracks.

This was the body shop where Valeria said her brother, Berto, worked. Valeria had dropped by one day to visit just before ICE agents pulled up to conduct a raid. Terrible luck. They arrested her but her brother escaped. He probably felt almost as guilty as Minoa did after she wafted Valeria away from a crime scene, setting her up to face a murder charge. Neither Berto nor Minoa had meant for Valeria to be arrested. Made no difference. Fate cared not one bit what you meant to do.

No sign of life and no information about a reopening. A woman at Berto's former address had said they'd rented his room to somebody else. How could she track down a Salvadoran young man who didn't want to be found?

She started walking around the perimeter of the yard. It was one of those brittle autumn days, vacuumed air swept by thinning sunlight. She paced down the side of the cyclone fence, turned the back corner. Along the backside of the lot ran an irrigation ditch, lapping as it headed south past sporadic buildings.

Her feet dragged. She slipped down and sat on the bank of the ditch, staring at the braiding flow. She would have to tell Valeria that her brother had disappeared. One more blow on top of the others. Ever since ICE arrested Valeria she'd been trying to help her. How did things go so wrong?

She stood and continued walking. Turning the far corner of the fence she spied someone hunched over in a garden behind a small adobe a little farther down the ditch. She headed over. An older gentleman with white hair and a walnut complexion looked up from his work. He held a spike in one hand. A garden hose ran beside his feet.

"Plenty of water in the ditch," she called out as she approached.

"*El repartimiento* is low." The old man smiled back. "I'm going to try drip irrigation, the high-tech kind."

He gestured at fuzzy holes punched in the hose.

"Are you worried about this Gavilan Mesa development using too much water?"

"Señorita, if the cistern is already low and you pull out more water, will the water that is left flow more slowly?"

"I guess so."

"And run dry before everyone has drunk their fill?"

"Probably."

He stared off toward the West Mesa.

"It's going to come to open warfare with the gringo capitalists. Just like the Mexican American War. I only wish I was young enough to fight."

"You heard about the ICE raid at the body shop?"

"I saw the ICE cars pull up. *Lástima.* We all carry the same blood."

He shook his head.

"Did you hear if ICE arrested everyone at the shop?"

"Oh, no, the only ones they picked up were customers. The *compadres* escaped out the back. They were ready for those *hijos de puta*."

"Do you have any idea how to reach the workers or if they are coming back? One of them is family to a friend of mine."

"I don't know them but I doubt they'll risk coming back, now that ICE found this place."

"Do you know of any other body shops around here? I need to find my friend's brother. She's in trouble."

He squinted at the auto body yard and then looked back.

"You could check some building materials stores where people look for day work."

"*Gracias. Muy amable.*"

She waved and walked back to the truck. Two home improvement supply stores showed up on a map of Albuquerque's valley and west side neighborhoods. Reassuring herself that two was her max, she headed out to the first, a huge chain store just over the Rio Grande. She arrived a moment too late. As she drove into the parking lot, she spied a police car on the far side, two officers staring into the desert beyond the asphalt where several men were scattering at a run. She squinted at the backs of the three runners shrinking in the distance. No way to know if Berto was among them.

At the second store, a local enterprise set among warehouses on the edge of Los Poblanos neighborhood, a small crowd approached the truck calling out 'I have tools' and 'work cheap.' No one responded to Berto's name but they tried to make helpful suggestions. One older gentleman with a silvering beard waited until she had said '*gracias, muy amable*' many times and the others had backed off. When he approached, he spoke perfect English.

"The easiest jobs to get are at car washes and tire stores. You could try those."

"That's a good idea. Thank you."

Though she knew it was hopeless, she found some addresses on her phone and started driving around. Berto must have fled to another state or another part of New Mexico, but continuing to search for him postponed that moment when she would have to tell Valeria her brother had disappeared. She tried four car washes, chatting with people as they wiped down dashboards and bumpers. Then on to tire shops. At a place on Barelas Road she found an older Berto with a silver tooth who said he did side jobs as a mechanic and guaranteed he could make her truck run better than it ever had. At Aztlan Tires a young Wiliberto looked terrified that a gringa was asking for him by name.

She turned up south Broadway and spied *Llantas El Tigre*. The fellow at the desk called out Berto's name. When he didn't respond, he told her she could look for him in the back. She walked out the back door into aisles of metal racks of used tires set on the bare dirt. After a moment's wandering, she spotted a young man with cinematic looks: a wave of hair tumbled over one brow, a dimple in the center of his chin softened a rectangular jaw.

"Are you Berto, Valeria's brother?"

He squinted, nervous, and gave a tiny nod.

"Who are you?"

"I'm Minoa. You called me when Valeria was detained in southern New Mexico, remember?"

"Oh, Minoa. Were you able to go to her hearing? Did she get out on bail? Is she free?" He dropped his eyes for a moment, kicked at the dirt. Then met her gaze again. "Of course I'll pay you back for any money you spent."

She waved her palm back and forth like a fan.

“That’s no problem.” Pause. “She was freed on bail and went to Santa Fe but ... there’s another situation.”

He scrutinized her eyes for clues.

“Is she hurt? Did something happen?”

She shook her head hard.

“It’s ... she’s in jail again.”

“Again? After she paid her bond? How can they do that?”

He rolled back onto his heels and slammed the toes of his shoes down onto the soil.

“She’s in a real jail now.”

His eyes widened, then squeezed like he was going to cry.

“What did ... why?”

“She was working at my landlord’s house when he was poisoned.”

“What?”

“The police charged her.”

“Charged her with what?”

“Murder.”

“*Ay dios mío.*”

He turned his face into the tires, started slipping down.

“It’s a weak case, Berto. They’ll never be able to prove it. But having police contact violates the conditions of her ICE bond, so they may detain her when she’s released.”

He punched his fist into the tires, which barely moved. Punched harder. Minoa noticed she wasn’t breathing and whistled in a filament of sandy air. When he turned around, holding his fist, his eyes blazed.

"Why do they blame her? Tell me what happened."

"Her boss drank contaminated liquor. She was working as his nanny but she touched the liquor bottle while helping in the kitchen. The authorities will figure out soon that Valeria had nothing to do with it. Plus, she's a victim."

"Victim?"

"She told police there was a sexual assault. They're trying to say that provided a motive to murder her boss which is ridiculous."

"Sexual assault? That bastard raped her?"

"Listen, Berto, I got her into this situation and I'm going to get her out."

He punched the tires with both fists, then spun around.

"Why wasn't I there to pick her up when she got out of the immigration jail? We could have escaped together."

"She's trying to protect you. She doesn't want you to have contact with ICE."

"I don't want her to protect me!" His yell drove Minoa back into the tires racked behind her. He froze at her startled expression, dropped his head, slumped over. "She can't protect me anymore. Please make her stop. Please."

His voice trailed off. Minoa swallowed.

"Berto, I thought, we all thought the nanny job was a great option. How could we know?"

His face squeezed in, slashing his broad cheeks with deep lines.

"She needs a lawyer."

"She has one. But the court process is slow. Listen, I'm going to do my best to turn up some information that will speed up this stupid legal process."

"I want to see her."

"Valeria's afraid ...."

"I've got to see her."

"Give me your new cell number and I'll give it to her. I'm so sorry about all this."

He gave her his number and then stared into the black tires as if the cut glass sky and lemony sun didn't exist. She held out the paperwork on immigration to Canada, rustled the papers to make him look.

"She sent this information for you."

He accepted the papers with one hand; the other tugged on his ear. When he dropped the hand, she noticed part of the earlobe was missing. He turned his back to her, walked down the aisle between tire racks, lurching as if drunk.

"I'll be in touch," she called out, watching him turn a corner and disappear.

She headed through the building. Out front she climbed into the truck and sat there waiting for her mind to calm. Instead, a spasm of horror traveled up her gullet and jolted her forward as if to retch. She banged her head on the steering wheel, then froze there. After a moment she levered her head up, stared weakly. Would police have arrested Valeria if she hadn't left Brent's house? Why had it seemed like a brilliant idea to help her flee police contact? Because escape was Minoa's specialty. She'd fled

New Mexico to go to college in the big city, then zoomed off to Ecuador to try out new cultures and new identities. Then back to New York thinking she could recreate herself as an eastern academic. That turned out to be a joke provoking yet another escape back to Santa Fe. Which left her in the here and now scraping up gig labor, late on her rent, drinking alone. And after all that she counseled Valeria to bet her freedom on the failed tactic of escape.

She took some long raspy breaths, then gave herself a figurative kick. Self-pity wasn't going to fix anything. Her mind stayed blank for a few minutes until an idea popped into it. She'd do a good deed. That would restore her confidence.

EIGHTEEN

A bit of phone searching revealed that the principal lobbyist for Big Sky Holding, the BBCC toads, as Carter put it, promoting development of Gavilan Mesa, was Terra Fuentes Trujillo. Minoa recalled that moment at Brent's party when Terra walked into the room all legs and arms angling out from that corn husk shift, her fine hair splayed over the neckline, sipping champagne like she hadn't just strolled out of one of Brent's spare bedrooms. And her husband, city council member Barney Trujillo, accepting Brent's taunt, tasting the scorpion mezcal no one else would touch. Was the exchange between Brent and Barney a macho duel over the woman they both sought to possess? Or was he establishing an alibi for later so people would think Barney Trujillo couldn't have poisoned that mezcal because he drank some himself? Terra's office was in Zia Tower, a fancy office building downtown, so she headed up Broadway to Lomas and parked on one of the shabby residential streets north of downtown. Then she walked to the plaza by the Convention Center and located the building nearby.

Terra's frosted glass office on the sixth floor breathed high overhead. Minoa walked in surveying walls plastered with cheerful artist's renderings of a future Gavilan Mesa mini-city with happy New Mexicans crowding streets lined by mock adobe retail strips. On a table beside a semi-circular couch sat a stack of brochures. She scooped one up, skimmed the illustrations. Looked up to see Terra enter the room.

"How utopian! When will condo units be available for purchase?"

"We haven't broken ground yet. But city approval is just around the corner. I can take your name for our mailing list if you like."

She sat at a small desk, opened a laptop.

"You're sure the project will go through? I hate disappointments."

"I'm positive."

"I saw on the news that people protested at the city council meeting and out at the site. You don't think they'll stop the development?"

"When people realize what an economic boon Gavilan Mesa will be for Albuquerque, the protests will quiet down."

Minoa set her phone beside the brochures, arranged herself on the couch, smiled at Terra.

"Then why are you arranging to sell the land?"

"Wh-what are you talking about?"

"Brent Harrison. Dead now. Supposedly poisoned. Negotiating to purchase Gavilan Mesa. A curious sequence of events."

"That's absurd." Terra straightened some papers on her desk. "Where did you hear that Mr. Harrison had any interest in Gavilan Mesa?"

"I saw it on the internet. Some blogger said a deal was in the works to sell the whole tract to him."

"People write all kinds of lies on the internet."

Terra batted eyelashes as straight as bristles.

"You would know the inside scoop. You were close to Harrison, very close."

Terra straightened, reared back her head.

"What are you talking about?"

"Brent's house, night of the party where he was poisoned. Just before the police arrived with the protection order. I saw you two together."

She shot to her feet, pointed a trembling index finger at Minoa.

"You're crazy."

"Did you wonder if Barney suspected the affair? And if he knows, think he would take revenge on Harrison for screwing his wife?"

"Get out of here."

"The blog said Harrison had a partner. Findley Malbore. Another rich dude. Is he still going to buy Gavilan?"

Terra picked up her phone and started punching, glaring at Minoa.

"I'm calling security."

"Just confirm if you're going ahead with the deal to sell Gavilan to Malbore. Then I'll leave and Barney won't hear a thing from me."

"Barney hear what?" She dangled the phone in midair. "How dare you? Don't threaten me."

"Okay, I'll get in touch with him. And the police will be interested to find out that a guest at the party had reason to hate Harrison. Seduction of an adored wife makes a strong motive for murder."

Terra started sliding around the office wall toward the entry, eyes nailed to Minoa, arms shaking.

"You're insane ..."

"Just confirm if the sale of Gavilan Mesa is still in process and this allegation will stay informal, at least for now."

Terra froze between steps with her mouth in a perfectly round 'O'. The ends of her hair stood out as if super-charged. Minoa stood, walked to the door, pulled it open.

"Stop."

She paused.

"If all you want to know is whether a purchase agreement is under negotiation with Mr. Malbore, I can say off the record that it is. Is that enough for you?"

"For the moment."

Minoa headed out leaving Terra staring with eyes wide. Turning a corner in the hall, she paused and began counting in whispers.

"*Uno, dos, tres...*"

After a minute she went back to the office, pulled open the glass door. Tara was holding a phone to her ear. Her expression went haywire.

"I forgot my phone."

"You!"

Minoa scooped her cell off the table by the couch as Terra choked on a chunk of sound chopped off from a scream. Minoa smiled and waved.

Once she was back in the truck, she clicked on Voice Memos and played the recording. After a sputtered series of curses and the sound of some object hitting a hard surface, Terra started a phone conversation.

"Hello, Mr. Malbore, I mean Findley? It appears there's been a leak about the Gavilan Mesa purchase ... Yes, some blogger ... Of course, I agree completely. The sooner the better ... Later this afternoon works."

Minoa messaged the recording to Carter with a comment: Confirmation of Gavilan sale by Terra Fuentes Trujillo. You owe me one.

Terra seemed sure her city-council-member husband didn't know of her affair with Brent. But there had been an ugly undertone to their conversation at the party when Trujillo tasted the scorpion mezcal. Could be relevant.

NINETEEN

Back on Santa Fe's south side she turned off Airport Road by Mercado El Campesino, passed a Western wear shop and bumped over the end of asphalt onto dirt. Where a scattering of structures dwindled to sagebrush-speckled empty lots, she spotted a house with a walled courtyard topped by a drizzle of broken glass Juarez-style. A handwritten sign hung from the gate: '*Abogada*' with an arrow to the left.

Passing through a gate around the side of the house, she came to a door with a plaque on it: Roxanne Armijo, Esquire. She pulled the cord on a bell hanging from a viga. A middle-aged woman in a broom skirt and concho belt, plump shoulders weighted by a squash blossom necklace with turquoise nuggets the size of ping-pong balls, let her in. They walked between dangling red chile ristras into a home office.

"You have a friend who needs an immigration lawyer?"

"It's complicated." Minoa slid into a Mexican loveseat with leather upholstery, launching into a summary of Valeria's situation.

"Her arrest constitutes a violation of the conditions of her release on bond, so she'll be picked up by ICE when and if she's freed."

"But when the judge finds out it was all a mistake?"

"No judge is going to look kindly on her involvement in a murder investigation, no matter the result."

"So she'll be jailed and punished even though she's innocent of this absurd charge?"

"Correct."

"What if ICE doesn't find out about the murder charge? Santa Fe is a sanctuary city, right?"

"As a sanctuary city Santa Fe has determined that local officials are not required to inform ICE about the detention status of an individual. But federal law says local governments can't prohibit officials from informing the feds."

"So it's up to the jail employees? Maybe if we pick up Valeria from jail the minute she's cleared for release?"

"If jail workers are anti-immigrant they may call ICE to alert them."

"There must be a way to save her from deportation. What if she marries a citizen while in jail?"

"USCIS has become cannier about marriages for the purpose of legalization. If a citizen requests residency for his or her undocumented spouse, the spouse is required to return to the home country. But once they leave this country after a year or more of living here illegally, they're subject to a ten-year bar on reentry."

"Valeria has almost finished her psychology degree at UNM. And I think she's scared to go back."

"My sympathies. However, the security situation in El Salvador has improved since they jailed gang members."

"Can you help her or not? And how much would it cost?"

"There are no guarantees but I could try. Although if she is tried for murder, all bets are off. I require a five thousand dollar retainer to take the case."

Minoa stood.

"You can divide it into three payments," said Ms. Romero, noting Minoa's expression.

"I'll get back to you."

She pocketed a card on her way out.

TWENTY

Driving downtown Minoa spotted the Gypsy Cafe partway down Montezuma Avenue. She cut a hard left, parked and walked over. Bought a coffee, then sipped while scanning walls plastered with over-colored posters of tourist destinations, waiting for the caffeine to kick in. A few people in rumpled polos and khakis hunched over pricey computers, probably New York City or Silicon Valley refugees researching the freedom lifestyle or the Sotheby's website or their broker's latest recommendations.

She sat herself down and told her mind to focus. Biegler had mentioned rat poison. Maybe she could find the name of the substance that killed Brent. She checked the website of the state medical examiner and found out she could order a copy of Brent's autopsy report for a small fee. Filled out the form and paid.

If the scorpion mezcal was contaminated during production, there would have to be more deaths or illnesses caused by the same liquor. Was that brand of mezcal sold mostly in Mexico? She ran some searches in Spanish and discovered that alcohol contamination in Mexico was a hot topic. Scores of Mexicans had died from drinking obscure brands of tequila. The *Consejo Regulador de Tequila* responded with raids. Of 18,700 gallons of confiscated tequila they found 235 gallons contained methanol, meaning windshield wiper fluid. No mention of rat poison.

Searching in English she found a few deaths of US tourists that received stateside coverage. One gringa vacationing in Playa del Carmen had died after downing five shots of tequila at a resort bar. A few other cases of tourists dying after consuming tequila popped up but none mentioned mezcal or rat poison.

So she scanned articles in the business press on mezcal production. Found a handful of financial analyses evaluating tequila and mezcal companies as investments. They rated stocks in this sector a buy. One described a Wall Street analyst's trip to Oaxaca to look for emerging investment vehicles. He termed the traditional fermentation process 'rustic and ripe for a margin-boosting upgrade.' *Mezcaleros* combined agave fibers, nectar and water in vats and used their nose and inserted sticks to test the fibrous muck for days while microbial yeast converted plant sugars to alcohol. Water was added along the way, whether from the tap or a well or the river. Looked like there were plenty of opportunities to contaminate the product. The analyst recommended automation and greater reliance on agrochemicals.

She pulled up the webpage for the only maker of scorpion mezcal she could find. The CEO appeared in a photo, a gringo with thinning long hair dressed in a Panama hat and a *guayabera*, smiling like someone was holding a gun to his head. A blurb boasted that this one-man startup provided jobs for local maguey technicians while serving the refined tastes of globe-trotting businessmen. No record of any legal suits against this guy or suggestions his product was tainted.

Product contamination had to be the cause of Brent's death. But Biegler named rat poison, not methanol, making the reports of deaths in Mexico traced to contaminated agave liquors useless. How could she prove Valeria hadn't funneled rat poison into a bottle of mezcal with her fingerprints all over it? She rooted around in her caffeinated brain for ideas. What came up was an image of that geeky PI with the sockless loafers. If he'd learned something surveilling Brent's property, maybe she could convince him to share it. He hadn't been too friendly when she saw him at Brent's house but she could give it a shot. Sucking down the dregs of her *au lait*, she stuffed the phone in her pocket and headed out, wishing the Santa Fe imports a whispered *buena suerte*.

TWENTY-ONE

She drove past a strip mall housing a food bank, hardware store, second-hand furniture shop and money transfer office to a tiny storefront at the end of the row. A sign in the window said Peewee's Confidential Investigations - Catch Cheaters Today! Pushing open the door she walked into a room fuzzy with desert dust. Vinyl upholstered chairs circled a wood veneer desk dotted with coffee cup rings and hunting magazines.

"Be right out. Make yourself at home," called out a girlish tenor.

Minoa perched on the edge of a chair and peered at photos of elk and mountain lion carcasses on the magazine covers. After a moment a blubber-faced man with an enormous physique stepped around the partition at the back and sat down with a 'humph' and a desperate creak in a tiny swivel office chair.

"Hey there. You in the market for investigative services? Got a divorce or custody case and want to nail that bastard to the wall? This is the best way to do it, guaranteed."

"I'm looking for a private investigator." She paused, trying to recall the appearance of the fellow she'd encountered at Brent's estate. "He's stocky, fair-haired, glasses. Said he does custody, divorce and child support cases. Do you happen to know who he might be?"

"Investigating an investigator? That's a twist. I can find the guy for you, $150 down and $65 an hour. Make it $55 for ladies."

"That's alright. I'll keep asking around."

"How about a one day flat rate of $100? No expenses, no add-ons. Results guaranteed by dinnertime."

"No, thanks."

She backed out as he pushed to his feet waving some brochure. Back in the truck, she checked the next name on a search for Santa Fe PI's and headed toward the historic section.

Kennedy Hanover, licensed private investigator, had an office in a tiny aged adobe crammed among other dollhouses just off Agua Fria near 285. She bounced across a rutted dirt lot, stepped out and knocked on a door painted the traditional sky blue. Heard a deep voice call out 'come in.'

Hanover turned out to be a middle-aged black guy in a rose shirt and silk tie. He sat erect behind a glossy antique desk.

"Good afternoon. What can I do for you?"

His voice flexed with hints of the Charles River. Minoa gave her description of the PI she'd seen at Brent's house. Hanover pondered.

"You must be talking about Derek Whitfield. He works mostly with legal firms. His office is near the taxi company." He grabbed a piece of notepaper, jotted something and handed it to her. "It's on All Trades Road. A green modular. Sign in the window."

She thanked him and turned to leave.

"Derek does excellent domestic surveillance. If you need other types of investigative services, I can give you a quote."

"Thanks. I just want to talk to Derek."

She found Derek Whitfield's office on a back street between auto repair shops and a tortilla factory. It was a metal prefab building with corrugated walls painted mold green, flecked gray where the paint had chipped. The door on the side of the building stood open. She peeked inside.

"Hello?"

The interior looked like an enraged husband had gone berserk. Papers, photos, manilla folders, document storage trays, coffee filters, plastic cups, even a few bullets lay strewn across the floor. A coat rack leaned sideways onto the desk. She stepped inside, peered around, listening. Silent except for the rustling of paper as she walked. Behind a reclaimed school desk lay a chair on its side and some dumped-out drawers. She poked a toe at a pileup of objects. Nothing but office supplies, packs of gum, lottery tickets, a few corn chips. A roll of toilet paper stretched across the floor from the back of the unit. A chill ran up her spine to needle her neck. She stepped back out to the sidewalk, peered up and down the street. It was dead as a Wild West town after the shootout.

Tiptoeing back to the unit she examined the door jamb. No damage, didn't look forced. She stepped around detritus moving through the office into a small back room. Two small windows were locked. More stuff strewn across the floor. She went back to the main room and scanned scattered papers and files. A few reports among the invoices and other correspondence but none mentioned Brent Harrison. The tabs of manila folders carried names: Thompson, Hernandez, Meyers, Rogers and others, a mixture of Spanish and gringo surnames. Didn't spot Harrison. What in the world in this muddle of discount office supplies could have motivated a ransacking? And where was Derek Whitfield?

She walked out without bothering to lock the door.

TWENTY-TWO

Deep purple seeped up from the rocky horizon circling Brent's estate, staining the azure sky. Minoa flipped on a desk lamp, sloshed B & B into a coffee cup, slid onto the stool at her door-on-cement-blocks desk. Resting her chin on one palm she peered out into the darkness filling up the space between her cottage and Brent's mansion. Questions flitted around her mind. Should she worry about Whitfield's untidy office? Maybe he was looking for something in a big hurry and rushed out when he found it without time to straighten up. Impossible. More likely some divorcing husband, displeased with Whitfield's discoveries about his affairs or hidden assets, roughed up the office. Even that explanation strained credulity. The scene at Whitfield's office felt scary, not messy. Her phone beeped and she glanced at the screen.

An update from Ron: Gavilan on hold. Police found human remains in mounds. Serial killer? Will let you know as soon as we're good to go. New project starting soon. Excavation near Crownpoint. Relevant to Turner cannibalism debate. Hot stuff!! Take care.

Take care? Too late for that. She'd spent days walking around alone on a tract of land where it turns out a serial killer was burying his victims' bodies. Now Ron had a new project up in the four corners area. Soon, he said. Given his use of the word 'soon'—next month, next year or next archaeological period—that made a shaky prospect for more work. Conclusion: she and her bank account were out of luck. She googled the Turner cannibalism reference. Some Arizona archaeologist claimed to have found evidence of Ancestral Puebloan cannibalism. That Crownpoint excavation job might be amusing, if it happened.

She forced her mind back to Valeria's predicament. Surveyed the situation: Brent dead, accused of rape, preparing a secret land purchase. Mercedes ecstatic, his mom chagrined, her caretaker anti-social, Derek Whitfield's office ransacked. Disparate facts with no logical connection, a grab basket of stuff more confounding than a Huaorani myth. She'd spent several years in Ecuador coming up with analyses of Huaorani practices, belief systems and myths and put it all in a dissertation that almost got published and almost earned her a faculty position. Hell, she ought to be able to sort out this mess.

Maybe one of Whitfield's surveillance targets became angry and wrecked the office. But how did he get in? A PI would have great locks. And if an out-of-control husband entered the office when Whitfield was there and confronted him, he could have stopped him cold. A PI would be armed, right? Regardless, this had nothing to do with Harrison's murder. There must be scores of people who had a motive to destroy Whitfield's surveillance documentation.

She took a sip and savored the weight of the brandy on her tongue, wondering if it was time to be concerned about her drinking. She brushed the thought away as another popped up. Maybe the police executed a search warrant at Whitfield's office looking for evidence in Harrison's murder case. Could that mean they were looking for other suspects, that they knew their case against Valeria was weak?

Something caught her eye out the window. Probably another coyote. She moved over to the window and peered out. Glitter speckled the basalt sky beyond Brent's house. She surveyed the lot in front of his palace, looked left and right into hulking junipers. Only a couple distant house lights flickered, a sparse scattering of fellow humans across the roomy lots on Santa Fe's north side. She glanced at her car keys sitting on a stool over by the door, considering escape.

When she looked back at Brent's house, reflected starlight on an upstairs window blinked, flashed, jiggled. A strange phenomenon. Maybe she should mention it to Ireni. She stared. The image clarified. A light was moving around within the window frame. Someone was in Brent's house.

Her spine went rigid. Could this be the same intruder who trashed Whitfield's office? Or one of Santa Fe's career burglars who read the obituaries and found out Harrison had died? On the stool by the door she spotted Valeria's house keys beside her car keys. Should she get the hell out, maybe call police once she was somewhere safe? But Eldon had offered her free rent in exchange for watching over the estate. What would he say if a house burglary occurred under her watch? She grabbed Valeria's keys and headed out, keeping her eyes on the upstairs window as she walked to Brent's house.

Inserting the key in the front door, she found it unlocked. She stepped inside and checked the control box for the security system. Dark. If a burglar had broken in, wouldn't an alarm have sounded? Maybe it silently notified police and they were on the way.

Padding through the entry to the staircase she mentally scanned for people who might have a key. Had Crystal come back for possessions she'd left behind? After tiptoeing up the stairs she continued down a hallway to poise outside the door of Brent's office. A dusky glow filled the space between door and jamb. Putting her eye to the crack she spied a figure moving from the wall to the desk and back again, carrying something.

"Eldon!"

She strode into the office. He shrieked and jumped, dropping something heavy onto the desktop. His hands flew to his cheeks.

"OMG in triplicate. I thought you were a robber."

"Eldon, what are you doing here? I almost called the police."

"I couldn't get the lights to come on. Maybe a fuse is out. I hope they didn't turn off the power. I'm inventorying the contents of Brent's safe."

She noted a stack of bars on the desk, a safe door hanging open on the wall behind. His cell flashlight striped the room with light and shadow.

"Brent kept gold bars?"

"Sure, he called it his after-the-apocalypse account, AAA for short."

"Is this how you cover your unpaid legal fees?"

"Questionable humor. Yes, my bonus for winning the custody case was pending at the time of death, but that's not why I'm here. I'm conscientiously carrying out my duty as executor to inventory Brent's holdings."

He carried a couple more bars to the desk, then typed on a laptop beside them.

"How much is one of those worth?"

"Given the lamentable state of the economy, gold is high now, so around fifty thousand."

"How many does he have in that safe?"

"Give me just a minute."

He typed away, furrowing blond brows over eye cavities shadowed from below by light rays spouting up out of the phone. When he looked up the shadow pools created a vampire face.

"It appears six are missing."

"Six? That's three hundred thousand."

"Brent never told me he was planning to cash in any of his kilobars."

"Did he tell you everything he was planning to do?"

"Luckily no. But I was essentially Lord Brent's chamberlain, meaning steward of the kingdom. That included legal defense, financial supervision, property management and disaster prevention in the personal realm. I doubt he would have moved this amount without my knowledge."

"Are you saying he was robbed?"

"I don't see how. This safe has Touch ID. Only he and I had access. An unauthorized person couldn't get in without blowing the door off. I must conclude he sold six bars for some purpose he preferred not to reveal, at least not to his overseer."

"Some woman?"

"Knowing Brent's proclivities ... probably."

"What about Crystal? She was living here. Couldn't she have taken it?"

"Would you give a pet access to a safe? Because that's how he viewed her."

"He trusted you."

"A wise decision you might consider adopting."

"Trust you when I find you with your hands in the *masa*?"

"Massah? You're beginning to talk like a southerner."

"It's a saying in Spanish, like catching you with your hand in the cookie jar."

"I most assuredly did not eat any cookies, if that's what you're implying."

He began restacking the bars inside the safe. Then he closed the safe door and picked up the laptop.

"What's that stuff you told me you sip for inspiration? I think you owe me something after terrifying me so much my hair turned white."

"Your hair was already light, Eldon. You can't blame that on me."

"How about this disturbing feeling in the pit of my stomach like a Georgia termite infestation? Can I blame that on you?"

She hesitated, momentarily at a loss for words. Her mind's eye traveled back to the cracked coffee cup sitting on her unvarnished pine desktop, the dream journal charting months of nightmares on a stand next to her unmade bed, the darkness outside looming over hills dusted by a few rich people's floodlights.

"Inspiration it is," she said.

TWENTY-THREE

The woven cedar base of their equipale chairs creaked, slicing up an awkward silence as they sipped from unmatched cups and stared out the window into mica-flecked blackness. Minoa scrolled on her phone.

"It says here you can use a gelatin impression, a photocopy or even a thumbprint picked up with a piece of masking tape to fool a biometric thumbprint reader."

"I suppose even Crystal could have figured that out."

"She might have stolen the gold bars to get her due share on the way out. Did Brent include her in his will?"

"Brent wasn't planning to die. And he figured if by chance he did, there'd be no more use for Crystal so why bother?"

"Does everything go to Leah then?"

"Eventually. He left a tiny bequest for his housekeeper."

"Dolores? Do you know how to contact her?"

"That's the rub. It's coffee money, so it hardly matters."

"You mean ...?"

"Five thousand."

"That may have been coffee money for Brent, but it would be a godsend for her."

"I suppose I'll have to locate the woman. Perhaps a notice in the newspaper will work."

"Eldon, she doesn't speak English. Look, I need to find her for Valeria's case so I can let her know."

"You're more than earning your compensation as estate custodian already."

She flashed him a sarcastic frown, wondering where this conversation was going or if it was time to invent some excuse.

"Why did you say Leah will get the money eventually?"

"The loving father directed me to create an interlocking series of trusts which will manage the fortune for Leah until she turns twenty-three."

"I suppose it's customary to manage wealth for rich kids until they're old enough to indulge themselves legally."

"Brent's main concern was to keep it away from Mercedes."

"Did Mercedes know what was in the will?"

"I don't know. She has covert methods of obtaining information."

"Meaning the private investigator?"

"Meaning ... I hesitate to comment."

She squinted at him over the lip of her cup.

"Brent's mom talks like she's about to be evicted."

"That's how she talks before the will is read. Wait till afterwards."

"When will it be read?"

"Tomorrow. I wanted to clarify the accounts before I hand out the bad news."

"Mrs. Harrison is certain Brent was a dutiful son. Is she about to receive a posthumous wake-up call?"

"Yes, well, that's an unfortunate aspect of this whole affair."

"Unfortunate?"

"Brent assumed his mother would be long gone when he met his fate."

"So she gets?"

"Not a dime."

"She said Brent's father was a successful Wall Street trader. Why is she living in Santa Fe claiming she doesn't have taxi fare?"

"Soon after she moved out here she was given a short time to live and put in hospice. Brent took over management of her affairs."

"But she didn't die?"

"Evidently."

"And Brent maintained control of her money?"

"He provided a generous allowance until his death interrupted payments."

"Why don't you give her back her money?"

"The will and attached documents provide no authority for that action."

"So you're going to starve her?"

"It will all have to be worked out in court."

"So Brent's mom and Crystal get nothing. Who will manage the trusts until Leah comes of age?"

"Your humble servant. The will names me as executor and trustee. If I survive the meeting tomorrow, that is. You wouldn't be available to read the will for me, would you?"

"LOL Eldon. What do you think they'll do?"

"Murder is possible."

She glanced at his profile: sprigs of yellow hair curved onto his forehead. His pale jaw and straight-edged nose looked cut in marble.

"What effect will Malbore's purchase of Gavilan Mesa have on all this?"

He tipped his chair back so far he had to sit up fast to keep from flipping over. Grabbed the armrests, straightened, looked her way.

"You're not supposed to know about that."

"Give up on the idea that this Gavilan deal is secret. The word is out. Why the secrecy?"

He turned back to stare out the night-blackened window of the guesthouse.

"It's customary to conduct negotiations in secret. It could affect the outcome."

"Because people in Albuquerque would realize the Gavilan Mesa development is robbing them of tax money and something more valuable than that?"

He glanced at her, eyebrows torqued with that customary sarcasm.

"There's only one thing more valuable than money."

"Water."

"I was going to say love."

The eyebrows dropped. Something vulnerable leaked from the ironic expression in his eyes. Longing? She looked away, swished her drink around the cup.

"Are you planning to keep Brent's money in the Gavilan deal?"

"As long as I comply with my fiduciary duty to the charming beneficiary I'm free to invest as I see fit. But let's talk about something more interesting. Tell me, what do you do for fun?"

"Fun?" She uncrossed and recrossed her legs. "When I'm not dealing with career and money disasters, I run cross-country to the point of exhaustion if it's daytime or dance and drink myself into amnesia when it's not."

"That shows both discipline and decadence. Commendable balance."

His ironic tone was back in control.

"I analyze dreams sometimes. It's a hobby. Reminds me of trying to understand Amazonian mythologies."

"How did you end up doing anthropology in the jungles of South America?"

"A scholarship to Columbia University. An inspiring advisor who specialized in Amazonian cultures. A fascination with shamanism. And a grant application funded to work with the sensationalized Huaorani."

"You shame me. How can I have wasted my life analyzing regulatory handbooks for loopholes?"

"Why did you become a lawyer?"

"It was that or teach Social Studies at Clarke Central High School in Athens. Not too many options for a General Studies major from the Deep South. No one suggested Amazonian mythologies or I might have jumped at the chance."

"How did you end up in Santa Fe?"

"'Go west, young man.' I thought it best to join the wagon train before 'young man' no longer applied."

"Did you consider theater? I have the impression you're perpetually acting."

"Now you wound me. I'm simply scouting the territory before I reveal my heart."

She shifted in her chair, rummaging around in her mental arsenal of self-defense quips.

"It's not safe to reveal your heart to me. I have the empathy level of a Huaorani warrior."

"Your fierceness is unconvincing."

She turned her head to meet his gaze, analyzing his tone of voice. Their eyes locked for an uncomfortable moment. Suddenly her phone pinged.

With a sigh of relief she read the text notification on the screen: I know Dolores lady you looking for. Meet for info?

She texted: yes. The answer came back: General Miles park half hour.

She stood up, knocking her chair over.

"I have to go."

He stood as well.

"Whoa! Wait a minute. What did I say?"

"Nothing. It's just ... business."

His mannequin-pale face morphed from incredulity to hurt puppy.

"I could provide free legal advice. No fees or taxes. No obligation."

A tone of pleading. She sighed.

"Any experience with juvenile delinquents?"

"We had a few at Clark Central High. I hid in the utility closet to avoid them."

"Alright. Here's a chance to improve your reputation."

He followed her to the door muttering, "What about I serve as a witness for any subsequent judicial proceeding?"

"Do you want to go or not?"

"Coming. I'm braver than I look."

"Let's hope so."

She walked to the truck. After a long chug to empty his cup, he followed.

TWENTY-FOUR

The truck pulled into a parking lot beside a playground. Lights and engine died. Minoa and Eldon stepped out. One streetlight spewed piss-colored light. A second burnt-out light buzzed like disheartened cicadas. Huddled playground equipment gave way to a scruffy field fraying into darkness.

"I assume we're not here to purchase illegal substances?"

His stage whisper from behind tickled her earlobe.

"I'm buying information. It will help you distribute Brent's estate, so pay attention."

She walked past slides and a swing set to pause by a mammoth rope pyramid. He dog-trotted to join her. They waited there a few minutes while the occasional lone car passed on Camino Carlos Rey, whooshing as it neared and retreating like a gasp followed by a sigh. Suddenly out of the interior of the park emerged shadows that sharpened into silhouettes as they approached. Three barely adolescent boys swaggered into the weak circle of light. Each had portions of their head shaved with clumps of hair spiked or tied back.

"So you looking for Dolores Orellana?"

"You said you know where to find her."

"For a price."

"What's the price?"

The boy sized them up.

"Two hundred."

"*Chistoso*."

Thumbs in her jeans pockets, she rolled on the balls of her feet. The other two boys fidgeted. One spoke.

"One fifty is good."

She glanced at Eldon.

"George Martinez here is a Santa Fe Police detective on the juvenile team. He can either take you into custody now in connection with a special investigation into illegal activities at the condos or he can forget he ever saw you, depending on how helpful you are."

The boys' eyes widened, they glanced at each other. As their bodies lurched to take flight, Eldon grabbed one by the wrist. The other two ran off into the darkness.

"Let me go, man! I didn't do nothing."

He twisted his forearm back and forth, leaning away for all he was worth. Eldon clamped both hands around his wrist and pulled hard.

"Where do we find Ms. Orellana, young man?"

The boy whipped his arm up and down but couldn't pull loose.

"She's in D330, *coño*. Now leave me alone!"

Eldon released his grip and the boy shot into the interior of the park. Minoa and he turned and walked back toward the parking lot.

"George Martinez?"

"The name just came to me."

They climbed into the truck, drove across the street and continued to the Cabeza de Cabra Condos parking lot. Parked and walked alongside parallel apartment blocks with spotty exterior lighting and overflowing dumpsters.

"I don't suppose you ever came over here to help Dolores get a work visa or sign her up for health insurance."

"That wasn't Brent's way. He liked to pay cash for the work around the house."

"You didn't question a multimillionaire paying day laborers with cash?"

"Brent considered it paying what the market allows. He believed in markets."

"Illegal markets?"

"It's a gray area. This may surprise you but he had a strong sense of ethics. He prided himself on his integrity."

"Really?"

"You remain unconvinced, I see."

No signs so they counted the fourth building down and climbed a hanging iron staircase whose bolts were working loose, provoking a humming tremor in the structure with every step. On the third floor at number 330 the sound of a TV filtered out the door cracks. After several bouts of knocking the door opened a few inches and a pair of dark eyes, rimmed by premature wrinkles, peered out.

"Good evening. This is Detective Millie Melendez. She's investigating a serious felony in this block of condos. We'd like to ask you some questions. Your cooperation is advisable to avoid unpleasant consequences."

The eyes blinked several times. Minoa glared at Eldon, stepping in front of him.

"*Disculpe la molestia, Señora Orellana.*"

She explained in Spanish that Brent Harrison left her a sum of money in his will and they'd like to ask her a few questions before turning over the money. The door stayed put.

"*Se trata de cinco mil dólares.*"

Minoa held up the five fingers of one hand. The door opened a few more inches. She asked whether the scorpion mezcal that killed Brent Harrison had come from his cellar or was brought by a guest. Dolores' eyelids clenched.

"*Mejor no decir nada.*"

Minoa's voice took on a pleading tone, reminding Dolores that poor Valeria was in jail accused of poisoning Harrison. Dolores stepped backwards, closing the door. Minoa put her hand out.

"*Por favor!*"

Dolores shoved the door toward the jamb. Minoa thrust her foot into the gap.

"*Cinco mil*!"

She held up the five fingers again, pushing against the door with her other palm. Dolores pushed back. Eldon telescoped his head in front of Minoa.

"If you force your way in, it's breaking and entering, maximum 364 day jail sentence."

Dolores whispered in a pleading voice.

"*Todos nos conocemos aquí. Venimos huyendo de San Gregorio en el departamento de Durango. Señor Harrison no sabía qué clase de gente tenía en su entorno.*"

"*A quien se refiere*?"

"*Con quién hablas*?"

A man's voice chopped through the open space like a hatchet. Minoa rescued her foot just as the door thundered shut. After a moment of silence she and Eldon turned to walk down the corroding staircase.

"Despite the language barrier I deduce that neither she nor her paramour want to talk to you. Translation, please?"

"She's scared. She said people around here are mostly from a town in Durango, Mexico, and that Brent didn't realize who he had around him. It makes no sense."

"It does seem irrelevant to the execution of a will. Although we didn't even mention the need for probate."

"Dolores wasn't worried about probate. I wonder what she is worried about."

"Maybe she feared I would turn her over to ICE."

"She's worked for Brent since before I moved into the guesthouse, right? Why would she worry about that now? And you always knew she was undocumented, right?"

"I suppose I accepted it as the southwestern status quo."

"Sort of like accepting slavery in antebellum Georgia?"

"Slavery was legal in Georgia unlike illegal entry in our time."

"She saw you, she recognized you and she looked scared. Why would she be afraid of you?"

"There's no call to draw me into this inquiry."

"Unless you're guilty."

"Me guilty? She's the one who violated laws. What would I be guilty of?"

"Of doing something that scared Dolores."

"As a well-mannered gentleman I do not scare ladies."

"And as Brent's lawyer you have no idea why his housekeeper would fear people in his orbit?"

"She may be a nervous personality type. Or perhaps general anxiety disorder?"

She glared at him as they stepped off the shaky stairs. Walking past the dumpsters a big rat ran in front of them, paused, stared with eyes glowing red in the streetlights. Eldon took her arm at the elbow. As soon as the rat ran off, she swung free.

"When Dolores mentioned people from San Gregorio, she wasn't talking about Valeria because she's from El Salvador. That would have been obvious even if Valeria didn't reveal it: the accent is different."

"The woman may simply live in fear due to her consort's violent nature."

"Could she have been referring to Mercedes? Do you know what part of Mexico she's from?"

"No idea. The only Mexican cities I recall are Puerto Vallarta and Chihuahua, the first because it appeared in *The Night of the Iguana* and the second because it sounds like a yippy dog."

"Mercedes hasn't gone to Brent's house in years, has she?"

"Officially she wasn't allowed to be there. In any case, I question the credibility of poor Dolores. She's likely confused by the trauma of watching her employer die."

"There's something else scaring her. Dolores spent time with Valeria. She knows she wouldn't hurt anyone. So why not defend her?"

"She's saving her own skin by staying silent while authorities accuse another domestic employee. It's not pretty but murder charges bring out base survival instincts."

"But if she's a witness for the prosecution and not a suspect, then she's not in danger. Why turn down an easy five thousand bucks?"

"An excellent question. As I've never met anyone who voluntarily turned down money, I'm dumbfounded."

They reached the truck and climbed in.

"Is this where we decide at which classy establishment to continue our interrupted drinking?"

"I don't do classy."

"Slumming is fine. Local color with an aroma."

"I wish I could but I have a date ... with some friends. I'll drop you back at your car."

As Minoa started up the engine Eldon glanced at her, his pale brows almost touching in the middle.

TWENTY-FIVE

A gnarly fellow with a brush of white hair tipped his head back to reveal a shimmying Adam's apple, crooning 'what kind of clown am I?' over the pianist's jazzy finale on the Steinway. Ireni slid into a chair at the table, smiled at Minoa and Carter.

"'What Kind of Fool Am I?' 1963 Song of the Year FYI. How many has Dan sung?"

"He's already done three from the Rat Pack." Carter pointed with the neck of a beer bottle. "Where have you been?"

"Running errands for the masterminds designing twenty-first-century plutonium triggers. They all think they're Oppenheimer. What's new?"

Retirees filled every other table at the piano bar. On a wall behind a grand piano hung a gigantic silver Longhorn skull. A woman with a gray pixie stepped up beside the piano and belted out, 'If ever I would leave you.' The pianist pumped out a few chords, the singer flung a hand wide. 'It wouldn't be in summer.' Carter beamed.

"Minoa started spying for the Stop Gavilan movement."

Ireni turned question mark eyebrows to Minoa.

"I'm not spying. Changing topic, I found out something shocking."

"What?"

"Turns out a serial killer buried some bodies at Gavilan. But I'm still here so don't worry about me. My boss sure doesn't."

"Minoa, that's terrifying. You can't go back to work out there."

"Yes!" Carter tugged an invisible cord down to pound her fist on the table. "This will stop the archaeological survey which stops the environmental impact statement which stops Gavilan development. We're saved."

"Carter, chill. This is a hiccup. Gavilan will go forward unless Malbore buys it and turns it into a prairie dog preserve or something."

Ireni leaned over the table.

"What about Valeria?"

Minoa shrugged.

"Some strangeness around Brent's death but nothing to get her out of jail."

"Like what kind of strange?"

"Like missing gold kilo bars strange. Like poor people turning down a check for five thousand dollars strange. Like a tornado touching down inside a PI's office strange."

"Hold on. One by one. Gold kilo bars?"

"Three hundred thousand bucks worth missing from the safe in Brent's office."

Carter rolled a beer bottle around on its bottom edge.

"Maybe Brent found out who took it so the thief decided to kill him. There's your motive."

She fired off a pistol shot with her index finger.

"What if the DA accuses Valeria of stealing the gold?" said Ireni.

"That would make things even worse, if it's possible to get worse."

Minoa frowned. Ireni waved at a passing waiter who kept going.

"We'd better think this through," she said. "Maybe someone in the household stole the gold bars and Brent suspected it. Maybe he confronted that person but didn't have enough evidence to go to the police. Maybe the thief decided to poison him at the party to eliminate a possible formal accusation."

"That's a lot of maybe's," said Minoa.

"That would clear Valeria, Ms. Science Whiz Bang, because if Brent thought she stole from him, he wouldn't have let her babysit his precious daughter."

"Listen, you two." Minoa set down her beer bottle with a thud. "Crystal is the obvious robbery suspect. Although if Brent suspected she took the gold when she left, why didn't he tell the police? He was furious at her so why not have her arrested?"

"I've got it." Carter pointed the pistol finger at her temple. "Brent had a gambling addiction. He used the gold to pay off his gambling debts."

"A gambling addiction?" Ireni shot Minoa a glance. "Let's table that idea for the moment."

"Agreed," said Minoa. "Why would the dude crave roulette when he spent his days playing the stock market?"

Ireni waved down a waiter, ordered a sprite with a maraschino cherry.

"What about that lawyer of his?"

"Eldon? I surprised him in Brent's office earlier tonight, safe open, bars stacked on the desk, in the dark. He jumped like a bunny. Told me he was inventorying Brent's assets and discovered six kilo bars were missing. But Eldon is clever. He could have made that up on the spot."

"Eldon acts nerdy and awkward, not like an astute embezzler," said Ireni.

"'Acts' is the right word."

Carter poised elbows on the table, propped her chin on her palm.

"You mentioned two more strangenesses."

"The housekeeper, a poor immigrant from Mexico, inherits five thousand from Brent but she won't open the door to receive it."

"Maybe she took the three hundred thousand in gold so she sees no reason to endanger herself for five more."

"She said she's scared of someone in Brent's world and that's why she doesn't want to talk."

Carter's trigger finger leaped back into action.

"She must know who the real murderer is."

"The list of suspects is getting longer," Minoa said. "It could include Brent's numerous sexual conquests and their jealous husbands or boyfriends. Barney Trujillo, for one."

"What?" Carter set her beer bottle down so hard it tipped sideways. She caught it just in time. "The Gavilan Mesa lobbyist was Brent's lover?"

"Yup."

"Wait till I tell the water defenders about that."

Ireni sipped her soda.

"This mess becomes more and more complex. I don't see any pattern emerging."

"All I have are questions," said Minoa. "How did rat poison get into a bottle of scorpion mezcal? Does the theft of gold bars have anything to do with Brent's poisoning? Would loss of custody drive an ex-wife to murder? What is scaring Dolores? Finally, why would a woman submit to rape by her boss and say nothing?"

"Lots of women don't report rape," said Ireni.

"Happens every day of the week," said Carter.

"But what if that woman has three close friends concerned about her and one of them got her the job?"

Carter and Ireni glanced at each other, then stared at Minoa.

"Oh, crap," said Carter.

"Same," said Ireni.

After Minoa explained what the PD had told her about Brent's alleged rape of Valeria, they sat glumly while a pot-bellied fellow with a shiny bald head ripped into "This Nearly Was Mine." He choked up over the final line, 'paradise once nearly was mine,' and the crowd went wild. Carter spoke as the applause died down.

"Maybe it wasn't rape. Maybe she was burned out on stress and fear and deprivation and she needed escape. That's no motive for murder."

"Or maybe Brent pressured her and she felt she had no option but to go along," said Ireni. "That still doesn't prove she poisoned him."

"Eldon swears Brent was super ethical. Still, his own mother criticizes him."

"Why didn't Valie tell us about the rape?"

"Maybe she felt ashamed. I hope she didn't cover it up to protect me from feeling guilty for arranging that job."

A zippy golden anniversary pair began to pantomime "I Can Do Anything Better Than You Can" using theatrical gestures to illustrate shooting a partridge, knitting a sweater, wearing a girdle. The retirees screamed and laughed. When the couple took bows and returned to their seats, Carter spoke up.

"It's just like the economy: rich capitalists rape nature like they rape vulnerable women. That's why I'm upping my game."

"Meaning what?"

Minoa squinted at her.

"Meaning aggressive action by our new eco-defense group."

"Carter, how much do you have left in your account for paying bail?" said Ireni. "Because I've already contributed twice."

"That money is not for me personally, it's for the cause. And the cause is going critical. The Albuquerque City Council just approved tax subsidies for the Gavilan Mesa development. So everybody in the city will have to pay to provide services for that sprawl monster. The water table will go down. Air pollution from exurban transportation will rise. South valley farmers will run out of water. The region will tip further into drought."

"Look on the bright side," said Ireni. "Oil will run out and then people who live at Gavilan Mesa will have to bike in and out of town for their jobs. A generation of fit cyclists."

"Hah. It will take decades more to exhaust oil and by then climate change will have turned the planet into a desert scoured by super-tornadoes."

"Carter, do you think any of the opponents of the Gavilan Mesa development might be so angry about the pending purchase that they would kill Brent?"

"Now you're accusing water defenders of murder?"

"I'm not talking about your friends. But if some unhinged environmentalist thought Brent's death would save the Gavilan tract from development, maybe he or she would view it as a worthwhile sacrifice."

"Maybe it would be."

"Carter," said Ireni, "ends don't justify violent means."

"So what's your excuse for working at a weapons lab?"

Minoa waved her arms between them.

"Ceasefire, you two. If we don't figure out who killed Brent, I'm afraid the judicial system will use their scanty circumstantial evidence to railroad Valeria to a murder conviction."

"What was the third strangeness?"

"Mercedes paid a PI to surveille Brent. His office has been ransacked. Or maybe the police searched it and made no effort to clean up."

"Police privilege, as usual," Carter growled.

"Are you suggesting this has something to do with Brent's death?" said Ireni.

"No idea. It's just ... strange."

"So what's the next move?" said Carter.

"Good question."

They paid their bill and filed out into the crystallized night as the retirees cheered a gangly fellow waltzing around the grand piano crooning "Cheek to Cheek." In the parking lot they agreed to visit Valeria at the jail.

As they headed to their cars Carter yelled out, "Watch yourselves. There was a cartel-style killing on the south side with the body dumped in an acid bath."

Minoa shivered with the image, the premonition of winter in the air and a sense of ominous forces at work outside the brittle light bubble in which she walked to the truck. She cranked up the rickety heater and sat there for a moment thinking as a spark of an idea flickered into her mind.

TWENTY-SIX

"We're worried about my brother-in-law."

Minoa tugged her cheeks down to feign distress. "He disappeared a few days ago and some of the guys he works with at the muffler shop are ex-cons. We don't know what he might have gotten mixed up in."

The young woman in a white lab coat leaning over a stainless counter in the forensic division of the state medical investigations complex looked sympathetic. She probably hadn't worked around autopsies for long.

"We have one body, or rather some remains, brought in yesterday morning. There's very little to view so it won't be easy to make a positive identification. And it could be upsetting."

"I understand. But the family is so worried, it would be a blessing to know one way or the other."

Minoa shifted her facial expression to resolve in the face of adversity. The lab tech flashed a smile of commiseration.

"Alright. Why don't you have a seat and I'll bring you some photos? There's coffee and tea by the mini-fridge."

Minoa glanced at a glass pot warming dirt brown liquid.

"Thanks."

Her stomach was percolating another blackish liquid, making her wish she'd picked up something more than coffee for the drive from Santa Fe. The waiting room was as blank white and chilled as the inside of a refrigerator. Rubbing her upper arms she took a couple turns around the room. The young woman returned and handed her a stack of 6x8s. Minoa sighed. At least she wouldn't have to walk past a line of corpses in stages of decomposition or watch while they pulled half dissolved body parts out of a cold vault. Her imagination had been running wild as she drove down the highway to the state violent crime autopsy unit at the University of New Mexico campus in Albuquerque.

"These photos display intact body parts. If you're able to identify your family member, or if you require assistance, push that button on the table. I'll leave you for now."

In the hush after the door clicked shut, Minoa stared at the first photo showing a section of skull sprouting a fringe of pale hair. She tried to recall what had been sticking out of the investigator's baseball cap as he scuffed around the grounds of Brent's estate. Possible. The rest of the photos showed grotesque body tidbits like pieces pulled at random from a human body jigsaw puzzle. She hit the bell. The technician came back.

"I can't be sure from these photos. Do you have any of his effects?"

"Let me see."

She disappeared and returned with a smaller stack of photos. The first showed shreds of a leather belt hooked to an over-large buckle. No memory tug. The second, a chewed up loafer. Within the leather folds decorating the instep glinted a silver coin.

"It's ... not him!" Her voice cleaved too far, too hard. She reined herself in. "I mean, he never wore shoes like that."

"That's wonderful."

Sunshine illuminated the attendant's face. Working in a morgue she likely heard precious little good news. But regret shaded Minoa's thoughts as she walked outside recalling Derek Whitfield trundling around Brent's property. She climbed into the truck and sat there staring out the windshield at a faded autumn sky. What could have happened in his life after that moment to lead to a horrific death at the hands of gang members or narcotraffickers or some maniac? Would a deadbeat dad or philandering husband, his usual trade, resort to an acid bath? Didn't seem likely. Whitfield did a surveillance job at Brent's estate for Mercedes. Then Brent was poisoned and Whitfield murdered. The methods were so different it couldn't be the work of the same killer, could it? Still, another murder within days was strange. Another strangeness. She cranked the stick shift and headed for the freeway north to Santa Fe.

TWENTY-SEVEN

A stray scooted up growling as Minoa pulled in beside the green modular unit that had served as Derek Whitfield's office. When she stepped out, the hound skidded sideways and loped crookedly a few strides before turning its long snout around to stare at her with dull eyes. Protruding ribs striped the scorched fur bristling off its body. The dog gamboled away at a lopsided trot.

She placed a tissue on the doorknob and twisted. At first her grip failed and the knob spun. On the second try the door fell open. She surveyed the room. Still looked like a couple wind gods had gone to war. Sitting down cross-legged on the floor she scanned labels on scattered file folders, picked up documents and skimmed. Ford, Goodwin, Harris, Herrera. The names on folder tabs and letter headings rang no bells. She picked up the Harris file and peered at the label. No, it didn't peter off into the ending 'son'. Mercedes probably used her maiden name given how much she hated Brent. She selected files with Hispanic surnames like Contreras Soto, Estrada, Castillo, Marroquin, Pérez Morales. Scanned more papers. No mention in any of them of Mercedes or Brent Harrison.

Suddenly she heard scuffling feet. A figure shot out of the back of the unit toward the door. On reflex she leaned sideways and stuck a leg out. The runner's ankle connected, flipping the blur to the floor to resolve into a tumble of jean-clad legs and skinny arms.

"Let me go!"

A girl scrambled to her feet, backing into the wall. Eyes wide with terror stared out of a pinched face. Minoa stood up, gesturing with her palms.

"Calm down. Nobody's going to hurt you."

The girl cut toward the door and yanked it open just as Minoa grabbed the back of her tee-shirt.

"Whoa, hold on a minute."

She held the girl's arm as she flipped and flopped like a minnow in a net.

"This is child abuse! You're going to jail, scumbag!"

"I just want to make sure you're okay."

The girl paused, huffing, calculating.

"You got no right."

"And you're trespassing."

"I didn't do this." She swept her free arm across the room. "It was like this when I found the place. The door was open anyway."

"It looks like you might need some help. I can buy you a meal or take you to a youth shelter."

"How about you give me some money and I'll buy my own food."

"Let me think about it. How long have you been on the street?"

The girl squinted at her.

"Are you one of those social worker types? Or are you with the court?"

"I'm not working for anybody. But I know you could probably use a hand. You know, I was a runaway too."

The girl twisted her forearm.

"Let me go and I'll talk."

She appeared to relax so Minoa released her grip on the girl's arm. Instantly, she dodged sideways and slipped out the door. Minoa ran out after her to see her thin frame pounding down the pavement, then swerving out of sight into an alley. The girl was fast.

"Oh hell," she muttered, returning to Whitfield's office.

She walked into the back area. More pages covered the floor. A formica-topped dinette table sat against the back wall beside a mini-fridge and a TV tray with a microwave on it. A fishing pole almost tripped her as she stepped around lures spilled out of a tackle box, open on its side on the floor. Photo contact sheets lay strewn about.

She gathered as many as she could find and scanned images. Found one series that showed Leah, running, jumping, hair flying sideways. Many of the contact sheets depicted men she didn't recognize, some taken through car windows, others fuzzy behind house windows, naked with partners. In several she spotted Brent's house as the backdrop. A couple in fancy dress stood waiting at the door. Another array of snapshots captured Crystal carrying shopping bags. Whitfield's surveillance cameras were motion-activated. Nothing incriminating here. Had the intruders found dangerous images and taken them away? But what would a dangerous image show? Could photos of Brent's estate depict anything that justified a ransacking? Or a murder or two?

Inside a coat closet hung a couple of jackets and a pair of gray coveralls. On the floor of the closet lay a ratty sleeping bag, a box of crackers and a half six-pack of Pabst Blue Ribbon. She lifted up a corner of the sleeping bag to reveal a makeshift sleeping pad of newspapers, documents and more photo sheets. She sorted through the pileup. The newspapers were recent editions of the New Mexican and the Santa Fe Reporter. Nothing marked, nothing cut out. Collecting photo sheets she moved over to a tiny window to review them. Found a few of Brent's estate. One showed the blood-drained redhead from the party stepping out of a small car. Another captured Findley Malbore on the entry porch, his gargoyle face crimped. Dolores appeared in two sets, sweeping the porch in one series, bringing out a tray of water cups in another with a scared look on her face. Why was she always frightened?

Even though they contained zero evidence of anything suspicious, she stacked all the photo sheets showing Brent's property and carried them out to the truck. She paused to sort a welter of feelings. Frustration that nothing here seemed likely to help Valeria, sickened regret over Whitfield's horrible end alongside a flush of pride that she'd identified the body in the morgue as Whitfield. Whitfield's murder was probably unrelated to Brent's poisoning and maybe even unrelated to the vandalism in his office. After he was abducted, some homeless vagrant might have broken in looking for cash or a place to sleep. Or maybe the runaway teen girl had drug or mental health problems and tore up the office.

It was conceivable Whitfield's murder resulted from an investigation that uncovered something someone wanted hidden, but the acid bath was a pesky detail. It suggested professional killers, not a desperate husband. Then there was the complication of Brent's murder. Whitfield's cameras might have captured something incriminatory from the day of the murder. He had told her there was no reason to go over recent recordings from Harrison's property, so he probably didn't even know what they contained or why somebody would want to kill him. What did the cameras capture? The delivery of the scorpion mezcal? One of Brent's secret lovers? But who would care? Brent's numerous affairs had already been exposed in court, so it wasn't news that he philandered.

Minoa set the photos on the seat and went back inside the office to the back room. She scooped up the sleeping bag, rolled it up and set it outside the door. Then she locked the doorknob. That girl would come back for her things, but this wasn't a safe place for her to sleep.

TWENTY-EIGHT

Mason Biegler's office smelled like weeks' worth of mummified lunch remains. He barely glanced up from the laptop he hunched over. Messy stacks of papers leaned in from both sides.

"You have information pertinent to your friend's case?"

"I tried to leave you a message but your office voicemail is full."

Biegler laughed.

"It's rarely not full. I'm covering 187 cases right now and that's only because I take the homicide and rape cases."

"Look, I don't care one bit what your caseload is. You have a legal obligation to provide effective representation for your client. And I need to talk to you."

Biegler glanced at his watch.

"Now."

"Ok, shoot," he said, and then laughed, "or rather, please don't shoot."

"I've found some leads that need to be investigated. First, alcohol contamination is a huge problem in Mexico. Did the DA's office even consider whether that scorpion mezcal might have been tainted during production?"

"How do you propose to prove this tainted product theory? Have you found reports on other deaths or illnesses from the same poison in this liquor?"

"Well, no."

"Next enthusiastic idea?"

"What about this? Brent's lawyer discovered that gold bars worth hundreds of thousands of dollars are missing from Brent's office safe. That would provide a motive for someone, wouldn't it, say if Brent found out and threatened to call the police?"

"How does this lawyer know Harrison didn't cash in the gold himself?"

"He thinks that's unlikely."

"And how did you find out about this?"

"The lawyer told me."

"He shouldn't have. The Supreme Court ruled that attorney-client confidentiality extends after the client dies, so he shouldn't have given you information about Brent's assets which Brent communicated to him as his lawyer. Still, my investigator could nose around to see if anyone is flaunting unexpected wealth." Biegler glanced at his watch again. "Got anything else?"

"The body of a private investigator, or what's left of it, is lying in the morgue in Albuquerque. It's the same guy Brent Harrison's ex-wife hired to investigate Harrison for the custody dispute. I caught him removing cameras from Brent's yard."

Biegler blinked several times, methodical blinks like a matador warming up his cape arm.

"Go on."

"His office was ransacked too. All the electronic equipment must have been taken because there's nothing in there now but a bunch of files, office supplies and some photo contact sheets. They must have found the incriminating material, but there could be copies in the cloud, right?"

"I assume the police are investigating?"

"The body hasn't been identified."

"I don't want to know how you know about this. But what makes you think the two deaths are connected?"

"They occurred within days of each other and both victims are linked to Brent's ex-wife."

"Pray explain, then, your hypothesis as to why the murderer would cannily poison a wealthy financier and then brutally knock off the PI in his child custody case."

Biegler made a loose cathedral with his knobby fingers and stared at her from under drooping lids.

"That's what we have to figure out."

"The police could put a computer forensic investigator on it, although I doubt they will."

"So it won't help to inform them of the latest victim's identity."

Biegler's eyebrows arched into a corrugated forehead.

"Be careful about that, although I'm not speaking as your attorney. If this case ultimately goes to trial, we could consider trying to get hold of the PI's file on Harrison. But we're not there."

"Keep in mind, Mr. Biegler, that if you pressure my friend to accept a plea deal, I will file a malpractice suit against you and devote my life to getting you disbarred."

Biegler laughed, a consumptive sort of laugh midway between a cough and water in his nose.

"While you're at it you might want to join one of the class action suits against public defenders currently being litigated in a number of states. I'm hoping the plaintiffs prevail. It might force state governments to put more money into legal services for the poor. I might even get a raise out of it."

"What can you do to speed up this process and get Valeria out of jail? This is a miscarriage of justice."

"Listen, Ms.... uh, the DA's case is weak. They were probably under pressure from Harrison's contacts in government to make an arrest. So this case may be a placeholder while they continue the investigation and try to figure out what really happened. It pries the governor off the attorney general's back and leads the real criminal to feel overconfident. If we're patient, the whole thing may fizzle some months down the road."

"Months? You've got to accelerate this fizzling process."

"Your zeal is admirable. Your friend's next appearance is set for Thursday. A preliminary hearing is scheduled but I'll likely waive."

"Waive? Why don't you force the prosecution to present their evidence? It will be clear they don't have a case against her."

Biegler sighed and frowned.

"There are strategic considerations. We don't want to enshrine damaging testimony in the transcript if there's a chance the witness will disappear before we finally go to trial in a year or two."

"A year or two?"

He stood, walked to the door and gestured out to the hallway.

"My client will make decisions about her defense in consultation with her attorney. Meanwhile, if you turn up anything else, leave a message with the front desk. And in the future, make an appointment, Ms ...."

"Diamond."

She stood and stalked out.

TWENTY-NINE

When Ricky Martinez walked into the waiting room at Santa Fe Police headquarters, Minoa started talking fast.

"I could have called the anonymous tip line, but I wanted to make sure I'm providing the police with all the information I have."

Martinez squinted at her.

"Weren't you at the Brent Harrison estate after his murder?"

"Yes."

"And, let me think, didn't you show up at an accident scene in the Ortiz Mountains?"

"That was a crime scene."

"No foul play detected."

"Detected."

"And now you have a murder to report?"

"A body to identify."

"You better step into my office."

He led her down a hallway lined with doors into an office furnished in particle board. She slid into a seat, stared at his lush lashes, chubby cheeks speckled with blue-black stubble, girlish flip of hair. Mu~!Qst have been hard to intimidate crooks on the street with that baby face.

"There's a body lying in the office of the Medical Investigator in Albuquerque that I can identify. Or rather, I identified his shoes. The remaining body parts are ... corroded."

"Corroded? Are you talking about the remains found off Camino Largo?"

"I'm not sure where you found it. I met him at Brent Harrison's house. He was a PI. Derek Whitfield."

"Derek Whitfield? At Harrison's? You were present when Harrison became ill and now you've identified a second victim? I'm going to record this interview."

He propped his cell on the desk facing her, told her to give her name and contact information. She squirmed, asking herself if she should refuse to speak until she could get Eldon to show up. He was her only option for a lawyer, yet what would be the payback if she asked for another favor?

"Now, what were you saying about Whitfield?"

"He was carrying out a surveillance job for Harrison's ex-wife related to their custody battle. I saw him picking up his equipment at Harrison's estate."

"He put surveillance equipment on Harrison's property? That's illegal."

Minoa shrugged.

"When his foot slipped into a prairie dog burrow, I noticed his loafers had dimes in the instep, not pennies. That's how I identified the body."

"Dimes in his loafers?"

"His office was ransacked. He may have captured incriminating images of Harrison's killer without realizing it. When he picked up his rock cameras he said he wasn't going to review the recorded images. But the killer didn't know he hadn't seen the tapes."

"Rock cameras? Ransacked office? Slow down. Why don't you stick with what you saw?"

"His rock cameras might have captured images of the poisoner. If there was a poisoner, I mean, if Harrison didn't just die from a bottle of mezcal contaminated during production. Which is more likely. But then Whitfield wouldn't be dead. Unless his murder stemmed from a different investigation. No matter which it is, Valeria Medina is innocent."

Martinez leaned back in his chair, lowered his curly lashes down to nearly obscure the pupils that remained fixed on her.

"What's your involvement in all this?"

"Valeria Medina is my friend. And she's innocent. The police are wasting valuable time trying to build a case against her."

"So you're trying to help your friend by finding a different theory for Harrison's murder. How does that explain your interest in Whitfield?"

"I never meant to get involved in Whitfield's murder. I went by his office to talk to him and somebody had trashed it."

"And that made you decide to drive to Albuquerque to identify a body?"

"I turned out to be right, so it was a good hunch."

"A burgled office made you suspect murder? That makes no sense."

"I heard about a murder. I saw Whitfield's office and wondered what had happened to him. Then I drove to the morgue to check."

"Why are you motivated to drive all over interfering in police investigations?"

"I'm trying to save my friend."

"Why do you think Whitfield's murder, if your identification is correct, absolves your friend?"

"The guy filming Harrison's house on the day of his poisoning ends up murdered a short time later. Isn't that suspicious?"

"Like it's suspicious that you're connected to both deaths?"

She sat up straight as if an electric charge shot up her backbone. Squinted at him, reevaluating the situation. Spoke with a frigid tone.

"I'm doing my duty as a citizen to let you know what I found out."

They battled stares for a long moment, then Martinez shifted.

"What else would you like to include in your statement?"

She tried to think. What could help Valeria's situation?

"Someone wanted information Whitfield had. If they found it, they took it, so it wouldn't be there now. The only way to figure out what was taken would be to locate his electronic backup."

Martinez gave her a condescending look.

"Whitfield must have had multiple targets. Probably most of them didn't like his spying. That's why people hire a PI, to get compromising information on somebody. All those people would have the same motivation to eliminate Whitfield's spy tapes."

"But Mercedes Harrison is linked to both deaths. She hired Whitfield to go after Harrison. When she lost custody she felt so enraged she might have poisoned Brent or murdered Whitfield because he failed to save her case."

Her voice faltered.

"The other problem with your theory is the loafers. A dime in the instep doesn't constitute a positive identification of a body. Whitfield may be out of town. The murder victim may also have put dimes in his loafers. And burglaries are high in Santa Fe, so there's no proof this one was motivated by anything other than an addict searching for cash."

Minoa stood up.

"Oh, alright. I've informed you of what I know. You decide what you're going to do with it."

She walked to the door, pausing when she heard his words.

"It's curious that you turn up at multiple crime scenes. How do you explain that?"

She gave him a withering look.

"I attract bad luck."

"Or maybe you're a serial killer with a compulsion to report your crimes to the police thinking you can fool us."

"Are you joking?"

Martinez returned her titanium squint, then relented.

"We'll check out the Whitfield ID."

She turned back around, strode out the office door and down the hallway of doors. Walked straight through the waiting area populated by one guy twirling a key ring around his index finger, glancing every few seconds at the door she'd just shut. Outside she paused for a deep breath. Biegler had told her she had to tell the police what she knew about Whitfield, but the interview hadn't gone well. Why did she bother? She checked the time. Oops. She'd almost forgotten. No time to go home to change. Jeans would have to do for a funeral.

THIRTY

Sunbeams like spears rebounded off the cemetery's neon grass, a glowing square bulldozed out of the yellowed prairie on Santa Fe's southern fringe. The golden casket, carried by six young men in white shirts and black bow ties, made Minoa's eyes water so much she stumbled into the red-haired woman walking beside Eldon, who shied away as if fearing contagion.

As they reached an open grave, a cell phone started ringing. One pallbearer, a dead ringer for a server at Brent's party, patted his pocket causing the coffin to lurch toward the hole. A desperate six-person juggle caught it just in time. Like some electronic version of a mourning bell, the phone rang over and over.

Minoa glanced at the Gavilan lobbyist of the Indian paintbrush dress, Terra Fuentes Trujillo, now in a dark gray version of the same, unaccompanied. Terra gave her a venomous look and then made a point of looking elsewhere. Findley Malbore, elegant in a navy suit and cantaloupe tie, stood beside and a few inches under his girlfriend, her black silk shirt and trousers billowing in a desert breeze. Mercedes wore a dress with a neckline like the Mariana Trench and Leah sported pink gingham check and ribbons, a billboard for her mother to advertise her refusal to mourn. Mrs. Harrison, looking desiccated within an over-large suit, stood beside Caitlin Romero, zippy in black-and-white polkadots. The gangly red-haired woman from the party shadowed Eldon. Minoa stood on the fringe of the group hoping no one would stare at her jeans and vintage bowling shirt.

As the rabbi spoke Minoa looked around at the mourners' faces, all lowered except for Mercedes. She shot bullets with her eyes at the rabbi as he extolled Brent's leadership of the community, his work ethic and integrity. When he described Brent's investment activities as sowing fertile prosperity in the arid soil of New Mexico, she looked like she was on the verge of an asthma attack. He concluded with, "May he go to his resting place in peace."

Under the supervision of an employee of the funeral home, the repurposed servers arranged straps around the casket and lowered it into the grave. Leah buried her face in her mother's stomach. When the rabbi told Leah to throw a spadeful of dirt onto the coffin, she didn't budge.

"You're traumatizing her," said Mercedes. "Leave her alone."

Caitlin Romero helped Brent's mom flick a few clods into the grave. As they left the gravesite Minoa had to skip a few steps to catch up with Eldon.

"What's your hurry?"

He paused, eyes flicking side to side.

"Ostensibly I'm a busy attorney now saddled with the execution of a complex will. But between you and me, it's wise to limit my exposure to this gang."

"Someone is unhappy?"

"The reading of the will occurred this morning. The only one truly happy with the will is Brent's eternal soul. He's looking down from heaven, thoroughly enjoying watching the conniption fits of those who survived him."

"You're sure of the location of Brent's soul?"

Out of the corner of her eye she noticed Mercedes heading with Leah to the parking area.

"I hesitate to slander someone whose fortune I'm taxed with administering."

"Isn't Mercedes happy that Leah receives most of it?"

"It will be years before Leah gains control of the fortune. By then Mercedes will be middle-aged and embittered, or at least that was Brent's intention."

When they reached the parking area Mercedes was standing alone watching them. She'd left Leah in the car. She walked straight up to Eldon and landed a resounding smack on his cheek.

"What the hell?" Eldon staggered, clutching his jaw. "That's second-degree assault!"

Minoa whispered into his ear, "It's accepted custom where she's from, appropriate behavior for a wronged woman."

"In Georgia as well before the Civil War."

"You thief! It wasn't enough to take a child from her mother. Now you're stealing her inheritance."

Minoa made a stop sign with her palm at Mercedes.

"*Cálmese.*"

"This criminal convinced Brent to impoverish his true heir. He's a *falsificador*. He forged the will so he could take control of Brent's money. You *monstruo*!"

She waved her fists. Eldon backed up.

"I'm an attorney, ma'am, and now the victim of a crime that carries a twelve-month jail sentence. You're free to seek legal advice if you have reservations about the will. Until then, you'd best stay away from my person or I'll be forced to seek a restraining order."

Eldon turned and tripped. Brent's mother had hobbled up from behind with Caitlin Romero. She swung a cane into the side of Eldon's calf. He jerked up his knee, wrapped hands around the calf.

"Ow!"

"Have you no shame, young man? You told my boy to take my money when I was ill and now that he's gone, you're trying to keep it all for yourself."

"Mrs. Harrison, I am a trustee and executor, not an embezzler."

Eldon returned his foot to the ground, straightened his clothes.

"You corrupted my Brent and now I'm all alone in this wasteland without a penny to my name. Gerald would ruin you, if only he were still alive."

Her head sank as sobs rippled through her. Without lifting her head she swung her cane at him again. He dodged it.

"I'm sorry you're unhappy with the will, Mrs. Harrison, but this will have to be worked out in a court of law." He backed up, whispering to Minoa. "It's prudent to flee this vigilante posse. How about we meet up later for a play-by-play?"

"Okay."

He pulled a card out of his pocket and handed it to her.

"Here's the address of my new office. Drop by anytime."

He jumped into a vintage luxury car and sped away. Mercedes turned to Minoa.

"It's a blessing Brent is gone, he did so much evil. But Leah is his only heir and now that *ladrón* says he put his money in trusts that won't pay out until she graduates from college. How am I supposed to raise her?"

"His only heir?" Brent's mom waved her cane at Mercedes. "That money came from his father's astute investments over the course of a lifetime. Brent was lucky he didn't lose all of it on gold-digging women. How dare you claim it?"

"You crazy old woman! You want to deprive your own granddaughter?"

"You Lorelei! You tricked Brent into marrying you by claiming you were pregnant."

"I was pregnant."

Mrs. Harrison hit her cane on the gravel parking lot.

"That pettifogging lawyer is worse than Bernie Madoff. But how will I pay a lawyer to fight the will in court?"

"That *embaucador* will live to regret helping Brent cheat me."

"Cheat you? How could my baby boy do this to his own mother?"

Mrs. Harrison shook and then stiffened as if shocked by electricity. Caitlin chopped hands under her armpits and pulled up so hard her feet left the ground. She turned her around in midair and started her walking by hauling on one arm. Mercedes turned to Minoa, her furrowed brows deepening a crease in her forehead that would cost her money she didn't have to Botox. Like flipping a switch, she transformed her expression into a beauty contestant smile.

"You rescued Leah after Brent died. I'm sure you don't want to see her harmed by this *huizache*. If you see anything suspicious at Brent's estate, or that lawyer reveals his evil plans to you, you will call me? It could be worthwhile for you."

"Well ..."

Mercedes turned and swaggered back to her SUV, prattling to Leah in mellifluous Spanish that stopped dead when her door slammed shut. Mrs. Harrison was hobbling back to the southwestern memorial chapel leaning on Caitlin Romero's arm.

Minoa slid into the driver's seat of the truck and stared out a dust-mottled windshield, past a serpentining hairline crack, at the south side tableau: stucco houses, asphalt expanses, clumps of yellowed bunchgrass bowed sideways, all of it ironed flat by wind and sprawl. Tried to think. Detective Martinez seemed smugly certain they had Harrison's killer in jail. Biegler was on his way to negotiating a manslaughter plea for Valeria like what he'd cooked up for the scissors murderer. Eldon was sorting pots of gold in order to execute the will. Mercedes and Mrs. Harrison were fantasizing Eldon's execution. Nobody cared that Valeria was sitting in jail accused of a murder she didn't commit.

So what should she do? She'd come back to Santa Fe to retreat from the disasters in her life. Yet all she'd found here were more problems. Maybe escaping didn't work. Maybe. Meanwhile, whenever she faced a perplexing situation, she had a fallback strategy. Research. Mercedes must be the link between Brent's and Whitfield's deaths, although the two deaths didn't look like the work of one killer. She'd start with a little research.

THIRTY-ONE

She headed downtown, parked a few blocks south of the Santa Fe River and walked to the district courthouse. Its tall glass facade reared up brazenly amidst a sea of squat earth-toned buildings. The deputies running the security check at the entrance gave her a nod of recognition. They probably figured she was a repeat drunk driver or maybe a domestic abuse victim who always recanted.

She headed to the clerk's office and tried her luck on a public computer, but digital case search only contained a bare bones case file with a few orders. So she sidled up to the counter and smiled at an elderly clerk with a snowdrift of hair puffed over peachy cheeks.

"I'd like to review the files for these two cases."

She handed over a scrap of paper on which she'd jotted the case numbers for Mercedes and Brent's custody and child support wars.

"You can view it in the reading room but it will take a little while to locate."

"I'll wait."

When the clerk returned she hunched forward, arms stretched around a bulging file that burst wide open spilling documents when she set it on the table in the reading room.

"Here's the custody file, honey. The child support case is sealed." She lowered her voice to a whisper. "You're not with the press, are you? I read this fellow got murdered and people care because he was one of those Wall Street high rollers. Do you think some mobsters offed him for the moolah? Or was it the conniving ex-wife?"

Her pale eyes glittered, her smile insinuated.

"I'll let you know if I find out."

Minoa sifted through the teetering stack. Brent's attorneys would have made sure the financial documents relevant to child support calculations were not public record. But they hadn't been able to seal the custody case. Maybe case documents would reveal what Derek Whitfield found out or provide some other clue relevant to the two murders. She started at the beginning.

There was the divorce petition filed by Mercedes five years ago requesting alimony and distribution of community property. An initial order conferred shared legal custody of Leah with primary physical custody to the mother. After a pinkie's width of paperwork came a motion by Mercedes requesting permission to take Leah to Mexico to visit relatives. Brent filed a flurry of motions to oppose and brought in some expert to testify at an emergency hearing on crime in Mexico. Motion denied.

Skimming another finger-width of documents she sensed resentments flaring. Mercedes filed a motion demanding supervised visitation for the father based on the father's alleged sexual harassment of a live-in nanny. A female judge expressed 'grave concern' over the father's behavior and issued a temporary order mandating supervised visits for three months at the Gemini Center. A subsequent two-day trial resulted in a ruling restoring regular visitation, as a male judge considered evidence of the father's inappropriate behavior inadequate.

Then father, through counsel, filed a motion alleging the mother was denying him visitation and requesting 50/50 shared physical custody, alternating weeks. More motions culminated in a three-day trial with experts of many stripes: child development, family psychology, even one who specialized in effects of the drug war on Mexican women. Judge ruled for the father and ordered all child exchanges be carried out in the parking lot of the police station.

In no time Mercedes requested sole custody based on the father's hostile behavior which made joint parenting impossible. At trial Mercedes' lawyer alleged Brent was leaving his daughter for long periods with an au pair. A surprise witness clenched the judge's ruling in favor of the mother: the twenty-year-old au pair testified, as summarized in an affidavit, that she felt guilty about sleeping with her former employer but admitted she couldn't turn down the expensive gifts or resist the psychological pressure.

The court file stank with the atmosphere of caustic loathing in which the next series of motions were filed. Finally, Brent mounted a full-scale siege, with Eldon's Notice of Appearance in the pleadings, alleging parental alienation syndrome. After a series of pre-trial duels, the trial kicked off with expert witness lists that wouldn't have shamed a high-profile murder trial. Minoa skimmed the expert witness reports summarizing the expert's credentials, area of specialization, payment and previous expert testimonies.

Dr. Gustavo Heidelberg MD Ph.D., Brent's highest paid expert at $50,000, listed ninety-seven other expert witness appearances. He stated Leah showed all eight of the diagnostic criteria for parental alienation syndrome where one parent supposedly influences the child to turn against the other parent. For example, Leah complained that her father liked other women better than her and never paid attention to her. Dr. Heidelberg labeled this Denigration Syndrome, a condition in which the child labels one parent negatively after absorbing criticism voiced by the other parent. Leah said she didn't want to visit her father because she was terrified black widow spiders in her room at her father's home would bite her. Dr. Heidelberg said Leah's reference to the black widow, a species in which the female kills the male after copulation, reflected the mother's expression to Leah of a wish that the father would die. Leah expressed anger towards the 'fully qualified, extensively investigated' au pair which her father had provided for her care and tutelage, proving the mother's destructive jealousy. And on and on.

Minoa jumped to the summary of testimony for Mercedes' prize witness, a female psychology professor from Northwestern who charged the bargain rate of $15,000. Her research focussed on how the extramarital affairs of a parent negatively affect their children. In Leah's case, said the professor, the child's heightened anxiety caused by her father's numerous affairs manifested as a phobia of spiders. She stated it was paternal neglect that made her reluctant to go with her father for visits.

The guardian *ad litem* recommended a change of custody to the father as the mother's expressions of anger toward the father led her to question the mother's ability to put the needs of the child first. The judge was persuaded by Eldon's case and jerked custody, awarding Mercedes only three hours of supervised visitation with her daughter each Saturday.

So this was the legal event that led to Brent's house party. Minoa rubbed her eyes and leaned back in her chair. There were enough revenge motives here for a Shakespearean tragedy, enough to lead Mercedes to scratch out Brent's eyes or worse. But there was no mention of Whitfield. That suggested his surveillance of Brent hadn't turned up anything to help Mercedes' case. Maybe the two deaths were unrelated, maybe she should stick with the obvious explanation for Brent's murder. Mercedes detested him and would have uncontested custody of Leah once Brent was eliminated. Plus she had assumed Leah would inherit. Mercedes was Mexican. Maybe Dolores saw her approach Brent's house on the day of the party with a bottle of poisoned scorpion mezcal. But why would Dolores fear Mercedes? Did she even know who she was? She packed the pleadings back into the file and hauled it to the counter, flagging the clerk.

"Did you figure out whodunnit?" the clerk whispered as she hefted the file with arms strengthened by a full-time schedule carting legal documentation.

"You may be right about the conniving ex-wife."

Minoa headed out, telling herself it was time to get tough with the main suspect in Brent's murder.

THIRTY-TWO

Squinting into curdling twilight as she drove up and down St. Michael's Drive, she spotted the sign: New Mexico Academy of Ballet and Theatre Arts. The building was a converted office suite with a pileup of high-end SUVs in the lot at one end. Inside she spied Mercedes breathing onto an observation window alongside a row of moms in yoga pants. Approaching, Minoa peered inside the room to see miniature ballerinas leaping across a hardwood floor.

"I had a chat with Derek Whitfield."

Mercedes' head spun around. Her cheekbones glowed, her lips glimmered desert honeysuckle.

"What does that have to do with me?"

"He was picking up surveillance cameras at Brent's house. Ring any bells?"

She swung her head back around, leaving Minoa to stare at waves of cinnamon-glazed black hair.

"My communication with my attorney is confidential."

"Did he hire Whitfield? Are you saying you had no contact with him?"

The head turned around again.

"Why did you want to see me? Did you find out something about that lying lawyer of Brent's?"

"This should interest you. There's been another murder."

She maintained eye contact although infinitesimal muscle adjustments twitched the line of eyeliner curling up at the outer corners of the eyes.

"What are you talking about?"

"Derek Whitfield."

Her eyes flitted back and forth.

"Derek dead?" she said finally. "How do you know?"

"He's in the morgue in Albuquerque, what's left of him anyway."

She looked down at the pointed toes of her suede ankle boots, kicked one a few times.

"*Qué lástima.* Have they found the killer?"

"It's under investigation. Do you have any idea who would want to kill him?"

"Why would I have any idea who killed him? Do you think all Mexicans are murderers?"

"It was a cartel-style killing."

"That has nothing to do with me. Derek's work was dangerous."

"Spying on cheating husbands and cheap ex-husbands?"

"Derek did all kinds of investigative work. I'm sure he knew plenty of bad men."

"Did he find anything incriminating in his surveillance of Brent's house?"

"I called off the job as soon as I heard Brent was dead."

"You mean, you ended the job at the custody trial, don't you? Or did you find something else for Whitfield to do after the judge awarded custody to Brent?"

"I ... I was going to appeal. But Whitfield's investigation turned out to be worthless. Judges in this country don't care that a father is *cogiendo* every woman he meets."

"You must have reviewed Whitfield's surveillance images to find evidence to present at trial. Did you discover Brent doing anything you hadn't expected?"

"I don't care what he did with his stinking *pene*. I just wanted my daughter back."

A few of the moms turned to stare at Mercedes. She smiled sickly. They returned to chatting, flaunting their salon-preened plumage and gym-molded thighs. The tiny dancers sprawled on the studio floor, twisting themselves into hieroglyphics as their teacher modeled stretching.

Minoa lowered her voice.

"How did you meet Brent?"

Mercedes flipped back her hair and gave Minoa a penetrating look.

"You want to know how a poor Mexican woman could marry an American millionaire?"

"Well ..."

"I'll tell you. I grew up in a tiny village in the state of Durango. One day when I was fifteen I was walking down the road toward town. A pickup truck stopped beside me. The door opened and two men pulled me inside. I thought they would use me and then kill me. But they were working for the man who wanted me. They took me across the border to a house in Los Angeles to serve as that man's mistress. He's a *traficante*. He told me he would kill my family if I tried to run away. So I stayed. I stayed until my mother passed on and my sister moved to *el DF* and married. Then I ran. In Santa Fe I found a job at a restaurant. That's where Brent saw me."

"Did you know any other people from Durango in Brent's household?"

"How would I know who worked in his house? We had mutual restraining orders."

"Did you know the housekeeper, Dolores, from the time of your marriage?"

"I don't recall."

"Dolores is also from Durango."

Mercedes flicked contoured brows.

"And?"

"She saw someone from Durango at Brent's house on the day he died. Was that you?"

The brows angled down.

"I thought you wanted to help Leah. Is someone paying you? Are you sleeping with that lawyer?"

Minoa huffed.

"How about the women he had affairs with? Can you name any of them?"

"Who knows? Brent was a *mujeriego*. He went after every attractive woman he saw."

"While you were married?"

"Of course."

Minoa paused to internally kick herself for throwing poor traumatized Valeria into a rapist's den.

"How did you find out he was poisoning the prairie dogs on the estate?"

"What are you talking about? I don't know what he was doing with his stupid *perros*."

"*Perros de las praderas*. Leah must have told you. I bet it upset her."

"Leave my daughter out of this."

"Or did Whitfield mention it to you?"

"I don't know what you're talking about. I don't have to talk to you."

"Better me than Detective Martinez."

"What do you mean?"

"I've been in contact with him about Whitfield's death. He knows you were Whitfield's client so you'll be questioned."

Mercedes' frown squeezed the pupils of her umber eyes into slits but she didn't respond. Minoa went on.

"Could Whitfield's murder be connected to the drug trafficker you ran away from? Maybe a warning sign for you?"

"He forgot about me a long time ago. He got what he wanted and he had no more use for me."

"But you knew about his trafficking operations, right? Wasn't he worried you would alert the police?"

"Don't be stupid. Nobody names people in the cartels if they want to live. And if he didn't come after me before, why would he bother now?"

She turned back to watch the ballet class. Minoa recalled Eldon's description of Mercedes. The woman was smart and tough. She tried to think of a line of questioning that might break through her bullet-proof complexion.

"Most Americans don't even know what mezcal is. So a Mexican must have gifted Brent the poisoned bottle."

Mercedes stabbed her with a look.

"You accuse me of poisoning him?"

"Wouldn't you do anything to get your daughter back?"

"You're crazy!"

Her arm shot out and slammed into Minoa's chest, shoving her backwards. As Minoa stumbled, flailing to regain her balance, the studio door opened and little pink projectiles whizzed to their moms. Leah threw her arms around Mercedes' waist. Over her head Mercedes glared at Minoa.

"Get out of here."

Minoa straightened, reviewed her options, decided she had none. She turned around and headed for the door. But before opening it she paused and called back over one shoulder.

"By the way, have you taken Leah to visit your hometown of San Gregorio?"

Mercedes' expression flickered from outrage to doubt back to outrage. No reply.

Stepping out of the building, humid with overheated young bodies and wet kisses, Minoa took deep breaths of crackling air. She'd exposed herself to Mercedes' hysterical aggression and hadn't learned much except that she was from Durango. But would the sight of her frighten Dolores so much she'd turn down five thousand dollars? If Mercedes knew the kind of people who would dissolve their victim's body in acid, she was a dangerous person to cross. Like Minoa had just done. Like Brent and maybe Derek Whitfield did before.

She scanned the parking lot leaking into black night. Where had they grabbed Whitfield? Was he at his office when the killer or killers burst in? Did they shoot him right away? She hoped so. She hoped they didn't do any of that sadistic violence she'd read about that Mexican traffickers used to terrorize people. It was awful to think something like that had happened here in her hometown. And could happen again.

Mercedes would come out of the building any minute. Minoa wanted to be gone. She headed to the truck, nerve endings pointy-sharp and attuned to the shadows.

THIRTY-THREE

Back home the dark window of the guesthouse reflected her face. She stared, wondering what she would do if another face appeared in the middle of the reflection. There was no escape from the guesthouse: it had only one door. What was she doing living at a murder scene while cartel assassins picked off people linked to the murder? Saving money, that's what. She could stay on here for free while waiting for a staff job to open up at the archaeology office or something better to occur to her. If she didn't mind being the only person under seventy within screaming distance.

She flipped open the laptop. The forensic medical report had arrived in her email inbox. The external examination noted extensive bruising while the internal examination described hemorrhages in various organs. Among the technical terms describing tissue samples and toxicology tests she spotted several references to Vitamin K-dependent coagulation factors. After evaluation for end-stage liver disease, hemophilia, disseminated intravascular coagulation and ebola virus, the autopsy attributed the cause of death to accidental or intentional brodifacoum poisoning.

A quick search revealed that brodifacoum was a super potent second generation version of an anticoagulant medication, marketed as a rodenticide under brand names like Gopher-Getter and Rats RIP. As a poison it led to death by bleeding out. It was lethal to humans in small doses and had been involved in many child and pet poisonings. There was no reliable antidote.

So Brent picked up this super-poison at a hardware store to annihilate a few prairie dogs? Or did exterminators bring the poison to Brent's estate and leave an unused bag in his garage? Maybe it was a coincidence that Brent had on hand a bag of the same poison workers used for the prairie dog kill and a murderer funneled into the scorpion mezcal. The key question was how the poison made it into that bottle. By accident or by intentional act? In Mexico or in Santa Fe? Did the police wonder how Valeria could have known Gopher-Getter would make an effective murder weapon? Nobody else was asking these questions and she wasn't coming up with answers.

She blew out a long breath in frustration. The prosecution in Valeria's case wouldn't investigate a possible contaminated production process and Biegler was already doing the plea negotiation tap dance. The mere fact of Valeria's arrest seemed sufficient to assure her conviction.

Ron's messages flashed across her mind provoking a shiver down her backbone. A serial killer's victims' bodies at Gavilan Mesa? She searched for news of it in the Albuquerque Journal. The police either had no leads on the killer or weren't revealing what they knew. She thought back over her days walking up and down the tract of land. Had the killer seen her? If he knew she was the one who found the bodies, he might blame her for the police investigation. Another shiver oscillated from neck to pelvis.

To distract herself, she skimmed online archaeology journals looking for references to the Turner cannibalism debate Ron had mentioned. She learned that archaeologists had found scores of sites across the southwest with Pueblo 3 era bones displaying evidence of cannibalism. Turner theorized that during the twelfth century bloodthirsty Aztecs from central Mexico, famed for ripping hearts out of living sacrificial victims, had established contact with the Anasazi at Chaco Canyon. They influenced an elite class to incorporate cannibalism into their rituals. Seeking safety, regular people fled and Chaco Canyon was abandoned.

Not everyone bought Turner's theory. Many believed severe drought led to the abandonment of Chaco. Some specialists said the markings on bones found at sites throughout the region could be explained with other theories. But no one could explain away all the evidence of cannibalism.

So this was what Ron had planned for her: digging up bones and pottery in northern New Mexico to see if a millennium ago some people ate some other people. If the job materialized. If not, she'd soon be back to tending bar at the casino, flying toward forty without a plan or a prayer.

She stood up, stretched, went over to the front door and opened it. Scanned the estate grounds, ghostly silent under a half moon. No coyotes, no prairie dogs and no assassins or cannibals. What was she expecting? This was Santa Fe's north side, a Disneyfied adobe village for the amusement of the super-rich. She locked the door, brushed her teeth, slid into bed and then lay there imagining how someone might have killed those victims she discovered at Gavilan Mesa. It felt like tossing and turning on a pile of cactus ...

THIRTY-FOUR

A long long time later she found herself striding through desert scrub, up a hill to pause at a ridgetop. In the basin below she sees two strange figures digging. A couple bodies lie on the dirt beside them. One looks up at her. His white face is splashed with black, flaps of skin hanging, hair in strings, antlers on top. His body is a skeleton. With a roar he runs toward her.

She spins and sprints back down the incline, pursued by crashing footfalls that grow louder. Stumbling, regaining her stride, tearing on propelled by terror. It's so close now she smells its foul breath. With a roar it grabs an arm, scrapes bloody trails down to the wrist, claws a bracelet of punctures. She trips, flails, falls onto the ground staring up at its monstrous face, buckling and squirming and choking on a scream as a skeleton hand pins down her throat. The figure looks up, loosening the suffocating grip of its bony hand. Wriggling free she jumps to her feet, spotting the other skeleton figure galloping toward them.

Then she's skimming across desert in a pell mell flight, a non-stop fusillade of steps that seems to take her out of danger until BAM! Toes catch in a hole flipping her forward to slam onto crusty ground. She twists around to sit up and finds she's in the midst of a prairie dog village, burrows and mounds all around. Coins lie scattered about, shiny golden coins. A prairie dog pops up out of one hole, then another from another hole, two little fur-posts, round eyes wide, turning to scan every direction. Little protectors, keeping watch, so cute, so huggable.

They freeze and blast ear-splitting squeals. Turning to look she sees the antlered skeleton creature hurtling toward her with a rollicking limping gait. She rolls onto hands and knees and leaps up, glancing back to see the other antlered hulk galloping to join the first. As she watches, they crash into each other spewing a cartoonish whirlwind of jerking shoving limbs, bone fragments flying, dust roiling to form a desert tempest that rolls toward her. Though she runs, the dust wave engulfs her, smothering, blinding ...

She woke gasping, struggled to her feet, bolted to the kitchenette where she flung open the window and sucked chilly breaths. Peered out at the sepia foothills of a bleaching morning as her mind caught up. The golden aspens circling the Sangre de Cristos towering over Santa Fe had tarnished. In a few days the leaves would flutter to the earth leaving bone-white branches to claw at the sky.

Another damn nightmare. A weird one. The skeleton creatures resembled a wendigo. She tried to remember what she'd read about it in a course on Native American mythology at Columbia. Drawn from Algonquin folklore, the wendigo was an evil figure with an insatiable desire to consume human flesh. In psychiatry wendigo psychosis described a compulsion to consume and destroy the environment. Ron's mention of cannibals must have suggested the wendigo to her dream mind.

But wait a minute. Golden coins scattered around a prairie dog village? That made no sense. They must have been aspen leaves. She'd watched the band of aspens circling the mountains above town every day, had seen it speckle with yellow, then turn into molten gold and now the vivid color was fading. Of course she would dream of that. Freud called it day residues that the unconscious incorporates into dreams. Unless ... unless the golden coins referred to Brent's missing gold? Or the money Mercedes had expected from Brent's death? Or the price being negotiated for the purchase of Gavilan Mesa? Questions about money circled Brent's death like vultures. But what in the world did prairie dogs have to do with all that?

Through the front window of the guesthouse the windows of Brent's mansion flashed like mirrors in the light of a rising sun. Suddenly Brent's SUV drove up the drive to the front of the big house and parked. She jerked as if shocked and then froze. How could Brent's car come driving home like any day before he died? Was Mercedes right about Brent faking his death? Had he taken the three hundred 'K' for the expenses of assuming a new identity until he could access accounts he'd set up overseas to fund his new life? Then who was driving his car?

She raced to the door, cracked it open, peered out through the gap. 'BULL01' said the yellow license plate with a turquoise Zia sun symbol.

She leaped to the dresser, pulled on a pair of jeans and ran outside. A fellow in a canvas jumpsuit was stepping out of the driver's seat.

"What are you doing with Brent Harrison's car?"

"Repairs are done, lady. He requested home delivery." A pickup truck was coming up the driveway. "Invoice is on the dash."

He walked over to the truck and climbed in. The truck did a 'K' turn backing into a piñon tree, trundled down the drive and disappeared. She retrieved the invoice. Six thousand four hundred sixty-five dollars for a replaced right fender, bumper, hood, headlight assembly, paint job and assorted details. Her eyes teared as morning dazzle rebounded off the white paper. Did Brent have a car accident shortly before his death? He hadn't mentioned it. Would he have any reason to hide a crash?

She stood there with bits of quartzite poking the soles of her bare feet, the sunshine pummeling her sleepy brain, trying to recall some mention of Brent's vehicle. At the party, Eldon had asked about it. No, he'd asked about Crystal's car. Was this relevant? She'd find out.

THIRTY-FIVE

Opening the door of Ultrathon Fitness, a gust of sweaty air slapped Minoa in the face. She found Crystal in one of the side rooms, chatting with gym members as they rolled up their mats and gathered blankets and resistance bands. She was wearing a crop top and workout pants and had chiseled muscles. She smiled a question as Minoa approached.

"Hey Crystal, I just wondered if your car suffered any damage recently?"

"My car? Somebody bashed it in the parking area."

"Check out this invoice."

She glanced over the sheet Minoa handed her.

"I figured it was Brent, but he went and died before I could get him on charges of assaulting a car, you know what I mean, and fleeing the scene of the crime. Not to mention harassment and stalking of a person, I mean, not a car. Big time violation of a PO. I would have loved to see his rich ass cooling in a jail cell."

"Was Brent violent with you? I knew he was pushy but I never thought ..."

"Brent was fine as long as I went along with his script. When I wanted out, he lost it."

"If you didn't know about the car crash, how did you get a protection order against him?"

Crystal turned her back to say goodbye to a couple of students. Then she headed for the door. Minoa skipped a step or two to catch up. Crystal gave her a frigid look.

"That's private."

"Sorry. Why don't you keep this receipt? Maybe you could file a case against the estate in small claims."

"It's not worth it at this point. I'm doing just fine without him."

"That's great. Where are you living now?"

"Ted and I are buying a place in La Cienega. It's beautiful. We'll have an apple orchard and room for horses."

"Wow. Ted is your new boyfriend?"

"I've known Ted since high school. He doesn't have money like Brent did, but he'd go through hell to get me a glass of iced tea."

"You must be getting a good deal on that property. I heard La Cienega is pricey."

"Ted's family is helping."

She squeezed the corners of her lips and turned to say bye to another student.

"You and Brent were together for a couple years, right? What finally made you decide to leave?"

Her expression twisted into an angry grimace.

"I found out he was screwing that anorexic lobbyist and probably every other woman he met unless they were too old to fit into stretch pants. Sorry, no offense meant."

"No problem. Is that what you and Brent were arguing about the day you left?"

"I got tired of his number one goal in life being to take down Mercedes. And he wanted me to become the unpaid nanny for that pampered little ski bunny."

"Take care of Leah, you mean?"

"He had some MCP idea that we were gonna be a happy little family, the three of us. That meant I do the work and he gets to tell his finance bro buddies about his pretty tax deductions waiting at home for him after a long day of chasing deals and tails. That's not what I signed on for."

"Surely he would have hired another nanny?"

"Duh, he had to keep up the flow of fresh meat. But I'd had it with the nanny trafficking."

"You and Mercedes had that in common."

"That and nothing else. Mercedes blew her chance. I never got one."

"You mean you wanted to marry Brent?"

Crystal squinted and looked away. When she turned back her expression was stony.

"Who gets more benefits? The temp workers or the permanent employees?"

"He didn't want to get married?"

"Mercedes screwed it up for all of us. I might've done better but Brent had wizened up by then. Realized he didn't wanna subject his investment proceeds to the whims of some family court judge. And the best protection in a community property state is never say 'yes.'"

"Do you know why Mercedes came out of their divorce without a chunk of Brent's money? She seems stretched thin."

"I'm sure the pre-nup would've won a Pulitzer. The only asset they let her keep was that little princess and she even lost Leah in the end."

"That would make a woman mad, don't you think?"

"That jezebel was born mad. I always figured she had cartel connections, but she ended up too poor for that. So I guess she was just trading on her tits."

"Do you think she had anything to do with Brent's death?"

Crystal walked out into the hallway. Minoa followed. Crystal turned around to face her.

"I wouldn't put it past her, but they're saying that new nanny did it. I always figured that oily lawyer and that stray cat accountant were planning a convenient accident."

"Stray cat? Accident?"

"That stick figure with the 'I Love Lucy' hair prowled around the house never making any noise. You'd walk into the study or the kitchen and there she'd be. Then the door swings and she's disappeared. Like something out of a slasher flick."

"You didn't trust the lawyer either?"

"Have you heard him talk? Nobody, I mean nobody talks like that in real life. Unless he's some Netflix reject or something."

"So you feared Brent would suffer a contrived accident? Instead, he was poisoned. Who do you think would do that?"

"That Mexican housekeeper gave me the creeps. You could've bribed her for a few 'K.' I made her taste everything she cooked."

"Crystal, are you saying you feared Dolores would poison you and Brent?"

Crystal peered down at Minoa's hand holding her phone.

"You're not recording this, are you?"

"No."

"Okay, Dolores had access and she was poor. Anybody who wanted him dead could go through her and it'd be a piece of cake to pay her off. That's why I wasn't surprised when I heard what happened."

"But they're saying the nanny poisoned him, not Doiores."

"What's the difference? Two illegals? They could have conspired the whole thing in Spanish and nobody would know."

"Have the police questioned you? Did you tell them your theory?"

"Course they talked to me. I'm an important witness. I know all about murder cases. I watch a ton of true crime shows."

Minoa glanced through a window at a room full of benches, racks of weights, leg presses, taking a deep breath.

"I suppose you know that Mercedes had a PI surround Brent's house with cameras? Those films will be full of images of the other women he saw and of you, too."

"That Mexican vulture never got her claws out of him. Come to think of it, he probably enjoyed the idea that she was watching movies of us doing it."

"You think Brent knew about the surveillance?"

"Brent was a *cabrón* but not a dumbass. If he knew she had him watched, he probably set up some shows to confuse her legal team. The real reason he wanted that spoiled brat was to torture his ex-wife."

"I imagine Brent told you gold bars were missing from his safe."

"Meaning what?"

"Was that the real reason for your fight?"

"You're accusing me? Of all the nerve. You could have been stealing packages off the front doorstep."

"Then who do you think stole Brent's kilobars?"

"I told you. That accountant. Plus I'm sure the nanny and the housekeeper and the landscapers were taking everything they could smuggle out. But me, dumb head Crystal, thinks this fund manager genius is in love with my ass and wants to acquire me along with his artwork and his fermenting liquor collection."

"Did he tell you he took control of his mother's money?"

"Supposedly he was trying to help her, but whenever Brent helped anybody his net worth went up."

"The police have arrested the wrong person for Brent's murder. So if you remember anything that might help?"

"When I move on I close and lock the door."

"Perhaps, but you'll be questioned about the missing gold."

"You got no right to accuse me."

"And if Brent found out about the theft before his death, the DA's office will figure out it provides a motive for Brent's murder."

"Why you traitorous snake!"

"What's going on here?"

Minoa felt the back of her shirt jerk up causing the shoulder seams to cut into her armpits. She twisted around to find herself looking down at a comically muscled guy grasping her shirt.

"What's your business with Crystal?"

"Ted, honey, it's okay."

"Nobody gonna harass Crystal."

Minoa shook herself loose from the muscle guy, stepping out of reach.

"Let her go, Ted baby. She's just Brent's tenant. She's harmless."

"See you around, Crystal."

Minoa walked down the hall toward the exit. Ted's words followed her.

"If somebody else hadn't taken out that rich stud I might be the one looking at a long sentence in the pen. What a gold-plated jerk."

A young woman behind a desk at the gym entrance smiled.

"Would you like information on a trial membership?"

"Thanks, but no thanks."

Walking out she paused to observe her image in a floor-to-ceiling mirror. She turned left and right, trying out a few poses. With a sigh she headed for the exit.

Outside, sitting in the truck, she took a moment to think over Crystal's spicy observations. She'd probably taken the gold bars, but at this point who cared? More pertinent was her suspicion of Dolores. If Dolores received payment to poison the mezcal, it was understandable that she'd try to implicate someone else and then grow nervous when questioned. That would explain her terrified refusal to open the door, even for five thousand bucks. But who would bribe Brent's cook to poison his booze? It sounded like something out of a gangster movie, not the wealth colony on Santa Fe's north side.

Crystal had suggested she knew how to solve murder cases because she watched true crime shows, so distinguishing fact from fiction wasn't her strong point. What's more she thought Mercedes, Eldon and that red-haired accountant were all capable of whacking Brent. What she didn't realize was that when she blamed a former lover for Brent's murder, she was describing herself.

THIRTY-SIX

Minoa parked beside Arroyo Mascaras in the confetti shade of Siberian elms, invaders a century ago who'd been crowding out native tree species ever since. A fitting metaphor for the wealthy who'd crowded out the traditional residents of Santa Fe's historic section, she mused as she walked four blocks to the Kearny Building to avoid paying the city's tourist-gouging downtown parking fees. Passing through the blue portico of the Kearny building, she spotted Eldon's office in a back corner of the interior courtyard. She crisscrossed the patio, ducked under a massive hanging pot of red geraniums and peered through a slab of glass. At the back of a waiting room done in chrome and cream sat Brent's accountant with the red chili hair, staring at a computer screen. She hauled open the door and walked in, noticing the nameplate on the accountant's desk as she approached: Gerda Grabowski.

"Hi, Gerda. Is this Eldon's new office?"

"Yes. Hello. Do you have an appointment?"

Gerda blinked washed-out blue eyes circled by pink rims. Either she spent a lot of time weeping or the desert dust didn't agree with her.

"He's expecting me. But I wanted to ask you something. As Brent's accountant, you must have paid his workers at the estate, right?"

"Not usually. Brent paid the temporary workers in cash."

She looked down, shifted papers on her desk. Maybe trying to convey that she didn't have time for chitchat. Minoa persevered.

"What about ordering supplies for the estate? I bet you could track liquor purchases to see if staff ordered that bottle of scorpion mezcal or it was a gift?"

Now she looked up, reproachful.

"I kept the books for Brent's investments and businesses, not individual grocery purchases."

"And did you work in his home office sometimes?"

She arched her eyebrows, stiffening.

"What are you insinuating?"

Minoa considered.

"It was obvious you excelled at managing the party preparations. I assumed you were in charge of Brent's domestic operations so you would have insight on what went wrong the night Brent was poisoned."

That fluffed her feathers.

"Although it wasn't explicitly one of my duties, I always made sure nothing lacked at Brent's house."

"Did you hire Dolores?"

"Dolores started working for Brent before I did."

"How about the landscapers?"

"Brent preferred to use temporary laborers for that. I arranged the major repairs and remodeling, plumbers, painters, furniture deliveries, things like that."

"Did you observe the deliveries on the day of the party?"

"Really, do you think I spent the day watching delivery trucks drive into the estate?"

"I'm sure you were busy."

Gerda clacked at her keyboard, frowning.

"Did you manage his calendar as well?"

She huffed.

"I'm not a secretary."

"Of course not. But you would probably know if Brent had an enemy. Maybe a woman he broke up with?"

She half stood.

"Excuse me? Brent's personal affairs were none of my concern."

"Photos at the custody trial showed he was seeing a number of women. You had an insider's view."

Gerda opened her mouth to snap a retort but instead squeezed her lips and slumped back into her chair. Her voice sounded husky.

"Women found Brent irresistible. He treated them kindly so as not to hurt their feelings."

Minoa skipped a beat. Gerda's secret infatuation had produced partial blindness. Just how far had her adoration of him gone? Could she be an emotionally repressed isolated individual whose inner pain finally drove her to violence?

"Okay, thanks."

She stepped past and walked through a doorway, Gerda's objection trailing behind. Eldon stood up out of a wooden armchair with brass-studded leather panels.

"Minoa, it's great to see you."

"Do you mind if I shut the door?"

"Not in the least. Does this mean we're progressing?"

She shut the office door and turned around.

"Gerda was in love with Brent. He rejected her, maybe even humiliated her. And she had access to the liquor at his house."

He furrowed his pale brows.

"It's wonderful to see you as well."

"Crystal suspects Gerda. And Gerda seemed super-attentive to Brent on the night of the party."

"I suspect her job has to fill the hole where a personal life would be. It makes her an excellent employee."

She slipped into a chair that looked like the little sister of Eldon's.

"What about enemies in finance or business, people who hated Brent or would benefit from his death? Brent's mom said his dad had enemies who would have been happy to cut his throat. Like father, like son?"

"Everyone from the governor to the mayor and his buddies praised Brent. He had a positive impact on New Mexico's GDP."

"Then whom do you suspect?"

"I incline toward the view that prosecution of an alleged murderer fulfills a societal need. So it hardly matters whom they accuse."

"Explain."

"We don't like to see a capitalist in the prime of wealth accumulation die unexpectedly. It undermines our faith in the power of money to protect us. So a malefactor, preferably someone from the deprived classes, must be made responsible."

"That's the most revolutionary thing you've ever said, Eldon."

"Perhaps I'm not the immoral legal shill you supposed?"

"Perhaps."

She glanced around the office: a historic adobe with foot-thick walls decorated to look like a Goldman Sachs coup in colonial New Mexico.

"So this is your new office?"

"Well, administering Brent's assets will be time-intensive. How's everything out at the estate?"

"I need a rodent mortician."

"That bad?"

"I step outside my door and everywhere I look bloody faces are staring at me."

"Sounds like you're feeling guilty about something."

"It's not a delusion. That poison holocausted the poor prairie dogs. I drive home and the vultures scare up like a scene out of Hitchcock. You've got to do something."

"Okay, I'll get someone out there right away. How about your job?"

"Job is on hold while suspicious mounds containing human remains are investigated by APD."

"It sounds like you need distraction from the cruel reality of death."

"Distraction? There's been another murder."

"Someone we know?"

"Mercedes' private investigator."

"Curious."

"Mercedes had him film Brent with women. She must have presented those recordings at the custody trial."

"I argued vehemently against the admission of those images into evidence. Brent had a reasonable expectation of privacy on his own estate."

"How did the judge rule?"

"Mercedes' lawyer tried to say that privacy doesn't extend to the front yard where people passing on the street could see you. But nobody could see the front of Brent's house from the street. Ergo, wealthy people have larger privacy zones."

She frowned. He leaned over and pulled something out of a desk drawer.

"I decided Dolores could use her bequest sooner rather than after the will is contested, which could take a very long time indeed. So I drew a cashier's check on the general expense account and I'll officially debit the amount designated for her when the legal battle concludes. I bet she'll open the door for a woman alone speaking her language."

He held out a check.

"Ok, I'll try."

As she reached out her hand, he retracted his.

"But you have to promise to meet me for dinner and a movie to tell me how it goes and celebrate Brent doing something positive with his money, even if it was postmortem."

Her hand hovered

"Is this a quid pro quo?"

"Not in the legal sense of the term."

She grabbed the check out of his hand.

"I'll consider it," she said. "The preliminary hearing is tomorrow at ten. Depending on how that goes I'll see if I'm up for celebrating."

"If I have to bribe the DA this is going to be an expensive dinner date."

"*Chau*," she said and walked out.

***

She headed over to Cabeza de Cabra Condos. After parking near the complex office, she glanced around scanning for truant teens. The place was deserted. She walked past the row of overflowing dumpsters and up the shaky suspended staircase to Dolores' apartment. There was no response to her knock, no sounds from inside. Moving over to the window she peered through the slit between curtains. In that slice of the room there was nothing to see. She tugged on the sliding window and it slid open, allowing her to push the curtains aside and see the entire living room. There was nothing in the room, no furniture, nothing. Looked like Dolores had moved out.

THIRTY-SEVEN

Minoa sat in the front row of the courtroom gallery, craning her head around every time the door opened. Finally Biegler shuffled in. He nodded to acknowledge her waving hand but continued straight to the counsel table. She stood and waved harder.

"I have to talk to you."

"Later."

"This is important."

Pretending not to hear, he began pulling papers out of his briefcase. She tried to pass through the swinging gate but a deputy stopped her. So she leaned across the bar and poked Biegler on the trapezius.

"This is inappropriate," he growled at her.

Deputies came out of a door in the back of the courtroom herding Valeria. They seated her beside Biegler. She glanced at Minoa, eyes crystallized. Minoa gave her a smile and a thumbs-up but she turned away without changing her expression.

"Biegler, I've got to talk to you before the hearing."

She aimed another poke in his direction but a deputy stepped in front of her. The clerk called out 'all rise' and the judge entered the courtroom.

"The first case on the docket is State versus Valeria Medina Ramirez. We're set for a preliminary hearing. Are the parties ready to proceed?"

"I believe we have an agreement to waive, your honor," said the DA, turning to glance at Biegler. Her gray suit with white-edged lapels mirrored the clean lines of her bob.

"Mr. Biegler?"

"Your honor, that's correct. The defendant would like to—"

"Your honor, I have information for the defense," Minoa yelled, standing up.

The judge peered at her. Biegler whirled around with a furious look on his face.

"It's important."

She threw an exaggerated scowl at Biegler.

"Is this person on the defense team?"

Biegler sagged as he turned to the judge.

"My apologies, your honor. May the defense request a five-minute recess?"

"Granted. Keep it short."

Biegler walked toward the door with a brusque gesture at Minoa to follow. The courtroom doors barely swung shut when he nailed her.

"You've gone too far this time, Ms. Desmond."

"Diamond."

"Whatever. This comportment will do your friend no good."

"Why are you waiving the preliminary hearing? That means Valeria will have to spend months more in jail before she has any chance of getting out."

"You do not understand how the court process in a murder case works. No one wins a case at the preliminary hearing stage. The DA only has to present enough evidence to show that probable cause exists to charge the accused. It's obvious they have something against her or they wouldn't have charged her in the first place."

"You're assuming they have a case against her when they can't have anything damning. I know because I was there and because I know Valeria. She's innocent. So why not put them on the spot and make them prove it?"

"Because, Miss Wannabe Attorney, it's not to our advantage. Time is our friend. With the passage of time witnesses forget, they get tired of taking time off work for an event that happened a long time ago. They move and forget to give a forwarding address. We don't want to enshrine their testimony in the judicial record while it's fresh. Better to wait patiently and watch the prosecution case corrode with time's passing."

"Even if one of their prime witnesses disappeared?"

"Which witness?"

"Dolores, the housekeeper, who would testify that Valeria was the only one to handle the poisoned liquor. Who knows what else she might say if it's in her interest to incriminate Valeria. She was terrified and now she's moved out. Maybe the real murderer threatened her. What do you bet she forgot to tell the DA where she was going?"

He stared at her.

"I'm considering using a forensic expert to testify on the fallibility of fingerprinting. But it would be a tough slog to get jurors to doubt fingerprint evidence. I was assuming the prosecution could back that up with eye-witness testimony that the accused handled the bottle. But if they can't, my strategy becomes more effective."

His gaze drifted sideways as if lost in thought.

"See? The case against Valeria falls apart without the housekeeper's testimony."

He looked back at her, frowning.

"Don't jump to conclusions."

"But her disappearance suggests that she's scared of someone else, which undermines the accusation that Valeria is the murderer."

"You're assuming this housekeeper fled out of terror. What if the prosecution hid her for protection?"

She gulped.

"But protection from whom?"

He tapped bony fingers on the other forearm.

"There are other things going on in this case we're not yet aware of, so we have to proceed with caution."

She burned holes into his flaccid cheek flap, dotted with moles, as he squeezed his face with apparent concentration. After a moment he spun around and entered the courtroom. Minoa followed.

"Are you ready to proceed, Mr. Biegler?" said the judge.

"Yes, your honor. Based on new evidence, the defense wishes to proceed with the preliminary hearing."

The DA stared hard at Biegler. When he refused to look at her, she turned to the judge.

"The prosecution was under the impression that the defense was planning to waive the preliminary hearing."

"It appears the prosecution was mistaken," drawled the judge.

She leaned over, whispered into the ear of the assisting DA while throwing glances around the public seating area.

"May we have a few moments to make sure all our witnesses are present?"

"You can have five minutes," grumbled the judge. "You knew this date was coming ever since you made the decision to bring charges. The court can't hold a person on a murder charge if you can't show probable cause."

"Yes, your honor."

The judge stepped out through a door in the back of the courtroom.

The DA began a frenzied conversation with the assistant prosecutor and another person who came to her table. The third person hurried outside the courtroom. As people whispered, swiveling heads, Carter and Ireni hurried in and squeezed onto the bench beside Minoa.

"What's going on?" whispered Ireni. She glared at Carter. "Ms. People's Revolution couldn't make it to my house on time."

"I wasn't going to buy coffee at some global chain."

Carter glared back.

"The DA is finding out that one of her principal witnesses disappeared."

"How do you know?"

"I'll tell you later," she said as the DA's investigator came back in and started whispering with the two DA's. Soon the deputy ordered all to rise and the judge returned to the bench.

"Ms. Maldonado?"

"Your honor, the prosecution would like to request a continuance."

Biegler shot up.

"The defense objects. My client has been deprived of her liberty, that most sacred right guaranteed under our constitution. Either the prosecution has a viable case or they don't. In this country we don't imprison people and then hold them indefinitely while we try to find enough evidence to substantiate charges. If the District Attorney cannot prove probable cause, I demand that my client be freed immediately."

"Objection sustained. You may proceed, Ms. Maldonado."

The DA leaned over to her assistant and had another whispered interchange. When she straightened up her face wore an expression of stifled misery.

"The prosecution would like to *nulle prosequi* charges against the defendant. We reserve the right to refile and present to a Grand Jury."

"Motion granted."

Valeria's head was spinning back and forth, her gaze flicking between the judge, the DA and Biegler, eyes elongated with fear and confusion.

Minoa leaned over the balustrade and patted her back, saying, "You're getting out," which earned an angry command from the officer standing behind the defense table. Valeria's eyes brimmed.

The deputies took Valeria out through a door in the back of the courtroom and the judge exited through another. Ireni, Carter and Minoa clasped hands together. Then Ireni and Carter headed out to the hallway. Minoa approached Biegler. He took a step backward as if to preserve the distance between them.

"Don't uncork the champagne," he said. "They'll refile charges and arrest her again unless it turns out this woman who disappeared is a *sina qua non* of the DA's case. And it's a good thing I'm nearing retirement because that DA is never going to negotiate with me again."

"But Valeria will get out today, right?"

"You can pick her up at the jail in a few hours."

She turned to leave but paused.

"Thanks."

"Don't thank me yet."

THIRTY-EIGHT

The three women leaned against the front end of the truck, arms crossed, staring at a long brown facade, mute against browned desert, striped at the entrance by white pillars. The wings of the detention center behind, two story walls peppered by tiny barred windows, were only visible on the drive in.

"I say we put her on a plane to somewhere that doesn't extradite to the US."

Carter shifted her squint from the door to her friends.

"Maybe if we fly her to Canada she could get temporary refugee status," said Ireni.

"Uruguay or Argentina is safer. Nazis hid out there for decades."

"If she flees, it will make her look guilty." Minoa took a walk in a tiny circle and returned to her spot. "I wonder if the conditions of her immigration bond require her to report this arrest to ICE. After all, the charge was dropped."

"I say let them find out on their own."

Carter made an angry gesture with her fist.

"So what do we do when she gets out? She can't just go back to normal life, can she?"

Ireni looked from Minoa to Carter and back.

"Valeria will have to decide for herself how to handle it."

Ireni pulled out her phone and Carter stretched. Minoa peered up at a raptor cutting lazy circles into a glowing azure sky, turned down a few volts, as October aged, from the zinging electric blue of high summer. Reminded herself to pull in a few deep breaths. Now she could relax and get back to the daunting task of reconstructing her life. She'd give Ron a call to see when she could finish the Gavilan survey and check on the timeline for the cannibalism excavation near Crownpoint. Although both of them knew her contractor spot at the archaeology office was likely a fling rather than a marriage. Even if he came up with the funds for a permanent position, was she willing to decline into her forties working a low-paid state government job with no future and high occupational risk for skin cancer? Plus traipsing up and down Gavilan Mesa had bored her to semi-consciousness. The most exciting thing to happen out there was discovering a few shallow graves.

What did she want to do next? She'd had some years to explore her fascination with shamanism, so why complain? Now it was time to accept that her youthful adventures were over. She should be mature enough at thirty-six to chain herself to a desk and be content with a regular paycheck. Just be grateful she wasn't paying off college debt and find an engrossing hobby. It wasn't anything she'd ever dreamed of, but so what? People rarely chose to become a shaman either. They'd fall mortally ill before understanding that the only way to heal was to heal others. Shamans were wounded healers. Minoa still ached with ancient and not-so-ancient wounds, so she had the wounded part covered. The question was: what path would heal her?

"Wonder how long it will take to release her?" said Carter.

"Same," said Ireni.

Suddenly a motorcycle roared into the parking lot and swirled around to stop hard beside them. The rider stepped down, pulled off his helmet.

"Whoa, am I dreaming?" Carter whispered.

"That's Valeria's brother, Berto."

Minoa greeted him and was making introductions when the detention center door opened and Valeria stepped out, blinking into sunrays rebounding off every surface.

"Vali!"

Berto ran to her. They embraced. Then Valeria moved toward her friends.

"How are you feeling?" said Minoa.

"I don't know yet."

Berto wrapped his arm around her shoulders, hugged her again.

"Vali, we've got to talk about your options," said Carter.

"Stay calm," said Minoa. "I have a hunch they won't refile charges."

"Do you think I have to notify the immigration court about my arrest?"

"Let's not. We can always say you didn't know," said Ireni.

"Ignorance is not a defense," Minoa began as a white SUV sped into the parking lot, skidding to a stop beside them.

Doors popped open and two agents in green clothing and black vests stepped out. They paused, scanning the four women, one blonde, one auburn, one brown-haired, one black-haired. After a moment's consideration the taller one, a crewcut guy with raspy cheeks, stepped toward Valeria revealing the wording on the back of his black vest: POLICE ICE.

"*Nombre*?"

"Don't say anything," said Carter.

Minoa stepped in front of him.

"Do you have an arrest warrant?"

"Get out of the way and you won't be harmed."

"She asked for an arrest warrant."

Carter moved to Minoa's side. The other agent, bald with a full beard, pulled a document out of the car and sauntered over.

"Here's the warrant."

He waved it in front of Minoa's face.

"Guys," Ireni whispered urgently, "there's nothing you can do."

"I can't read that if you're moving it."

Minoa pushed the document back, scanned it and then looked at Valeria.

"Valie, you may have to go with them for now but we'll get a lawyer right away."

Valeria sobbed, slapped a hand to her mouth.

"Wait a minute," said Carter. "Let me see that warrant." She grabbed the paper. "I don't see a judge's signature."

"Carter, don't make this worse," Ireni pleaded.

"Ladies, you're all risking charges. Now step aside."

The taller agent pushed a hand past Carter's and Minoa's shoulders. Valeria shrunk back. Minoa froze, glanced at Carter, then back at the red-cheeked agent.

"Can you give us a minute?"

"Min, a warrant has to have a judge's signature."

"There's a smudge. How are we supposed to know if it's legal? She needs a lawyer."

"You know damn well this isn't right, even if it is legal. Valie didn't do anything wrong."

"Time's up. Step aside."

No one moved. Minoa was looking through a wallet she'd pulled from her pocket.

"I put that lawyer's card in here, I know I did."

"Now!" screamed the bald agent.

Ireni wrapped an arm around Valeria's trembling shoulders. She choked, reached out a hand to Berto.

"*Berto, no te preocupes ...*"

The bald fellow stepped behind them, flung Ireni's arm into the air and grabbed Valeria's shoulders. She shrieked. Berto strode over to face off with the agent.

"Leave my sister alone."

The bald guy squinted at him.

"Looks like we may have another one, Mike."

Carter's face exploded with outrage.

"How dare you? You're profiling him and threatening him with arrest just because he looks Hispanic? This is New Mexico, you cretin. The governor is Hispanic along with half the people in the state."

"Carter, chill," said Minoa.

"Every one of you is breaking the law. Move aside now or face arrest."

"ICE arresting citizens? You're going to regret this."

"We don't have to take this shit from you femoids," muttered the bald officer.

"Chill out, Frank," said the other. "I'll deal with this."

He walked toward Valeria dangling a pair of handcuffs from one hand.

"Arms behind your back."

Valeria blinked at him, lowered her gaze and turned around.

"Wait a minute," Carter said, stepping in front of Valeria. "What do you think you're doing? She may be pregnant. You can't cuff her behind."

Minoa and Ireni threw Carter a horrified glance. Berto's expression broke into pieces. The bald agent hip-checked Carter making her stumble sideways. She regrouped and side-shoved the agent. He crossed one ankle over the other and tripped himself to splatter onto the ground. Shot up like a rocket.

"That's it!" he screamed. "You assaulted an officer."

"You fell down because you assaulted me," Carter screamed back.

"Everybody calm down," Minoa yelled.

The taller officer locked a hand around Valeria's wrist and hooked on handcuffs. Valeria blurted an exclamation of fear. Berto's face glistened with tears, his body shook.

"Stop hurting my sister!"

He grabbed Valeria's other wrist and tried to pull her away.

"No, Berto, no!"

The taller agent made a stop gesture with his free hand while continuing to haul on Valeria.

"Back off!"

A few feet away the bald agent now stood with feet spread wide, brandishing a revolver.

"Hands in the air, now!"

All four women froze, staring. Berto kept tugging on Valeria.

"Let my sister go. She hasn't done anything wrong. Take me instead."

"Berto, *levanta las manos.*"

The taller one clasped Berto's fingers trying to pry them off Valeria's forearm. Berto swiveled his arm while pounding his other fist on the agent's hand holding the handcuffs.

"Back off or I shoot," yelled the bald agent

"Christ, don't shoot me," yelled the taller agent, pushing Berto away with an elbow.

"Vali, *llévate la moto y vete.*"

Valeria was shaking her head, crying.

"No, Berto, I can't."

Ireni took off running for the detention center door. Minoa waved her hands like a desperate crossing guard.

"Everybody stop. We can resolve this."

The taller agent jerked the handcuffs toward himself while shoving a hand into Berto's chest. He stumbled, then charged forward launching a wild hook that the agent dodged. At that instant a shot rang out, reverberating off the stucco face of the jail to echo across the plains. A shocked silence followed. Berto crashed forward pushing the taller agent backwards to stagger and fall with Berto on top.

"Oh, my God!" Valeria fell to her knees beside Berto. "Call an ambulance!"

Minoa and Carter stepped to Berto's side.

"What the hell are you doing?" Minoa yelled at the bald agent.

"Assassin!" Carter screamed.

"Get me out of here," came a muffled cry from underneath. The taller agent wriggled out from under Berto, rolling him onto his back. Blood welled up from the neck of Berto's shirt. A wail tore out of Valeria. She laid her forehead on his, sobbing hysterically.

Two guards came running out the detention center door with Ireni close behind. They paused when they saw the scene and one started talking into the microphone protruding from his collar. Ireni, standing to the side, punched at her phone.

"A man has been shot outside the county detention center. We need an ambulance right away."

Valeria smoothed her brother's hair over and over, pouring out a lamentation. Berto coughed out foamy blood onto the pavement. More guards came running out of the detention center with a stretcher, a medical kit, a defibrillator. Carter moved to Berto's side.

"Have you got a chest seal or occlusive dressing?" she said to the person carrying the kit.

"I don't know."

She reviewed the contents of the first aid kit and pulled on a pair of surgical gloves. Everyone watched, paralyzed, as she crouched over Berto and tore open his shirt. Blood formed a crimson pool on his chest. Carter mopped it up with gauze and covered the wound with an adhesive dressing. A siren, first faint, grew louder. The bald ICE agent started talking into his phone. One of the guards stood in front of him.

"Officer-involved shooting. We'll have to carry out an investigation."

The agent lowered the phone and glared at the guard.

"That illegal attacked a federal officer in the line of duty. Arrest him or we will."

Then he went back to his phone call. The taller agent took a couple steps their way.

"That's right. He attacked me."

His rough pink cheeks carried stripes of blood. The bald agent put a hand over the mouthpiece.

"This never would've happened if you'd let us execute our detainer. Federal law takes precedence over state and local law. You can't interfere with our mission."

He went back to his call.

"Nobody goes anywhere," said the detention center guard. "I'm calling Sarge."

They stood in silence, eyes flitting back and forth. After a siren wound closer and closer, an ambulance roared into the parking area. EMT's jumped out, glanced at Berto and unloaded a stretcher. Valeria hovered as they checked Berto and slid him onto the stretcher. When they started carrying him toward the ambulance, she followed. The bald agent ran over and grabbed her dangling handcuff.

"Don't move! You're under arrest!"

"No, please, I must go with my brother."

He locked the dangling half of the handcuffs onto her other wrist. The taller agent strode into the ambulance while the bald one led Valeria to the SUV.

"Hold on just a minute. None of you are free to leave."

The EMT's turned to look at the detention center guard.

"Not you."

He motioned the EMT's to leave. The bald agent paused with one hand on the driver's side door of the ICE SUV.

"That's a federal detainee. He's got to be accompanied by an officer. And I'm taking this one into custody."

He climbed in, shut the car door and zoomed out of the parking area as everyone stared. The sound of the retreating car fizzled, restoring the afternoon's silent brilliance. After a moment the guard turned around.

"Uh, everybody else inside. We got to write this up."

Another guard held out his arms and herded them toward the detention center entrance.

"Unbelievable," Carter muttered.

"I just hope they don't take Berto to St. You-Know-Who's." Ireni inserted herself between Carter and Minoa as they walked. "Even healthy newborns have trouble getting out of there alive."

Minoa couldn't speak.

THIRTY-NINE

It was late in the day when she pulled up in front of the guesthouse and stepped out. She paused, leaning against the truck, to survey the estate and surrounding hills, dusty and yellowing after another day of solar gales. Pulling out her phone, she sought the immigration lawyer's number and dialed.

"I'm calling about Valeria Medina Ramirez. I came by for a consultation, remember? She's been picked up again by ICE, even though the murder charge was dropped. What can we do to get her out now?"

She listened.

"But it was a bogus case, a ridiculous accusation."

Her eyes rose from the blue brown foothills of the Sangre de Cristos up to emerald ridges, up up the mountain past its sash of tarnishing aspens to a snow-lined crest incised against buffed blue.

"Are you saying her case is treated differently because of where she lives? ICE may not send her back to a sanctuary city even if the DA refiles the murder charge?"

She glanced over at the prairie dog burrows. No corpses evident. Maybe Eldon had sent out the prairie dog cleanup team. If it were possible to feel any sicker, the sight of the deserted prairie dog village would have done it. But she was already past the zero point.

"So there's no way to get her out of ICE detention? Ok, thanks. I'll be in touch."

She dropped her phone hand to dangle at her side while her gaze returned to the cactus-speckled estate. A dead landscape. Nothing moved. Nothing had moved in a while, not since the last Porsche or BMW or Range Rover barreled past churning up a layer of dust first laid down in the Pleistocene. She felt like sliding down to the ground and taking a long nap. Or escaping. Running as fast and as far as she could go. And just not coming back. Her mind felt like a bulldozed lot, scraped clean of life, devoid of water. A couple unwanted tears squeezed out distorting her view of the landscape, probably the only liquid in sight for miles. She wiped them away with angry swats. There was no use crying at this point.

Finally her feet started shuffling across the parking area in front of Brent's mansion, dragging her along with them. They continued up the incline to the east side of the house and stopped by the prairie dog village. Empty now. Heaped up piles of dirt among a cribbage board of abandoned burrows. Would the rattlers move in? That would be a joke on Brent, poetic justice for his entitled manipulation of nature.

A lightning bolt of grief stabbed her desiccated emotions, grief for the cute little murdered prairie dogs, not for Berto or Valeria. Was she heartless? Those creatures had been her companions out here at the estate. Nobody else to talk to. She'd watched the hijinks at Brent's manor house like a reality TV show. Sure, she'd savored the panorama; the wealthy had carved out a whopping portion of beauty and freedom and fun for themselves. Sadly that included raining poison on a village of innocents. Along with a lot of other crimes Carter could detail. Right now (what kind of malcreant was she to think of rodents when Berto might be dead and Valeria jailed?) she missed her pop-up furry friends.

She heard tires rolling up the drive, a raspy sound peppered by little pops of kicked-up pebbles. Then a car appeared and stopped in front of the guesthouse. Low and wide, maybe Lincoln or Caddy, circa turn of the millennium. The driver's door opened and Eldon stepped out. He looked around, spotted her by the prairie dog village, waved. She walked over.

"What brings you out here, Eldon?"

"Well, I thought we had a quid pro quo, or rather, an agreement falling short of the legal definition but still moderately binding."

"This is not a great time."

She spun around, walked to her front door, opened it and went inside. Eldon followed. At the door jamb he stopped with both hands on the threshold.

"Perhaps my arrival was inopportune. I certainly don't intend to take advantage of my position as your *in loco dominus.*"

Minoa paused with her back to him, forced herself to relax. Turned around with a mannequin face.

"Loco? No dispute there. Dominant? Don't think so."

"It's Latin for landlord. You see I'm a highly educated—"

"Spare me. I can fill in the blank: a southern gentleman. Eldon, what are you like behind that Ashley Wilkes mask?"

"You mean, what am I like in the morning before I've had my bourbon-laced latte? Perhaps you'd like to find out? In that case I'm even willing to start the day with a cup of that Argentinian brew you favor."

She walked over to the kitchenette, pushed a cup of water into the microwave, stared out the window, thinking. Hoping something would come to her. What came was a feeling like somebody drove a fist through her abdominal wall. Delayed grief, she thought. The idea came a few seconds later. She looked at him.

"Here's my offer: I'll meet you for a shot of southern bourbon later if you'll do something for me first."

"As long as it doesn't involve the commission of a felony."

"All you've got to do is call Mercedes and ask her to come over to pick up Leah's things from Brent's house."

"And you?"

"I'll meet you at your place for that drink later."

His palomino eyebrows arched.

"Keep in mind that as I'm not your attorney our communications are not confidential."

"Understood."

"I'm subjecting myself to another possible assault at the hands of that Mexican Mama."

"You'll survive."

"Alright, seven pm."

He took a business card out of his wallet, wrote something on the back and handed it to her.

"Here's my address."

"Deal."

"For the record, this conversation didn't happen."

"Give me twenty minutes before you call."

"Please don't set me up for any more emergency visits to the police station. My heart can't take it."

He headed toward the big house. She grabbed her keys, paused, then ran to the bathroom for a pair of surgical gloves. On the way out she stepped around the side of the guesthouse to the pile of two-by-four cuttings and selected a two-foot chunk. She placed it on the passenger seat, climbed into the truck and drove off.

FORTY

She parked around the corner from Mercedes' place, a mock adobe townhouse stretched taller than nature intended, squeezed in a cluster of similar tipped-up shoe boxes with little garage cubes between. Peeking around the edge of the last condo in the row, she saw no movement. She speed-walked to Mercedes' driveway and slipped into a niche where trash bins sat next to the garage.

She waited, fanning that sense of outraged resolve that had powered her into the truck and through the drive over. Brent's death along with police and prosecutorial incompetence had ruined Valeria's life. Poor sincere Valeria who had wanted to finish her psychology degree and maybe aspire someday to become a social worker. Back in ICE detention with no way out but a flight to San Salvador. And her brother might die. He might already be dead. Maybe she shouldn't have told him Valeria was getting out of jail. Or anything at all. Because everything she touched got worse.

The guilt smothered her fire of outrage to sputtering embers. Now she could hear Eldon's imagined warning in her head: 'Burglary, a something-degree felony with so-and-so many years of prison.' But would she give up and just accept the mess fate had made with a little help from her? No way. The pilot light of righteous determination in her belly flared up again. Mercedes must be responsible for the poisoning blamed on Valeria and she wasn't going to get away with it. Minoa would find a way to prove her guilt even if it cost her a jail sentence.

Anyway, if she didn't take anything the charge wouldn't be burglary, it'd be trespassing. A few months max. Carter would laugh at a few months locked up in service of the greater good. And despite her perpetual early mid-life crisis, Minoa wouldn't let a twenty-something self-righteous rebel outdo her. She tugged on the surgical gloves.

Within five minutes a rumble indicated the garage door was sliding up. She moved to the corner of the house, peered around. Heard a car engine. Ducked back, then spied out again. A sedan backed into the street, shifted from reverse to drive. She spotted Leah in a booster seat in the back as it drove away. As the garage door rolled down, she leaped around the corner, positioned the two-by-four underneath. The door landed on the chunk of wood, wheezed and stuttered. After glancing up and down the lane of condos, she rolled under and kicked the board.

By the door to the house she flipped on the garage light and surveyed items on a couple wall shelves. No super warfarin or other rodenticide in sight. She stepped inside, passing through a laundry room to a kitchen bright with flowered Mexican tiles. The place was silent. She glanced in the living room—antique furniture in the gauzy light of sheer curtains—and padded up some steps. Upstairs she passed a couple bedrooms, one with a canopy bed and photographs of puppies and horses on the walls, another with a king-size with velvet upholstered headboard.

At the end of the hallway she spied a room with a desk in one corner and yoga supplies in baskets in another. She ducked in, scanned the contents of the top desk drawer and flipped through manila folders in the bottom drawer. The majority contained legal paperwork relating to five years of custody and child support battles. A few held financial documents, tax forms, invoices. Toward the back she found a file labeled 'Derek Whitfield.'

Inside were a group of five-by-eights, more lurid than what she'd seen in Whitfield's office. One spied through a window frame to a fuzzy image of a naked Brent with a woman plastered to his chest. Another showed Brent in the open front door kissing a woman. From the back of the head, draped with fine straight hair, she guessed it was the lobbyist. Another caught Brent out in front of the house, kissing a woman mostly off camera. Beyond his silhouette, in the background, two prairie dogs posed at alert, erect above their burrows. And on and on.

All this documented sexual activity had failed to defeat Brent's custody bid. Probably Mercedes came off in court as a jealous ex-wife bad-mouthing her child's father to the innocent child.

At the back of the file was Derek's invoice for $7643.96. Someone had scribbled an 'X' over the page. Did that 'X' signify the bill had been paid? Or did it show that the invoicer had been 'Xed', killed and dumped in a barrel of acid?

She glanced around the room. Near the baskets of rolled up yoga mats, foam blocks, folded blankets and a rainbow array of resistance bands stood a statue of the *Virgin de Guadalupe* on a stand, framed by a radiating gold aura under a bright ceramic arch. Devotional candles flickered before the statue. Framed photos sat on either side. She approached.

One photo, a black-and-white, blurry with age, showed a *campesino* couple, the man in white shirt and broad sombrero, the woman in a drab shirtwaist. The other was a full-body image of Brent in swimming trunks at some Caribbean beach. It was stuck full of sewing pins. There were pins in his eyes, nose, mouth, throat, heart, genitals, feet. Against the photo frame leaned a ceramic icon of a female figure in a long red robe, skull head crowned by flowers.

Nuestra Señora de la Santa Muerte, Saint Death. She'd read about the cult as she tried to keep up on journals covering folklore, cults and indigenous religious practices in Latin America. Worship of Saint Death had spread among the impoverished masses in Mexico and was a particular favorite of cartel members.

So Mercedes had been asking Saint Death to torture Brent. Maybe *Santa Muerte* had suggested to Mercedes that she funnel some brodifacoum into a bottle of scorpion mezcal. Maybe Our Lady of Holy Death instructed Mercedes to pack the poisoned mezcal into Leah's suitcase when deputies showed up to enforce the judge's reversal of custody, with instructions to her *hijita* to leave the bottle in the cabinet as a secret present for daddy.

The doorbell rang out. She rushed across the hallway into a bedroom and peered out a window overlooking the front of the condo. A man with rippling black hair stood at the door. Below that she saw print sleeves rolled up onto forearms, jeans flared over needle-toed cowboy boots. After a moment he pulled a key ring out of his pocket, inserted a key into the door lock. She heard the door swing open.

She dashed back into the office, scurried to the window and looked down. It was a two-story drop to hard rocky ground. The man was moving around downstairs. Tiptoeing back to the door, she pushed it shut and scanned the contents of the room again. A small open closet held a stack of boxes. The windows had Venetian blinds.

Then she heard steps climbing the stairs. She took a couple of long strides to the window, pulled it open, climbed onto the sill. Pausing, she jumped back into the room and ran to the resistance bands. Taking the longest one, she looped it around the strut of the window frame and scooted off the sill. She bounced, slamming into the stucco wall. Twisting her torso she landed her feet on the wall and walked down rappel-style until she was hanging by her hands from the strap. At that moment the strap slipped off the window frame. She fell to the ground, rolling across her shoulders in a Ukemi breakfall straight out of her teenage years studying judo. Leaping up, she realized with a shock that she'd instinctively recalled the move without planning. She sprinted to a gate in the back fence and ran down an alley toward where she'd parked the truck.

At the end of the block she peeked around another condo garage to where she could see a green pickup truck parked in front of Mercedes' condo. A graphic with words was painted on the driver's side door. She trotted closer until she could read the words: Ted's Landscaping Services. Hurried back to her truck.

As she slid into the driver's seat she realized the pink resistance band still looped around her wrist. She flung her hand out and shook it as if she'd spotted a scorpion crawling up. The band flew to the other side of the cab and dropped to the floorboards in a heap. She hadn't intended to take anything from Mercedes' house. Could they get her on theft charges for stealing a resistance band? She'd have to get rid of it, burn it, bury it. Then self-reflection kicked in. Was she going nuts? She rubbed her arms, peeled off the surgical gloves and brushed down her clothes as her breathing slowed. Back on course.

She hadn't found anything to incriminate Mercedes, unless invoking avenging spirits to kill an enemy was illegal. But who was the muscled Latino guy with a key to Mercedes' house? She searched on her phone. Ted's Landscaping was owned by Teodoro Garcia Melendez. According to the website the company offered landscaping, irrigation, deck construction and pest control. Pest control. Her memory soared back to that Friday afternoon when she'd driven home after another long day trekking up and down Gavilan Mesa to find Brent and Crystal tussling and a couple Latino guys shoveling poison into the prairie dog burrows.

She dialed the number. A woman with a heavy accent answered.

"Hello, I'm interested in landscaping and pest control services. You provide that, right? Could you give me the addresses of some homes where your company does landscaping and pest control? I'm particularly interested in extermination of prairie dogs. I'd like to see examples of your work, places where you've gotten rid of the prairie dogs—they're such a bother—before I decide which company to use. Preferably on the north side."

She waited.

"Lejano Lane? And Upper Canyon? That's great. But do you have any homes near Stagecoach or Thunderbird? That's my neighborhood."

"No? An estimate would work. I'll get back to you."

She tossed the phone onto the passenger seat and was about to drive away when she heard an engine start. Easing to where she could spy around the corner she spotted Ted in the green pickup. When he took off, she trailed behind.

FORTY-ONE

She followed him onto the relief route heading south. He curved all the way around town to exit onto the frontage road alongside the interstate heading to Albuquerque. Then he turned at Los Pinos, a country road that wound past the usual mix of the struggling, the privileged and the artistic amidst buffalograss speckled with cyprus where water leached to the surface.

Finally he turned down a short dirt lane. She swerved off onto a spur leading to a trailer on a big lot. After stopping where a shed blocked her truck from Ted's view, she jumped out and ran over to a board fence missing chunks. She peered over at the yard of Ted's Landscaping, a bare dirt lot encircled by sagging chicken wire. He walked past scattered pieces of equipment to a tiny office, a prefab shed with a handwritten sign on the door, and disappeared inside. Maguey plants in pots dotted the area behind the shed. She waited, watching a turkey vulture circle overhead, its bald red head tracing lazy loops on the vellum October sky. Her train of thought spiraled up into the boundless blue, viewing events on the earth's surface from a bird's-eye perspective.

Ted must be Mercedes' current boyfriend, permanent enough to have a key to her place. Was he a *paisano* of hers from Durango, Mexico? In his landscaping company he likely hired people from his home region. That was typical in Santa Fe. Maybe he plotted with Mercedes to get pest control work at Brent's estate so they could plant a poisoned liquor bottle. Or maybe he gave his workers the order to liquidate Brent and, spotting liquor deliveries as they shoveled rodenticide, they improvised a method.

Could Ted's workers be the people from Durango who scared Dolores so much she turned down five thousand bucks and ran for her life? The guys she'd seen shoveling brodifacoum into the prairie dog burrows when she came home that Friday evening after discovering the mounds at Gavilan Mesa didn't look like assassins, just workers following orders on a job. Still, Durango was next door to Sinaloa, former home of El Chapo and headquarters of the Sinaloa Cartel. Could business-owner Ted be a friend of cartel members? Or was Mercedes the link to Mexican traffickers, even though she'd scoffed at Minoa's insinuation that she still had contact with her trafficker ex- or his colleagues? Mercedes claimed not to know Dolores and she might be telling the truth. But Dolores might have known Ted's laborers from her hometown of San Gregorio, Durango. And she might know they worked for the cartel when they were in Mexico.

None of this explained why Brent had articles on his desk about cartel money laundering. Perhaps he'd hoped to accuse Mercedes at the custody trial of having links to drug traffickers. He must have decided against that tactic as she didn't remember any mention of it in the custody file documents she scanned. Of course the file didn't include a transcript of the trial. Maybe an allegation of links to drug traffickers was the ultimate weapon that assured Brent won the years-long custody battle. The question remained why Eldon hadn't mentioned it.

Ted came walking out of the office and loaded a piece of equipment, perhaps a tiller, and a chainsaw into the back of the truck and drove out again. She ran to the truck and hurried back to Los Pinos where she caught sight of the green truck just before the road curved out of sight. She caught up at the frontage road and followed Ted all the way back into town, past Museum Hill and St. John's College, up into the foothills of Atalaya Mountain where wealthy homes occupied huge mountainous lots. He pulled into a drive and parked behind another Ted's Landscaping truck. She passed the house, parked by a cluster of piñons and hurried back to spy.

Ted dropped off the equipment with a couple of workers, one tall and skinny, the other small and portly. Both wore western hats. She thought back, trying to recall that moment when she'd glanced out the window at two workers shoveling poison into the prairie dog burrows. Hard to remember exactly but she thought they'd been more or less of middle stature, slender, wearing jeans and western hats. Not one big and one small like these two workers. Ted climbed back into his truck and drove away.

She strolled along the road as if out for a mid-day walk. Nearing the two workers, who were fiddling with the equipment, she cut over.

"Hi."

They looked up and stared.

"You work for Ted's Landscaping, right?"

The two of them exchanged glances.

"I saw your truck over at a neighbor's house on Stagecoach Road on the north side. Was that you working there?"

"*Disculpe, señora. Solo somos obreros.*"

The accent was northern Mexican. She continued in Spanish explaining that she'd seen them at a friend's place on the north side. She explained she had a problem with praïrie dogs at her house and had heard they carried out an effective extermination at her friend's.

"It's a big long house with a guesthouse and a circular drive on Stagecoach Road," she prompted, forging ahead despite their clueless expressions. "Do you remember?"

The large fellow made an 'aw shucks' gesture with his hands, the small one twirled a shovel handle between his palms.

She thanked them and left. They were good liars if they were covering up a special job for their boss leaving poisoned mezcal at Brent's house. More likely they had zero idea what she was talking about and considered her a typical crazy rich American. She drove back down the mountain.

At the stop sign where the road intersected Camino de Cruz Blanca a green pickup pulled into the opposing lane and the window rolled down.

"Hey, I hear from my workers you looking for landscaping," Ted said. "I can give you more information."

She looked across a few feet of road into his round brown eyes set in a face of thick skin, thick stubble, thick black brows. Even the wavy hair was thick. Was there anything more in his expression than an eagerness for work? Had he spotted her in her truck at Mercedes' condo and was putting two and two together? His eyes betrayed nothing but a touch of wariness.

"Yes, I heard your company did an excellent job exterminating prairie dogs at Brent Harrison's house. He's my neighbor."

"We could come by your house and give an estimate."

"That might work. You did do the job at Harrison's house, didn't you? I thought I saw one of your trucks there."

"I no remember the name but I can check."

She thought his eyes narrowed.

"Alright, I'll get back to you."

She let her wheels roll.

"Wait!"

He backed up fast, angling the rear corner of the pickup across her path, forcing her to stop.

"Here, I give you a card. You call me. I give you a good deal."

She took the card and waited. After a moment the window rolled up and he sped away. She mulled as she headed downtown. Was Ted an overzealous salesperson desperate for a new client? Or was the act of backing in front of her car a subtle warning? He'd acted like he didn't recognize Brent's name, but any friend of Mercedes would have heard it countless times. So he lied to her, and now he knew what she looked like and what kind of truck she drove. Maybe Ted had Brent killed to appease Mercedes' hatred or maybe they conspired to kill him to get access to the fortune through Leah. Either way, finding out Brent constructed a will to keep Mercedes from ever controlling his money must have burned.

If you included Crystal, Mrs. Harrison and Caitlin Romero, that made a lot of people who were mad as hell over being cut out of the inheritance. Who would they take it out on? Eldon, the messenger bringing bad news? But Eldon had come out of this better than anyone else. It was time to figure out exactly what he'd gained from Brent's death.

FORTY-TWO

She stumbled out of Probate Court onto Palace Avenue, her visual field shimmering like pixel popcorn from an hour deciphering a minuscule font. After walking up a portico lined by hand hewn posts, she slid onto a decorative park bench in the plaza and let her tired eyes wash over the flow of late season tourists. October days were growing shorter. The late afternoon light carried an aquamarine wash of approaching night. As tourists headed to their dinner destinations, she sorted out the implications of the last will and testament she'd just read.

Leah would receive a pitiable monthly disbursement until the age of twenty-three. Brent's mom wasn't mentioned. Ditto for Crystal. (Had he changed the will after Crystal moved out or was he always intending to stiff her?) Net proceeds were to be reinvested. The overall effect of constructing a set of trusts designed to keep everyone's hands off his money was to turn the will's executor and trustee into sole controller of investments, proceeds and accounting for many millions during the next decade and a half. On top of Eldon's liberal fees there would be oodles of opportunities to profit from moving that kind of money. The real beneficiary of Brent's will was Eldon. Yet all he did was complain about his unpaid bonus for winning the custody case.

She pulled out her phone, launched a search on the name Eldon Bohnefeld III. Found an old facebook page with photos of Eldon, a few years younger, posing with a dark-haired woman against a variety of backgrounds. There was a LinkedIn page listing his areas of legal specialization as tax law, civil suits, real estate, contracts, trusts and wills. An Albuquerque Journal article on a New Mexico Bar Association conference mentioned his name as a panelist. She scrolled past search results until the name Bohnefeld in the text caught her eye. Clicked on the article:

New Jersey Investigating Tax Credit Scheme.

New Jersey offered tax breaks to corporations to persuade them to relocate to cities with high unemployment rates. But an in-depth investigation by the Newark Star-Ledger discovered that companies falsely claimed they had been planning to locate elsewhere in order to claim the tax subsidies.

A report by the governor's special task force reveals that one company alone, Shurken Properties Inc., benefited from $327 million in tax subsidies after it certified to the state government that it was planning to move to Philadelphia at a cost of 384 jobs to the state of New Jersey, but would agree to stay in exchange for the subsidies. The investigation found that Shurken Properties never applied for any permit in Philadelphia.

Eldon Bohnefeld III, counsel of record for Shurken Properties, stated at the task force hearing, "Shurken Properties takes its civic responsibility to contribute to the state economy seriously, and projects creation of over 300 new jobs in Camden."

New Jersey? Could there be another Eldon Bohnefeld III Esquire? Doubtful. Eldon was far from transparent.

She looked up. The pine-forested mountain above town glowed blue-green in the last beams of a sinking sun. She rose and paused, noting a familiar figure approaching the square. Ron was walking beside a woman in a pastel linen dress. She was smiling at him, clasping his arm. About twenty feet away he saw her and approached.

"Minoa."

"Hi Ron."

"It's great to see you. This is Elsie."

"Hi."

"Hey, there's news. Which do you want first: the good or the bad?"

"How about the bad."

"APD says the human remains found in those mounds at Gavilan are recent, so the killer is likely still active. Check out the coverage in the Albuquerque Journal."

"So I've been walking around Gavilan alone while some psychopath dumps his victims' bodies there?"

"If that wendigo wanted your flesh you would have seen him by now. You run more risk of encountering a rabid porcupine."

"Did you say wendigo?"

Ron smiled at her while patting Elsie's hands clasped around his forearm.

"I thought a cultural anthropologist would know that reference. It's from Algonquin–"

"I know what it is. Did we mention it before?"

"Not that I recall. We usually confine ourselves to archaeological techno-talk. But maybe there will be a little space for you to delve into the cultural perspective up at Crownpoint."

"Crownpoint?"

"You know, that site I mentioned that we hope holds evidence relevant to the Turner cannibalism debate."

"Do you think that project will start soon?"

"That segues to the good news. Funding's falling into place. Might even start surveying this fall, take a break for the cool weather and then get those pickaxes swinging after the last frost."

"So I go from contemporary serial murder to ancestral Puebloan cannibalism."

"You know what we say: never a dull moment at Arch Studs. And don't forget to vote. Of course I can't tell you how to vote. Just remember what I told you about which party will use their majority in the statehouse to up our funding enough for a new staff position."

"I remember."

"I'll let you know as soon as we've got the okay to finish Gavilan. Should be coming soon. Enjoy your evening."

He and Elsie strolled away. Elsie had never unclamped her hands from Ron's arm.

She watched them walk down Water Street, street lights coating them in a fuzzy glow, mentally recalculating. She'd imagined Ron spending his evenings after work with a tumbler of brandy in one hand and a tome on geochemical analysis of ancestral Puebloan potsherds in the other. Not going out to dinner with the love of his life.

The sun had set, staining everything a wistful teal. She started walking back to where she'd parked the truck, aware of a hollow feeling in her belly. She told herself to ignore it but it lingered, like a place marker for something that disappeared a long time ago.

FORTY-THREE

She escaped a glut of luxury vehicles on Paseo de Peralta and drove up Bishops Lodge Road through prime Sotheby's territory. After pausing atop a hill to gaze at a glittery tapestry of city lights, she turned onto a dirt lane lined by custom adobes on huge lots speckled with juniper and prickly pear. Eldon's house clicked all the Santa Fe style boxes: rough hewn lintels, protruding vigas, carved door. Knocking scraped her knuckles and she raised them to her lips as the door swung open. He invited her into a living room where everything appeared swollen—thick plastered walls, massive wood frame furniture, huge southwestern paintings.

"Before you say anything, I rent this place furnished. The owner shows up every summer for opera season so I have to skedaddle for a month or so."

"You'll be able to buy yourself a nice place now that you're managing Brent's fortune."

"My quite reasonable fees are specified in the will. Overall, I'm bound by my fiduciary responsibility to the beneficiary, that is, the adorable Leah Harrison. I'm not expecting to get rich."

"A six-year-old won't be an exacting client."

"Mercedes will perch on my shoulder. Knowing what that will be like, most attorneys would refuse to serve in this trusteeship. And given the extensive nature of Brent's holdings it will create forbidding conflicts of interest with other potential clients. In reality, I'm entering a tunnel of enormous career limitations if I see this thing through till Leah reaches the age to gain control. Please have a seat. Chips and salsa coming up along with scotch whiskey."

He stepped out of the room. Minoa took a turn around, peering down a dark hallway, then sat in a bulging geometric print armchair. She pulled a folded check out of her pocket and smoothed it flat on a coffee table. After a moment he returned with a platter and placed blue corn chips, salsa and two tumblers of amber liquid on the coffee table. He eyed the check.

"Ms. Dolores still won't open the door?"

"She moved out."

"Curious."

"Speaking of moving, uh, was it a big change when you moved from Georgia to Santa Fe?"

"My first taste of western freedom. Exhilarating."

"I moved back here from New York. I don't suppose you've spent time there, or nearby?"

He squinted at her.

"Have we reached the happy stage where we share life stories?"

She looked away.

"You heard that Valeria's brother was shot?"

"Lamentable. But at least your friend is out of legal jeopardy."

As she turned back to look at him her tone of voice shot up.

"Out? She's in an immigration detention center with no way to avoid deportation."

"Has she considered Canada?"

"She has."

He poked at the salsa with a chip.

"Perhaps we should converse about something more cheerful. At least you can stop chasing murderers now."

With a sigh she dropped her tensed shoulders.

"The ridiculous murder accusation against Valeria went away. But it ruined her life and may have murdered her brother. And I'm the one that got her into this. Giving up is not an option."

"I see. I would quote some famous football coach celebrating perseverance, but I never watch football. Do you have any new suspects?"

"Maybe Mercedes' boyfriend. He has a landscaping company so his workers could have delivered the poisoned bottle while doing a job at Brent's estate. Do you know if Brent ever hired Ted's Landscaping?"

"Unlikely if Mr. Ted charges sales tax."

She dipped the point of a chip in salsa and nibbled it.

"Who do you think killed Brent?"

"If the poisoning wasn't accidental, it's obvious. Mercedes hated him as if he'd stolen her only child, which I guess he did."

"With your help."

"I wasn't paid to advise Brent on parenting."

"So you did whatever he told you to do?"

"Your criticism would apply to all attorneys. We're the servant of the client."

"But attorneys decide which cases they will take. Are you saying Brent bought your compliance?"

Eldon sighed.

"Brent bought everyone's compliance. What else is money good for? Why do you think he offered you below market rent on that guesthouse?"

"What do you mean?"

"You didn't think a man who manages millions of dollars worth of investments would fail to check comps on a rental property, did you?"

"I just thought ..."

"That was one of his favorite strategies: offer something you can't afford to turn down, then collect a favor in return later. He must have sensed your financial stress when you came by to see the place, so he offered a low rent to make you amenable to future requests."

"But what favor did he plan to—?" She looked at him with eyes on fire. "You mean you knew all along what he was thinking and said nothing?"

"I viewed technicolor screenings of Brent's tragic flaws on a daily basis. As you saw with the protection order, I was working hard to contain him. And there was no remuneration for that extra job duty."

"Still, you've come out of this better than anybody else."

"That's due to Brent's acute perception that everyone else, with the possible exception of Leah, hated him."

She stared straight ahead, mouth clenched.

"Perhaps I've spoken too baldly." He slipped into his *Gone With the Wind* drawl. "My manners as a gentleman have faltered. I beg the lady's forgiveness and vow to devote myself to her service. Let's toast to something positive. Perhaps the reuniting of Mercedes with her charming daughter?"

She glanced at the two tumblers of scotch.

"I can't stomach straight whiskey without a water chaser."

He stood and headed to the kitchen.

"And I thought you were a seasoned bartender."

She watched him disappear through a doorway, then looked at the two whiskey glasses. Heard a cabinet open and close, water flowing. Suddenly she grasped the glasses and switched them. In a moment he walked back in with a water glass in each hand and sat down.

"I'll indulge in a water chaser as well. My tolerance for strong spirits has declined while out here in the land of watery Mexican beer."

"And by your time in New Jersey?"

He paused with his glass in midair.

"A contaminated environment in every sense. Brent was pure western air after that."

"I just wondered why you didn't mention that you'd lived there."

"Being from Georgia sounds romantic. New Jersey dirties that image."

"As does misuse of tax subsidies?"

He smiled.

"Alleged misuse. Vigorously contested. Obviously wealthy people don't want to pay taxes. Nobody does. But they have the resources to avoid it."

He pushed her whiskey tumbler toward her.

"Why don't you have a drink and try to relax? It's Glenfiddich fifteen year. Straight out of Brent's cellar. I figured he had no use for it now."

She lifted her glass.

"To a future without murder."

"Or other serious felonies."

They clinked glasses.

"Did New Jersey prepare you for the tax subsidy negotiations for the Gavilan Mesa development?"

"Whoa there." He sat up straighter. "Your investigation has taken you in unexpected directions. Those negotiations, by the way, are supposed to be secret."

"I guess there's a need for secrecy when you're trying to make taxpayers pay for utilities for a private development while losing their water rights?"

"That's short-term thinking. In the long term, the community benefits from development."

"Do you believe that? Or are you saying what Brent paid you to say?"

He sipped the scotch, then tipped the glass side to side before meeting her gaze.

"Brent had a strong sense of ethics in business and finance. He never asked me to lie."

"He was negotiating to buy Gavilan Mesa from the British Bank of Commerce and Credit, a bank that's notorious for accepting laundered money."

"Tax subsidies. Water rights. Now you're concerned with money laundering?"

"You must know Brent was researching cartel money laundering. Why?"

"I hesitate to ask how you know that."

She lifted her glass to her lips, then set it down.

"You have no idea why he was concerned about dirty money?"

"Perhaps because he invested in a southwestern state that borders Mexico. Let's talk about something more interesting. Books? Movies? Perhaps golf?"

She placed her palms on the wooden arms of the chair and paused. Then she stood.

"Eldon, I think I better go. I'm tired."

He stood as well.

"Please don't leave. I've been looking forward to your visit."

"To be honest, I may have miscommunicated."

"Miscommunications are to be expected. It doesn't matter. I find you so witty, so appealing. I don't even mind your political correctness grilling. It's as stimulating as a high stakes motions hearing."

Stepping toward her he reached down and grabbed her hand. She wriggled her hand free.

"Eldon, no."

"Despite these affluent trappings I'm lonely. I suspect you're lonely too. Why should we suffer alone? Let's have another whiskey, converse and take things from there."

He wrapped an arm around her shoulders. She shook free. She walked around a chair and headed to the door. He took long strides to cut her off, planting himself between her and the door. He grabbed both her hands.

"Pretty please pretty Minoa."

"Eldon, let me go."

They started struggling, arms levering up and down.

"Minoa, calm down. No one's going to hurt you. Just sit down and we'll talk this out."

"Let go of me."

"I won't let go until you agree to talk. Then you can do whatever you want."

She froze with her arms in midair. Finger by finger he released his grip on her arms. He paused a few inches from her skin.

"Okay, are you going to sit down and be reasonable?"

She nodded. He let his arms return to his sides. At that instant she jammed her knee into his testicles. He doubled over with a deep throated cry and she shot to the door. She pulled it open, spun around to slam it shut and caught a fingertip between door and jamb. Jerked open the door to free it, slammed the door shut again and raced to the truck.

FORTY-FOUR

The Cross of the Martyrs retained a ghostly glow against the night sky. Standing on the observation deck overlooking downtown, Minoa pulled the aching finger out of her mouth, stretched her arms wide and leaned out over the railing to pretend-fly. Imagined herself as a hawk zooming through magenta-hued evening, vision panning the Paiute country rolling west to the Rio Grande, sparkly now as lights flipped on in the Las Campanas mega-homes of filmmakers and IPO winners. Then soaring southward over the array of city lights that ended in a tawdry cluster on the underprivileged fringe.

She navigated with her widespread wing-arms, teetering over the railing as if taking off, teasing gravity, daring it to crush her onto the rocky slope below, until she gave up and dropped the soles of her tennies back onto the cement slab. Then she walked to the truck, spooking a cottontail out of brush and causing a pair of lovers in the only other car in the parking area to turn and stare at her.

Back at the guesthouse she turned off the motor, pulled out the keys. As the truck cooled she stared out the windshield into night, imagining she could see the earth mounds by the prairie dog burrows. Her mind flew back to that Friday afternoon when she'd driven home and seen workers shoveling poison into the holes. So much trouble had followed that one act of killing prairie dogs.

Stepping out of the truck, she headed up the drive toward the prairie dog village. This murder wasn't going to be solved. A lot weren't, she'd read that. Just like those bodies out at Gavilan Mesa. The cops likely wouldn't find that perpetrator either. She walked around, toe-testing to avoid twisting an ankle in a hole like poor Derek Whitfield. If she'd never done anything this whole situation would have turned out better. Detective Martinez might have looked harder to find Brent's poisoner if he didn't have the easy target of a Salvadoran woman with immigration problems who fled the scene of the crime. Berto wouldn't be in intensive care. The Gavilan Mesa sale appeared unstoppable, but even if Findley Malbore bought the land, it might turn out better than leaving it in the hands of a foreign bank motivated to do any and everything to turn red ink black. Would Derek Whitfield still be scuffing around New Mexico placing rock cameras? Hard to say. But he must have known his occupation carried dangers.

When she turned around she caught sight of a figure moving up the drive. The intruder walked onto the porch of her guesthouse and leaned against the glass of the front window. She scanned short-term memory and concluded nobody had a reason to enter a dead man's estate at night. Squinting at the figure she couldn't distinguish a weapon. This was probably one of those drug-addict burglars Detective Martinez had mentioned, high as a kite and looking for something to grab to cover the next fix. What if he broke a window or door? Damn if she'd be a helpless victim.

Moving through piñon and juniper she cut a wide swathe around the natural area at the front of the estate to come up on the side of the guesthouse. Peered through the side window to the front window but saw nothing. Where had he gone? She stepped around the corner of the house, saw the figure at the door, leaped over. Grabbed his shoulders, lifted his hip with hers and swept his feet out from under him in a fair rendition of *Ushiro Goshi*, rear hip throw. Laying a patio chair across his chest she pinned him to the ground.

"Help," Eldon screamed. "Don't kill me!"

She blinked, discerning fair features from the gloomy background.

"Eldon, what are you doing here? Why were you spying on me?"

"I wasn't spying. You're crushing my chest."

She stood up, righted the chair, stared down at him.

"Why were you peeking through my window?"

"I was coming to apologize."

He scrambled to his feet, smoothed his clothes, coughed.

"Apologize? By spying through my window?"

"I didn't want to wake you if you were asleep. Listen, I know I overstepped. Despite my gift for words I'm awkward with women. I don't seem to find the best road to closeness."

"As a lawyer you would know that grabbing a woman is the road to incarceration, not closeness."

"Look, I'm sorry. I thought we had a chance but forget it. I'll leave and never bother you again."

He spun around and stomped down the drive into the night. She listened to the whine of his car motor diminish into the distance, then slumped into a patio chair and pondered. Was Eldon's southern gentleman persona confected to camouflage clumsiness in personal relationships? Or was he a crafty dissembler, always ready with some clever excuse for sneaky behavior? He presented as so respectable, so educated. She must be insane to distrust him. She propped her chin on her palm. Had she just thrown away a chance for companionship? There'd be no more free-rent-in-exchange-for-keeping-an-eye-on-the-estate either. Was she self-destructive or emotionally damaged? She honestly couldn't remember the last time she'd trusted anybody completely. Certainly not herself.

After a moment she stood and put the key in the lock, trying to twist the door handle while arching the pinched finger above the others. The knob slipped out of her grasp. She froze, on the verge of tears. At that moment her phone vibrated. She pulled it out, read the text flashed on the screen.

Whr r u

Oh, no. The new eco-defense group meeting. She'd promised Carter she'd attend. She pulled out the keys and hurried back to the truck.

FORTY-FIVE

A bonfire raged in an empty lot at the end of the dirt lane off lower Agua Fría, crimson flames clawing at night. Minoa parked and waved at Mr. Jaramillo, tending the fire with a grass rake. Mrs. Jaramillo's home daycare trailer was dark while the stucco house where she and her husband entertained an endless string of grandchildren, great grandchildren, nieces, nephews and various first or second or third something-or-others glowed cheerily. She walked around the side of the house to the remodeled garage Carter rented and pushed the door open without knocking. Inside four people, sitting on an assortment of second-hand chairs, leaned into a circle. Carter slid her a chair across the tile floor. A gray-haired woman in a blue button-down and jeans looked up from a laptop.

"What if we flood the emails of the city councilors, the county commissioners and the Water Authority bigshots with complaints? Make their system crash."

"We already tried overwhelming the complaint box, Frankie. We've exhausted the legal avenues of protest, in the strict sense anyway."

Minoa recognized a tall fellow with a blond ponytail from the protest at the Paseo de Pradera construction site.

"Oh no, Jude is going to propose blowing up something again."

A plump young woman with dimples and French braids frowned at him. Carter leaned forward in her chair.

"Jude is just stating facts, Marta. We've organized letter-writing campaigns, picketed meetings, showed water usage projections to every politico who would meet with us. Remember that guerilla theater at the public comment meeting when we poured pitchers of water on the council members' heads?"

Frankie chuckled.

"That heights councilor was spluttering so hard I thought he was having a seizure."

"I still think we should have narrated with the megaphone," said Carter. "Nobody realized we were enacting the La Llorona legend."

Frankie tried to tamp down the corners of her mouth but a laugh popped out.

"I'm afraid people thought we were wearing white sheets because we escaped from a mental hospital."

Marta joined her in a shared giggle.

"The public doesn't have to understand the symbolism for guerrilla theater to work, Frankie," said Jude, his Adam's apple bobbing up and down his long neck. "What people remember is seeing two cops wrench a water pitcher out of a young woman's hand, throw her to the ground and cuff her while driving a knee into her back."

"I agree with Jude," said Carter. "And hopefully they remember those cops were soaking wet by the time they cuffed me."

She threw Minoa a smirk.

"But none of it has made one bit of difference," Jude went on. "Those city councilors just keep raising their sticky little hands in the air to vote yes on every phase of the Gavilan development plan despite us filling the auditorium with opponents."

"And that shameless Barney Trujillo refused to recuse himself."

Frankie ended with an outraged humph.

"Even though his wife was sleeping with Brent Harrison."

Everyone turned to stare at Carter uttering cries of shock. Carter winked at Minoa.

"That's the gossip anyway."

"The Gavilan developers and the fat capitalists are in bed together whether it's literal or figurative."

"Well said, Jude."

Carter and Jude exchanged a high-five.

"I think we should focus on endangered species." Frankie tapped her pen on a stack of printouts under her laptop. "The fate of helpless animals can galvanize public opinion more than projected acre feet of water usage and groundwater recharge. What about the banner-tailed kangaroo rat?"

"Nobody knows what that is, Frankie, and everybody hates rats." Marta twirled one of her braids like a lasso. "If we're going to focus on animals harmed by the Gavilan development, we should use the prairie dog. Everybody loves them because they're so cute."

"Marta, both white- and black-tailed prairie dogs are off the endangered list," said Jude.

"But their numbers are greatly reduced and they're a keystone species."

"And endangered black-footed ferrets depend on them for survival."

Carter brought her chair down with a crunch.

"Their burrows provide habitat for burrowing owls too. I read that," said Marta.

Jude sat up, brought a fist down on his thigh.

"Guys, we don't have time to launch another campaign, particularly if this secret purchase goes through without a hitch. Besides, species survival is irrelevant when there's money to be made. This has been studied. Out of tens of thousands of development projects approved nationally in the last decade only two were delayed or halted to protect an endangered species. The law is close to useless."

"Jude's right," said Carter. "We need more aggressive civil disobedience."

"I say we lie in the road in front of the bulldozers," said Jude.

"What if they run us over?" Marta's eyes widened. "Anyway, I want to go to medical school and I don't want a criminal record to ruin that."

"Not everyone has to be on the front lines, Marta. Minoa prefers to work in the shadows too."

Carter flicked eyebrows at her.

"BTW where's Nellie?" said Marta.

"She said she'd be late," said Carter. "She may have to catch up with us later at the Sustainable Futures coffeehouse."

"What did she learn about Malbore with her latest undercover mission?" said Jude.

"She said she found some curious info about his venture investments in Mexico. When she shows up we can get more details, see if it's actionable."

"Where is Nellie?" Minoa asked.

"She's been on location at the venture capitalist's house." Carter tilted her cellphone so Minoa could see a photo on the screen. It showed a classic washerwoman with a babushka plastering her hair and a peasant blouse over jeans. "She got a job as a housecleaner."

"That's her? She's working in Findley Malbore's house?"

"Scrubbing her ass off while somebody's watching, photographing everything in his office when they're not."

"Carter, the house is likely full of surveillance cameras."

"Dogs. She said the dude has a sociopathic guard dog. But she's only seen cameras outside. Don't worry. Nelly's smart. She'll figure it out."

"She's crazy brave as well."

"Devoted to the cause, Min. We're the underground resistance. Who else is offering to save the planet from the profit hounds?"

Minoa gave her a thumbs up, tried to focus on the discussion, failed. Out the front window of Carter's dwelling she spied the bonfire furling and unfurling scarlet tongues. Destructive fire scouring a void ... it felt like the inside of her stomach. She'd ruined her free house sitting gig at Brent's place by kneeing and throwing Eldon. Maybe he'd been telling the truth, maybe he was a rule-bound lawyer who just wanted some human companionship. Why was she so suspicious? And why did she follow Ron around like a well-trained house dog waiting for her next contractor assignment? He would spend the winter pleasantly with Elsie while she begged her old boss at the Buffalo Thunder casino bar to take her back. Why was she so desperate and clueless at 36 after devoting her entire youth to education?

On top of it all, despite spending a lot of time pondering Brent's and Derek Whitfield's deaths, she had no solid theory of how it all went down. Not to mention no way to help Valeria or Berto. She must have missed some crucial factor. The moral of this story was that she should focus on saving her own skin and forget trying to save others. Although Carter always told her the opposite, that she was too self-centered, that she should sacrifice for a cause. She realized Carter was waving a hand in front of her face.

"Hello? Anybody home?"

She looked around. Marta and Frankie were going out the door. Jude was hoisting a backpack.

"Send out a crypto chat when you hear from Nellie," he said, heading for the door.

"Ok. Viva Gavilan."

Carter punched a fist up.

"Viva Gavilan."

They went out. The door shut.

She turned to Minoa.

"Short on sleep?"

"Just brooding."

She stood.

"C'mon. We're gonna pick up Reni and head to Sustainable Futures. Nellie will meet us there."

Minoa went over and opened the door, looked out. The bonfire had died down to a smoldering city. Carter gave her a playful push from behind.

FORTY-SIX

After an hour's drive down I-25 to Albuquerque, Minoa exited onto Central Avenue and cruised a zone of seedy motels offering week-to-week housing. Spotting the sign for Sustainable Futures, she parked on a side street and the three of them headed over. The glass storefront was painted over with a mural depicting pueblos, hogans and freeways in harmonious coexistence with corn fields and frolicking goats before a backdrop of mesas and alpine peaks. Inside she picked up a coffee at a counter and paid five dollars to pass through a door into the back part of the building. On a low stage at the back of the room two women, one on acoustic guitar, were singing a folk revival song.

"What is this place?" said Minoa as they occupied a table.

"Progressive performance space," replied Carter. "It's open mic night. Maybe you could do one of those shamanic chants you showed us?"

"I thought you said Nellie was coming."

"She must be on her way."

"I'm excited to meet her," said Ireni.

Carter angled her phone screen toward Ireni showing the photo of Nellie in a babushka and peasant blouse.

"That's her current disguise."

"You mean for Halloween?"

"She's undercover at Malbore's place. She said she found something sus."

"Sus?"

The sparse crowd started singing along on the chorus, so Minoa had to repeat herself.

"Why sus?"

"She broke into some of his accounts. The dude is making big money off his Mexican investments."

"What's suspicious about that? Investors invest to grow their capital. That's how the system works."

"Venture capitalists don't hit it right with every project they fund, do they?"

"I wouldn't think, but what do I know?"

"There are ways to sum different probability estimates to—," Ireni started.

"Stop, Dr. Keynes. The point is: nobody wins all the time unless they've got an in."

"Sounds valid," said Minoa.

"Plus the dude has plenty enough to buy Gavilan on his own. So why'd he partner with the deceased?"

"Who knows, Carter? Maybe to spread the risk or because Brent's regional fund gave them a local footprint. How are we struggling gig workers supposed to understand how finance capital operates?"

"I have a full-time job."

Ireni crossed her arms and huffed.

"Don't let the robber barons of capitalism mystify you, Min. The basic mechanism is suck it up from below, then splash it around on top."

"Well now that's a helpful image."

Ireni frowned at Carter.

"The point is Malbore is doing better than he should. It's probably a racket conspiring with corrupt politicos down south."

"Maybe."

Minoa was staring off into space. The song ended followed by sparse applause. A young woman in black stepped to the microphone, began droning a poem about the seven tribes of Aztlan, her voice rising as she ended each stanza with 'Their land is our land.'

As she stepped off the stage to a couple people clapping and cries of '*Órale*,' Carter's phone bleeped.

"That's weird. Nellie's phone just sent me an emergency notification."

"Call her," said Ireni.

Carter punched away.

"I hope she didn't get arrested."

"You see?" Ireni said. "Breaking the law is not the way to deal with the environmental crisis, Carter. Science can save us."

"Science in the service of corporations is not going to save anybody."

"Did you get a response?" said Minoa.

"I've got her location. It shows her on I-40 west near Coors Road. What's she doing over there? That's not the route from her house. Maybe something came up and she didn't have time to explain?"

"That's irrational," said Ireni.

Minoa blinked.

"Did she pass Coors Road?"

"Uh, yeah, heading right on past. There's a casino out that way. But why would she ..."

Minoa stood up slamming a fist down on the table.

"Why didn't I see this before?"

"See what?" said Ireni.

"Nellie's in danger. We've got to find her."

She spun around, raced out the door. Carter and Ireni stared at each other. Then they jumped up and ran after her.

FORTY-SEVEN

The truck raced west on I-40 past thinning city lights glittering like the scattered crystals of a broken chandelier. Minoa sped so fast the truck's dented passenger door buzzed.

"I put Nellie on my SOS Tracker," Carter said. "It looks like she's heading up the access road to Gavilan. She wouldn't go out there to monkey wrench alone."

"She's not alone," said Minoa, leaning into the steering wheel.

"Somebody is kidnapping her, right?" said Ireni.

"If she's still alive."

"What do you mean, if she's still alive?"

Carter slammed a palm on the dashboard, turning to look at the profiles of Ireni and Minoa, outlined against the weak glow from the dash lights. When no one answered she hit the dash again.

"Will somebody talk to me?"

For a moment no one spoke. Then Minoa's voice was a low drone.

"I didn't see the connections. The prairie dogs. Gavilan Mesa. What Brent realized."

"Oh, I get it," said Carter with an exaggerated drawl. "The prairie dogs conspired with Brent's ghost to kidnap Nellie to Gavilan Mesa."

When no one responded she slumped back into her seat.

"Brent was a chronic womanizer," said Minoa. "That's what most people saw in him. He pressured his daughter's nannies to sleep with him and seduced every attractive woman he saw. On top of that he underpaid his domestic workers and never stopped fighting with his ex-wife. But he considered himself ethical in his business dealings."

"You're saying he was a sociopathic predatory vulture capitalist who followed accounting rules? How comforting."

"Relevance, Min?"

Minoa met Ireni's glance for a moment, then squinted into the night as she drove on.

"Nellie must have found out what Brent found out."

"You mean that Malbore does too well in his investments down south? That he's engaging in some kind of fraud or bribery?"

"Money laundering."

Carter and Ireni ping-ponged looks.

"You think Malbore works for a cartel?" said Carter.

"The purchase of Gavilan involves a massive stateside investment with a respected financier for a partner. Money pulled out down the line would be clean as the snow piling up on Santa Fe Baldy."

"But Brent is dead."

"He's dead because he figured out Malbore's game. And now Nellie found out the same thing."

"OMG," muttered Carter suppressing a sob.

She pounded a fist on the door's armrest, causing it to ratchet down.

"But honestly Min-min, you really think one super-capitalist would rat out another, even if his investments smelled bad?"

"Why else would Brent have been researching how Mexican cartels launder money? His desk was covered with info on the subject."

Ireni looked from Minoa to Carter, her eye whites gleaming in the dim light of the cab.

"Nellie made a big mistake going into Malbore's home."

"Don't blame me. This isn't the fault of our radical action group. Nellie wanted to do it."

Ireni grabbed the dash with pale elongated fingers.

"There may be men with guns out there. We should wait for the police."

"Would APD respond if we tell them our friend's phone is heading west-southwest and we're worried?"

"We can call 911 and say she's being kidnapped."

"I told you two I discovered some shallow graves out here. They're planning to put her in another one."

"Graves?" Ireni sputtered.

"Where's her phone now?" Minoa said.

"East-southeast about a mile."

"That's more or less where those graves are so they could ... any second."

"Oh no!"

"We can take these bastards," Carter said.

"Take? What do you mean by 'take?" Ireni coughed out.

No one answered. After speeding up the dirt track Minoa crossed the cattle guard into the lot by the Gavilan gate. She turned the truck around to park facing outward and cut the engine.

"Reni, why don't you wait in the truck? You can be the getaway driver."

Ireni's voice was a single strand, barely oscillating.

"I'm not a ... a coward."

Carter patted Ireni on the top of her head.

"Look, Rain-rain, if we don't make it out of this alive, I want you to know I don't really blame you for working for the military-industrial complex. We're all pawns of the system."

Ireni just stared straight ahead, blinking.

They stepped out and paused there feeling a wave of heat radiate out from the truck motor. A brittle silence coated the desert, poised to fracture. Carter leaned around Ireni to whisper at Minoa.

"Have you got a knife in that toolbox?"

Reaching into the truck bed Minoa opened the box, fumbled inside and handed a lug wrench to Carter. Carter turned the wrench in her hand.

"You're kidding, right?"

Minoa gave Ireni a few flares.

"It's called bricolage."

She stuffed a wad of twine into one pocket and a flashlight into the other. Pulled a spare shirt from under the seat and tied it around her waist.

"Reni, why don't you follow the fence up to a span where the wires are cut? Draw back a bit and light some flares, then run for the truck. You can drive until you're out of reach. That will distract them."

"What if these guys run faster than I do?"

"Make sure you have a good head start. Carter and I will circle around and approach from the far side. When they get distracted by the flares we might get an opportunity to free Nellie. If not, we can create another distraction. Let them know they're being watched."

Carter scratched her back with the lug wrench.

"They might just shoot."

Minoa gave Carter a look.

"Do you have a better idea?"

Carter jogged, shifting her weight side to side.

"Keep dodging and faking like a soccer player."

"But I don't know how to play sports."

Ireni ducked her head and started walking along the fence line. Minoa watched her slip into darkness as she held down the top strand of barbed wire so she and Carter could step over. They scuffed up the slope, blinded by a stripe of city lights on the horizon that contrasted a black miasma smothering the ground. After climbing a long rise they came to a ridge top and paused. Minoa's whisper ruffled the silence.

"This reminds me of a dream ..."

"We shouldn't have left Reni alone."

"She's a braniac. She'll think of something."

They walked along the ridge. The great rift of the Rio Grande valley appeared in the distance, a blackened gash in a land speckled with pinprick lights. Suddenly a murmuring surfaced, disappeared, emerged again. They froze. Carter raised the lug wrench over her head. Minoa waved her index finger back and forth in front of her face as a caution and then beckoned. As they tiptoed downhill, voices clarified. They paused, seeing nothing, listening.

Whispers surfaced, disappeared, then a laugh and a woman's muffled scream.

"C'mon!"

Carter lurched downhill. Minoa grabbed her shoulder. Spoke in a hoarse whisper.

"It won't help to run down and get shot."

"Goddamnit! I'm not just standing here."

"You circle left, I'll go right. I make a noise. As soon as they focus on me, you make a noise from your side. We keep alternating while moving around a perimeter."

"Okay."

Carter held up the lug wrench like a torch. They took off jogging, Carter veering left down the incline, Minoa traversing the ridgeside. After a short run she turned downhill, scanning textured blackness as she trotted on tiptoes. Suddenly a shape bulked out of the night. Making a split-second decision, she sprinted over and leaped onto someone piggyback style. She locked arms around his neck and started throttling him. Something glinted flying through the air.

He whipped his torso back and forth, bellowing, jerking her wrists loose. She jackknifed her elbows around his shoulders, trying to stay on. Another figure shot out of the night and Carter was suddenly beside them, hitting him anywhere she could with the lug wrench. He stumbled forward taking Minoa on a wild bronco ride. Carter hopscotched back and forth following and landed another blow on the side of his head. He collapsed to the ground. Minoa scrambled to her feet and the two of them stood over his prone body, panting.

"Do you think I killed him?"

He groaned and shifted.

"Don't think so."

Minoa dropped her knee onto his back, pulled the twine out of her pocket and started wrapping his wrists. At that moment his back arched and he jerked his arms free, torquing to his feet.

As she tripped sideways, he snapped arms around her. Carter raised her arm to rain down another blow with the lug wrench.

"Drop it or I break her *pinche* neck."

With an arm around Minoa's throat, he jerked so hard her legs kicked up. She clawed at his arm, a ghastly sucking noise spitting out of her mouth, until his other fist punched her stomach and she hung limp.

"Okay, okay."

Carter dropped the lug wrench.

"Get down."

He gestured with his head toward a shadowy lump on the ground. Whimpering sounds filtered out of the nearby darkness.

"Run," Minoa croaked.

The guy squeezed her neck again, forcing a sound out of her throat like metal dragging on asphalt. Carter spun around, ran into the night. The guy hurled Minoa to the ground beside a prone figure. On the other side of her body where she lay face down, mouth crammed into the dirt, she wormed her hand under her hip, grasped the flashlight sticking up out of her pants pocket. As he reached for her wrists, she rolled toward him swinging the flashlight toward his head.

The thud on his forehead made him stiffen, then tumble backwards. She thrashed her way to her feet as he recouped. Thrusting a foot into his sternum she shoved him back down. He scrambled up and charged, grabbing her shoulders, slamming her down to plank onto hard soil.

Suddenly a shot punctured the night. The man skittled sideways like a buckshot sidewinder, bouncing on one leg, grabbing the other thigh with his hands, expelling a serrated cry. Minoa heard footsteps as she pushed to her feet. She saw Carter rush out of the night and come to a stop over the wounded man, who was moaning as he tried to drag himself away. She stood there, legs in a wide stance, pistol dangling from one hand.

"I found the gun," she said in a breathy voice. "Should I shoot him again?"

FORTY-EIGHT

"I'll tie him up."

Minoa scuffed around, found the fallen wad of twine. The man was folding and unfolding his upper body, moaning, grasping the thigh with both hands. When she grabbed his wrists he cried out, jerking and convulsing, until Carter stepped on the ankle of his injured leg. As he blubbered bloody misery, Minoa wrapped the twine around his wrists, then pulled the tail down to his good ankle and tied it off short. He lay there moving like a nutcracker, ribs pumping, jaw working. She stood, rubbing her neck.

"You've never shot a gun in your life. Weren't you worried you'd hit me?"

"I did archery in high school. I know how to be still and aim."

"In the dark?"

"I hit the right target. What are you complaining about?"

A blood red flare slashed the darkness farther down the slope. Then Ireni's yell split the night.

"I'm going down. See if you can free Nellie and come help."

Minoa raced down the hill into darkness until a hulk emerged out of deep gray. She stopped short. The shape clarified into a guy holding a semi-automatic rifle with a short barrel aimed at Ireni's temple. His other arm encircled her neck.

"*Párate.*"

She went still.

"Please, no," Ireni dribbled.

"Do what I tell you or I kill her."

He waved the gun barrel up the slope.

"Walk."

She hesitated.

"Now, *perra*."

She turned around, started walking up the slope with the guy hauling Ireni behind. Partway up the hill she yelled out, "Man with gun coming." He kicked her from behind. They reached the other fellow, bound and groaning on the ground. Carter and Nellie had vanished. He shoved Ireni to the ground.

"Get down."

Minoa crouched a few feet away. He kicked her on the hip, launching her sideways to crash into Ireni. Keeping the gun trained on them, he bent over, pulled a knife out of his boot, cut the twine off his buddy's wrists.

Boom! As he stood a shot hit the ground kicking up a spray of dirt between Minoa and Ireni and the two men. Ireni shrieked.

The man with the gun pivoted around spraying bullets into the darkness as Minoa and Ireni dove for the ground. Minoa grabbed Ireni's wrist, pulled her into a crouch. As the man spun around firing, they bolted up the hill amidst cracking gunfire coming from everywhere. It was like running through a fourth of July free-for-all except they knew they could be killed at any moment. The outburst of shots fizzled as they stumbled over a rocky ledge lining the ridge top. Standing on top, panting, squinting at a horizon smudged by distant city lights, they rubbed their arms, listening.

After a moment of gaping silence a peal of curses in Spanish reached their eardrums followed by moans, exclamations. The sounds diminished, moving down the hill. Then a car started at the foot of the ridge. The whine of the motor traveled toward the cattle guard at the Gavilan gate punctuated by a tiny pop. Then headlights followed the dirt track down the Gavilan border, scratched across the blackened plain below switching to tiny red pupils inching toward the interstate.

Ireni crumpled onto the ground.

"Are you okay?"

"I ... I think I was hit."

"Oh no. Where?"

Ireni tugged on the neck of her shirt to reveal a shoulder. Minoa adjusted her position to allow Ireni's pale skin to catch the faint glow of lights from the Rio Grande valley.

"Can't see much but I don't see blood. Is it worse when you move your arm?"

"A little."

"Maybe a shot grazed you or that bastard punched you. We've got to find Carter and Nellie."

"They must be dead. That guy was firing everywhere."

Minoa put two fingers to her mouth and whistled as Ireni staggered to standing. They listened hard, heard nothing.

She whistled again, then called out, "Carter! Nellie!"

As seconds passed with no response, she sensed her organs inside her belly starting to shrivel.

"Maybe they ran too far to hear us."

"They're dead. They're both dead."

Ireni doubled over and heaved a string of sobs.

Minoa moved her head back and forth as if she could see, as if she had a plan, as if she didn't feel like the world she knew was teetering on the edge. She tried to think of reasons why they would be unhurt yet fail to answer.

"They may be wounded. Or maybe they ran to the truck."

But she knew sound carried for miles out on these empty desert plateaus. Inside her abdomen a sensation of downward suction grew stronger. Ireni wiped the backs of her hands across her face.

"We better start looking."

Her words made sense. Ireni always made sense. She'd wanted to hang back and wait for the police. That had made sense too. If they'd done that at least three of them would be alive.

"We can zigzag back and forth down the hillside," she said.

"Okay."

Minoa didn't budge.

"C'mon, Min. Help me."

Ireni took hold of her arm and tugged.

Minoa started shuffling across the slope pulled along like a recalcitrant child. Internally she was scouring her brain for words. What would she say when they found Carter dead, riddled with bullets? What would she say when they had to meet her parents flown out from northern Virginia to pick up the body of their adventurous daughter? Not a single word congealed.

Ireni pulled her along criss-crossing the hill, calling out every so often, tripping over clumps of bunch grass. They came to the barbed wire fence and found the cut span. Out of the periphery of her consciousness Minoa noticed tire marks churning the dirt. What evidence would they have to prove that two undocumented *sicarios* working off the books for a venture capitalist shot their friends? Had those killers picked up the bodies to haul them away and dispose of them? Would Carter and Nellie get dumped in a barrel of acid like Derek Whitfield?

Nearing the fold at the base of the hill Ireni froze and shrieked. Minoa assumed ready pose, scanning the night, aware how ridiculous it was to think she could protect them from anything.

Two silhouettes emerged.

"Don't shoot," Ireni screamed.

"Min! Reni! Are you two okay?"

The sound of the voice melted what was left of Minoa's insides. Carter and Nellie came to a stop in front of them.

"We thought you and Nellie were dead," said Minoa. "Why didn't you answer?"

Carter waved the gun like repeated exclamation points.

"Answer what? We followed those cowards as far as we could. I got a shot off when they turned out of the Gavilan entrance but then this thing ran out of bullets."

Minoa lurched forward and locked arms around her.

"You idiot."

She touched the side of her head to Carter's cheek, felt a moment of blessed communion. Then Carter's jaw muscles lurched.

"Idiot? That's what you call me after I hit one of those bastards and saved Nellie?"

Minnoa straightened, feeling a silly grin on her face.

"Carter, how did you avoid getting shot? That guy was shooting everywhere."

"You think I don't know how to dive? I was team captain of my high school soccer team and a damn good goalie. No way I'm gonna stand there and let somebody drill me."

Ireni moved to Nellie.

"Are you hurt?

"I ... I don't feel great but I'm not dead. That's a plus."

Carter clasped an arm around Nellie's shoulders.

"You're a hero for the resistance. You've survived the first attempt on your life. You'll be in the history books written after we found a sustainable society."

Minoa, Ireni and Nellie burst out laughing.

"Carter's one of a kind," said Nellie.

"We better call the cops," said Minoa. "I should have listened to Reni."

"Wait a minute. I don't want to be questioned," said Nellie. "If they find out I was in Malbore's house, they'll arrest me instead of him."

"What did you find out?"

"The guy launders for a cartel. He invests in businesses in Mexico, then places the proceeds, always excessive, in stateside investments. He'd already participated in a couple of Brent's investments, some fracking firm and a coal mining company. Plus he owned properties like a ranch near Tucumcari, an apartment building in Albuquerque, lots of stuff."

"Did you find any evidence he had Brent Harrison killed?"

"No. But those two Mexican goons do dirty work for him. Including getting rid of me. If you guys hadn't showed up I'd be dead."

She brought a fist to her mouth and choked. Ireni patted her back.

"Luckily they hauled you out to Gavilan Mesa before killing you."

"They ... they were getting ready to rape me when you guys showed up."

"Those two killers are warning Malbore right now," said Carter. "What's he going to do?"

"Now that he knows I'm on to him, he can't let me live."

"We're calling the police." Ireni's voice squealed.

"There's no way we'll convince police with a phone call that a rich dude living in a mansion in Santa Fe is a money launderer responsible for murder and attempted murder," said Nellie.

"Plus the murders of those victims found in the graves out here."

"I agree with Nellie," said Carter. "Besides, they better not find out I shot a man even though it was self-defense."

"You fired first," said Minoa.

"And they're the only ones that came out of this with injuries," added Nellie.

"Those criminals won't report it, so we just agree to keep our mouths shut, right?"

"We have to report this to APD to help their supposed serial killer investigation."

"Anonymously."

Minoa focused on Nellie.

"Can you go into hiding for a while?"

"I can stay with Jude. He's great at going dark."

"I'm going to try to stop Malbore from fleeing."

Carter waved the gun around.

"How are you going to do that, Min? The gun's empty."

"I know where he lives. Something will occur to me."

"We could buy ammunition."

"God save us," Ireni muttered.

"Let's drop Ren and Nellie at Jude's. I'm going with you, Min."

Minoa gave Carter a look but didn't comment. They started walking back toward the truck. When they reached it and crammed into the cab, Carter spoke up.

"Now that I won a shootout with cartel killers, I guess you guys will have to show some respect."

"Don't get your hopes up." Nellie elbowed her.

"Wait a minute. I saved your wrinkly butts."

"Safer for you if we just decide this never happened," said Minoa.

"Well, I'll keep my gun as a souvenir."

"Your gun?"

"Wipe it and toss it," said Nellie.

"We'll be passing over the Rio Grande," said Minoa.

"Hey, how about I snap a selfie with the gun?"

"Oh shut up."

FORTY-NINE

After dropping Ireni and Nellie at Jude's house in Rio Rancho, Minoa and Carter took I-25 north. They drove fast all the way to Santa Fe, then took the relief route around town to come out on the north side. Sped up Hyde Park Road into the mountains, squinting out the window for a glimpse of that circular mansion poised on a ridge point. A few cars meandered down the highway, probably clients of the Japanese hot tubs located farther up the mountain. Finally Minoa spotted Malbore's place high above, dotted with lights around the circumference like a spaceship lowering to land.

Unmarked dirt lanes branched off from the two-lane highway, most leading to a mountain-style home. She spotted one dirt drive with no mailbox and began following it. Soon she was traversing hairpin switchbacks along the walls of a ravine. Emerging onto a saddle, a break in the pine trees revealed the lights of Santa Fe far below, glowing like a network of microcircuits.

She continued along the ridge until she spied lights ahead. Pulled the truck off the road and parked. She and Carter moved through the forest paralleling the drive, then huddled behind a cluster of Ponderosa pines looking out at Malbore's house. Banks of floor-to-ceiling windows and glass doors covered the circular walls, opening onto a concentric deck that ended on both sides of the front door. A tennis court jutted out over the canyon from one side of the structure, suspension wires glinting in the house lights. A black Porsche, a silver BMW, the royal blue sports car and a dark blue SUV sat in front.

"Let's scout around the house to see what's going on," Minoa whispered. "If it looks like Malbore isn't leaving, we'll have time to try to persuade the police to take action. If he's fleeing, we'll have to think of some way to slow him down."

"I'll take the left side, you take the right." Carter moved along the edge of the clearing, pausing to tie a sneaker.

Minoa trotted around to the other side of the house where the land fell away from the foundation toward a rocky canyon, steep banks rough with rocky outcroppings. The only way she could spy through the windows on this side was from the circular deck. How was she going to walk on that deck without being seen from inside? As she hesitated the front door swung open and a Doberman Pinscher barreled out, angling straight toward Carter. The dog crashed into her flying up into the air over her head like the prow of a ship crashing into the hull of another.

Carter and the dog rolled around in a flurry of legs and barks and yells. Malbore came out the door. He wore a polo shirt and trousers, thin blond hair gelled back.

After watching for a moment, he called out, "Let go, Giovanni."

He aimed a handgun at Carter. Giovanni crouched to the side, teeth bared, growling.

"Why don't you come inside and explain the reason for your visit?"

Carter stood up, brushing off her limbs.

"That dog should be tied up. Anyway, I just wanted to get a picture of this place. It's pretty awesome. Is it a Frank Lloyd Wright?"

"Good try. My men advised me of the problem at Gavilan Mesa."

"Cavalier Mesa. What's that?"

"Inside. I will shoot. New Mexico law is serious about trespassing."

"I thought this was national forest land."

With a crack, a puff of dirt mushroomed up from the ground beside her feet. Carter jumped sideways. Malbore motioned with the gun toward the house. As Carter started walking toward the front door, the hand dangling at her side gestured furiously signaling Minoa to back off. Minoa plastered herself against the house, then peeked around. Malbore was scanning the surroundings. She ducked back, then looked again to see him use a hand command to order the dog inside. He disappeared pulling the door shut.

She stood there cursing, asking herself if the best course of action was to back off, call the cops and wait for help. But driving up here from town would take fifteen minutes. Malbore had a gun. He employed *sicarios*. He worked with drug traffickers. They'd be angry about what happened at Gavilan Mesa. She didn't want to imagine what they might do in fifteen minutes.

She stealth-walked along the balcony to the first window, paused, craned her neck around to peer inside. Beyond an unlit room, the doorway to a kitchen glowed yellow. She sprinted to the next post defining another bank of windows. Inside sat a dining table. Through an opening into another room, she saw a blond woman walk by. She dashed to the next group of windows, pausing at the edge.

There in a living room stood Malbore's girlfriend, blonde hair in a twist on top of her head, wearing some linen outfit, wine glass in hand, turning her head to speak to someone out of sight. She turned back and continued toward the windows. Minoa backtracked to where the curvature of the house wall concealed her. Heard a sliding glass door open followed by footsteps on the deck. A moment later the woman called out.

"I wish we didn't have to travel now, Finn honey. I love Santa Fe in the fall. Couldn't we put it off till it gets cold and dreary here?"

"The weather will be perfect in Mazatlan this time of year, Janine dear. Not too hot."

Malbore had moved onto the deck.

"But is it safe to fly at night?"

"Much safer. That's why we're doing it. Very little traffic, air currents are calmer. You can sleep on the way."

"Alright, but you have to promise me we'll come back for the spring."

"Of course, dear."

Minoa heard the front door open. She spun around to see a Latino man in jeans and cowboy boots walk out to the Porsche carrying suitcases. His back was to her but when he turned around he would see her. If she moved out of his view she'd be visible to Malbore or Janine. She glanced around, took a deep breath and lowered herself over the edge of the walkway, dangling by her hands from the edge. As she felt her fingers slipping, she swung by her arms to an angled strut that allowed for a better grip. She hung there, feet dangling into space, wondering how long she could hold on.

"Who is that person in the study?"

"Giovanni caught a trespasser. Francisco will hold her here until the authorities arrive to take her into custody."

"Maybe she's just a hiker who got lost. She doesn't look threatening."

"It's best to be cautious. We'll let the police sort it out after we've left."

Minoa swung her legs back and forth and after a few tries hooked a foot over the crosspiece. She pulled herself up and over to rest her belly on the slanted metal bar, legs hanging, hands under her cheek.

"Should we have supper before we go?"

"I don't think there's time. Hilda's preparing something for us to take."

The sliding glass door shut. Somewhere down in the ravine an animal scurried through brush. Then the sound of a car door shutting, steps on gravel, the house door. Silence. She glanced down into the ravine, up at the deck above her head, wondering how she was going to get out of this. Resigning herself she slid off the bar, dangled by her hands swinging her legs back and forth and let go. Landed on the steep bank of the ravine on all fours but started skidding down on a rolling carpet of pebbled dirt. Her limbs flew out from under, hands clawing at the ground and then the air. In an instant she was scooting like a bobsled. She zoomed down the incline to fly off a rocky abutment into an instant of airborne terror, then crash land rolling over and over to smash into the trunk of a fir tree.

For a moment she didn't move. As pebbles stopped rolling, she lifted her face, spat dirt. Bit by bit she pushed up to sit leaning against the tree, arms and legs trembling, heart racing. Her cheeks burned, her shirt and jeans had rips all over, the palms of her hands bled onto ruffled flaps of skin. Hugging the tree trunk she pulled herself to standing and leaned there taking balloon breaths, smelling the tree resin. The forest was invisible in the darkness yet teeming with creatures, aromatic with oils of pine and fir. She shifted her weight, flexed joints. Everything moved despite the scraped skin and bruised muscles.

She noticed a fluorescent dot near her feet. On the bed of pine needles at the foot of the tree sat a fluorescent green tennis ball. She picked it up, almost flicked it into the canyon but stopped and stuffed it into a pocket. Then she traversed sideways a few paces and started scrambling up the slope through scrub oak, grabbing one branch after another for balance.

At the ridge top she paused, scanning, listening. She trotted to the Porsche. No keys in it and the suitcases were in the trunk. For a moment she considered letting air out of the tires but concluded it would take too long. Should she break the windshield? That would force a showdown with armed men. So she circled around the other side of the house where she spied from behind a tree. In an illuminated room she spied Carter sitting on the floor, hands tethered to the leg of a desk. A Latino guy sat in a chair, gun in his lap, staring at his phone.

She ran into the forest, scouted around, picked up a cantaloupe-sized rock and carried it back. Cradling it in one arm, she stepped behind a divider panel, pulled the collar of her shirt over her mouth and called out in her best imitation of Janine's fluted voice, "Francisco, could you come in here for a moment. I need help. Francisco!"

The man stood, looked from the door to the windows and back again.

"Francisco!"

He shot a look at Carter and walked out of the room. Minoa jumped over and pulled hard on the handle of a sliding glass door. Didn't budge. She crashed the rock against the glass. It shuddered but held. Carter jerked on the rope anchoring her tied wrists, swiveled them back and forth, tried to haul the desk but it barely budged. Again she smashed the rock into the glass. Instantly the glass sheet filled with a spider's web of cracks. She kicked at it. An alarm went off as the glass sheet avalanched to the deck to form a heap of shards.

Shouts were heard from the rest of the house. She leaped inside and raced to the interior door, but it had no lock. From a shelf she grabbed a metal statue of a cowboy lugging a saddle and crouched behind the door. As Francisco burst in, gun waving, she brought the statue down on the back of his head. He crumpled to the ground. She grabbed his gun off the floor just as Malbore ran in and aimed at him. He backed out fast. Rummaging in a desk drawer she found a pair of scissors and sawed the rope binding Carter's wrists.

The last fiber of rope frayed just as Malbore appeared outside holding a rifle. He started spraying the room with bullets as Minoa and Carter dove behind furniture. The shots stopped. After listening for a moment, they ran onto the deck toward the front of the house and stopped cold. Malbore was beside the Porsche with one foot inside and the rifle in one hand. He raised it and fired another barrage at them as they ducked back. They heard the car door shut and jumped around the curve of the house to see him peel away.

They found Janine huddled in a corner of the living room. Giovanni was barking hysterically from the other side of the house, seeming to choke on his own slobber.

She shrieked over and over, "Don't hurt me. I didn't do anything. Please don't hurt me."

Minoa made pacifying gestures with her hands.

"Just calm down. We're not going to hurt you."

Janine screamed, "Findley! Help!"

Carter approached, took a wide stance in front of her. She held Francisco's gun in one hand.

"He's gone."

Janine went silent. Minoa glanced at Carter.

"We'll never catch up to him in the truck."

"So we take his bimmer."

"That's my car," said Janine.

Ignoring her they went to the kitchen and opened drawers and cabinets. Inside one they found a few sets of keys. One fob bore a circle with blue and silver quarters.

Minoa grabbed it and they ran for the car.

FIFTY

She backed out spraying a wave of pebbles across the front of the house as she took off. They raced along the ridge crest for several minutes with no sign of the Porsche.

"Do you think Janine is calling the cops right now?" said Carter.

"I'd bet she's figured out this is her chance to clean out every account she can access and drive herself to the Sunport in that futuristic sports car."

"Think we should call 911 for Francisco?"

"Let her deal with it. We probably don't want to advertise our presence up on this mountain."

"If he dies you could face a murder charge, Min."

"Breaking and entering. Assault. I hope it doesn't come to homicide."

Careening around hairpin curves, she spotted Malbore several switchbacks down before his Porsche disappeared into the pines. She skidded around the V-shaped turns nearly crashing the back end into trees lining the road.

"Maybe I should drive," Carter said. "My dad had a bimmer. I learned to drive on it."

"You're carrying the heat."

Carter turned the gun back and forth, then held it up to aim out the windshield. Minoa flashed her a look.

When she pulled onto Hyde Park Road she caught a glimpse of the Porsche before it disappeared around a curve farther down. They slalomed down the serpentining mountain road, raced the straight stretch to downtown and then wound up and down narrow historic streets, wheels screaming on the turns, pursuing blips of the Porsche up ahead. On the other side of downtown they followed Malbore onto the relief route that circumvented Santa Fe. The Porsche picked up speed. Minoa edged up to keep it in sight, reaching seventy, eighty, eighty-five.

"C'mon, old timer. I hit a hundred-and-five one time in my dad's bimmer on the George Washington Memorial Parkway."

"Reckless driver. Gun crazy. And I thought you were a peacenik nature worshipper."

Carter sighed, looked out the window at charcoal-hued desert flying by beyond the road shoulder.

"You think I'm a hypocrite?"

"What I'm thinking is we have no plan."

"If he's driving all the way to the Mexican border, he'll have to stop for gas and we can jump him at the gas station."

"That's an amusing idea."

The black asphalt strip stretched through dark desert silvered along the shoulder by the headlights. Far ahead they glimpsed reddish lights shrinking into night.

"There's something I never understood."

"You figured out most of this, Min."

"Brent was concerned about laundered money when the party happened, but he still invited Malbore. That means he hadn't confronted him."

"The guy is dangerous so I can see why he wouldn't risk it."

"But at that point Malbore had already ordered his men to kill Brent. So if Brent hadn't tipped off Malbore to his suspicions, how did Malbore become aware Brent was on to him?"

"Who knows? I doubt cartel types worry about due process. They just kill anybody whose loyalty they doubt."

"Maybe. But that means Malbore found out what Brent was up to without any communication between them."

"Think that lobbyist was playing off one against the other?"

"She wanted the deal to go through so she had no motive to break up their partnership."

"What do you think?"

Mina gripped the scalloped steering wheel harder, squinting down the road.

"It had to be Eldon."

"The nerdy lawyer?"

"Eldon wrote up Brent's will so he knew how he would benefit. He could have suggested to Brent that Malbore was planning to wash dirty cartel funds in the Gavilan Mesa purchase. Then all he had to do was mention Brent's suspicion to Malbore to assure Brent's death. Eldon must have been the conduit of information manipulating everyone's knowledge for his own benefit."

"Geez! He's like that *Breaking Bad* lawyer that worked for narcos."

"There's another thing I never understood. Malbore must have lent his men to Brent for the prairie dog extermination and maybe other yard work so they'd have a cover while they found a way to kill him. But how did they find out Derek Whitfield had cameras trained on Brent's house that would have captured them preparing or leaving that poisoned bottle of scorpion mezcal on the day of the party? Derek used camouflaged rock cameras. I live there and I had no idea the estate grounds were bugged. Only people involved in the custody trial would have known about the surveillance. Neither Brent nor Mercedes would have told Malbore so it must have been Eldon."

Carter swiveled around to stare at her.

"And I thought you might be falling for him."

Minoa's voice was tight.

"I don't fall in love. It's not in my nature."

Carter reached out a hand and patted her shoulder, retracting it quickly.

"Hey, me and Rain-Rain love you and don't you forget it."

Minoa huffed. After passing the intersection at Airport Road, continuing past low hills south of the city, Carter spoke.

"I think we lost him."

"Crap."

Minoa swerved left into the strip of desert separating the two sides of the highway, rocking the car like a boat as she bushwhacked across the wide median. Carter clawed the interior of the car to regain balance. They accelerated heading back to town. At Airport Road they turned west and veered onto Aviation Drive to race to the Santa Fe Airport terminal, a hacienda-style building with a glass air traffic control tower perched on top. The place was deserted. A hangar to one side gaped open. No sign of the Porsche.

Down at the far end of one of the airport's two runways a small jet was turning around revealing a strip of four round windows along the fuselage. Minoa gunned the BMW across a paved expanse to the middle of the runway and stopped the car. She and Carter jumped out and ran to the edge of the pavement. The plane was coming down the runway toward them, picking up speed.

Carter aimed Francisco's revolver as Minoa scanned the ground for rocks. Just as the plane lifted off she remembered the tennis ball. As Carter fired, she threw. One of Carter's shots hit a tire at the same time as a flame shot out of one jet engine. The aircraft sputtered and dipped overhead causing them to dive to the ground. Carter rolled onto her back and pulled the trigger again but the gun clicked empty. The plane recovered and started ascending, one wing tipping higher. They scrambled to their feet and watched as it climbed, banking around to head south, shrinking against soot-black sky, flashing lights on each wing dwindling to stars, then blinking out. They stood up brushing off.

"Dammit."

"Agreed."

"Maybe the plane won't make it."

"At a minimum he'll have a bumpy landing in Sinaloa."

"Think he'll come back?"

"Doubtful. He knows we know."

"Maybe Nellie can turn over what she filmed and get him indicted."

"Maybe."

"What if he sends those hirelings to silence us?"

"After they recover?"

Carter smiled.

"We whupped 'em pretty good."

They continued to stare south into a dark sky bleached at the horizon by a faint glow of Albuquerque city lights. Finally Carter walked back toward the BMW.

"Thank goodness we saved Nellie."

Minoa joined her.

"I wish we could have saved Valeria and Berto."

"Maybe Berto will make it. Maybe Valeria won't be deported."

"Maybe again."

"This may stop the sale of Gavilan Mesa. But BBCC's local lackeys will still push to develop, so we've gained nothing."

"You've gained time. What else is there?"

"And I thought all these rich people exploited workers and poisoned the environment to get rich. Turns out they're murderers and rapists as well."

"Maybe not all of them, Carter. We don't have enough evidence for generalizations."

"If we had democratic ownership and universal health care and sane drug laws, none of this would have happened."

"There's the Carter we know and love."

They slid into the BMW.

"Think we could keep the car?"

"Don't even go there. Back to the land of the normal, Carter."

"What about the gun?"

"You're going to keep an illegal weapon?"

"Okay, okay."

"We better pick up the truck."

"What if the cops are there when we show up?"

"She won't call them."

"Ya think?"

"What good would it do her?"

"If she splits, nobody would know if we keep the car."

Minoa flashed her a look.

"Alright. Who wants a bimmer, anyway? It'd be worthless in the backcountry."

They drove out of the airport and headed back to the highway north.

FIFTY-ONE

Her sneakers squeaked as she walked down the buffed linoleum at St. Peter's Hospital. Where the hallway angled left she spotted a police guard leaning against the wall. Pausing in front of him she pulled Eldon's card out of her wallet and flashed it.

"I'm here on behalf of his legal counsel. Attorney visit."

The cop squinted at her, opened his mouth to speak. She ducked through the door and shut it behind her. The door opened again and he stuck his head in looking fierce.

"Door stays open."

"Absolutely not. Attorney-client communications are confidential."

He pulled his head back in time to avoid getting pinioned between door and frame. No further reaction from outside so she figured she'd won that round. Berto lay in a hospital bed with tubes coming out of one arm. The other wrist was handcuffed to the bed frame. He turned his head as she entered.

"Berto, don't try to talk. I don't want to tire you. I just wanted to come by and say how glad we are that you're doing better."

He looked at her for a moment, then turned his face away to stare out the window. When he spoke his voice sounded under water.

"Did they arr—... her?"

"Yes, they did. But she's safe, like you, so there's hope."

"They'll deport ..."

"Listen, Berto, I contacted someone I know from graduate school who's doing research in El Salvador and has an apartment in San Salvador. If it comes to deportation, she can pick her up at the airport and give her a place to stay while she sorts things out."

"It won't hlp ..." He coughed, convulsed, went rigid, face muscles stretched. Finally relaxed back, eyelids fluttering.

"Please don't tire yourself."

A growling sound leaked from his throat.

"Look, I understand this is awful. I can come back when you're feeling better. I'm just so glad—"

He turned his face to her.

"Listen."

He choked, glared. She leaned over, putting her ear near his mouth. He spoke in a choppy whisper. Some words made it out, some caught in his throat.

"*La mara*.... raped her... She... taking care of me... and that *hijo de puta*... cut my ear... she was begging..."

He convulsed at the abdomen like he'd taken a punch in the stomach, squeezed his eyes shut. Minoa straightened, glanced at the monitor beside his bed, scanning for a call button.

"Wait."

His eyes were wet, pleading. She crouched again putting her face near his mouth. At first she heard little gagging noises, then words dribbled out.

"I ... stood there ..."

He moved his head, stabbed her with eyes so taut with pain she feared they would burst and spew blood.

"... like a stupid baby."

She grimaced.

"I'm so sorry. That's horrible."

"They were laughing ..."

She met his gaze. His eyes seemed to claw at her as if he were falling off a cliff and hoped she would save him. When the visual contact became unbearable, she glanced out the window. Above the clustered flat rooftops of Santa Fe's historic section, mountain peaks poked snowy cones at the sky. The belt of golden aspens had turned to bone and cinders. It left a burnt taste in her mouth just to look at it. She braced herself and turned back to him.

"She never told us what happened."

Now his face hardened to stone. She waited, glanced around the room. Tried to think of something to say or, failing that, an excuse to leave. The thick glass of the hospital window drained the desert landscape outside of its usual blinding vibrancy. She turned back as he sputtered out more words. His body straightened hard, his expression exploded.

"... my fault."

He choked, then fell back, formless as a jellyfish, to stare at the ceiling. The air in the small room seemed to oscillate with wild waves, her body as dumb as a post.

"No, Berto, this mess is my fault. I set her up to work in a rapist's house. I made things worse. I'm ... I'm sorry."

She slapped her palm against her forehead several times. He didn't budge, his eyes staring unfocused.

"With that kind of story I'm sure she could win an asylum case."

He shifted his head, blasted her with his eyes, gargled a few words. His eyebrows spoke sarcasm. Turned his head away.

She stood there without moving while her mind flipped somersaults trying to think what she could say, what could be done. When she came up with nothing, she commanded her heart to send empathy his way. Still nothing. No sign. Waited a few more. As he refused to look at her, she went out the door. The guard didn't shift his gaze from his phone screen.

Outside in the parking lot she leaned against the truck, crossed her arms and gazed up at pure blue. Her head tipped back to rest against the top of the cab, eyelids drifting down, lulled by October sunshine, not too hot, just the warmth of the hearth after the fire of summer dies out. It'd be so nice to sleep, to dream. And why not? She couldn't fix the mess left in the wake of Brent's passing. He'd selfishly exploited the world for his own gratification. Then paid with his life for someone else's crimes. Maybe he'd planned to turn in his money-laundering partner. Everybody had some good in them, right?

So what now? Carter still had the Gavilan Mesa development to fight. Ireni was tired of working at the lab but she'd come up with something. Valeria was going back against her will but Salvadoran gangs were in prison so she'd face less danger there now. Looked like Berto would survive but jail was his next stop after the hospital. How much time would he get for jumping an officer? Would getting shot soften the sentence?

He'd sit in jail while Findley Malbore drank margaritas in Mexico. Unless the plane crashed or his trafficker bosses no longer trusted him. What a world.

Ron had given the go-ahead to finish the archaeological survey at Gavilan. A few more days of paid work, then back to scrounging. And she had no idea where she'd be living next month or what she would use for money. But still you never knew. You just never knew what might pop up in the headlights next. She climbed into the truck, started up and headed out.

THE END

Oñate's Blood

A preview of the third Minoa Diamond novel

The face of the church was dark, the courtyard full of hulking shadows under an ebony sky varnished with moonlight. She waited, leaning into a wooden arch, stiffening against a freeze-dried norteña night. Nothing moved. Was this Churro's idea of a joke? Make the nosy gringa drive a couple hours for nothing? She should have demanded money to cover her wasted time, not that this investigation was doing much to salvage her bank account. But faithful crickets chirped an unceasing rhythm that muttered over and over, 'clock-time is an illusion,' 'the only reality is flow.' It lulled her to linger at the courtyard entrance, sensing chilly breaths saw at her throat, eardrums ruffled by a distant murmur of lapping water. The space felt crystalline, sacred. What difference did it make if Marcos showed or not?

The sound of an approaching car jolted her. Would it turn into the parking lot? Of course not. The place was closed. The noise died out. She walked to the middle of the courtyard and paused by a rough-hewn cross on an adobe base.

"Marcos?" she called out. "Churro sent something for you. If you want it, you've got to answer a few questions."

Her words seeped into the night. Chill air rising off the flagstones numbed her fingertips.

"Marcos? I'm leaving with the key Churro sent for you if you don't come out."

A misshapen overfull moon shot beams at the courtyard leaving the facade of the church in deep shadow. After another pause she turned to leave.

"Wait."

She spun around, peered at the church facade, perceived nothing. A moment dragged by and then a dark form emerged around the corner of the church.

"Are you ...?"

"Yeah, Marcos, I'm the one who nearly took the hit for you when that *sicario* showed up at your smoke shop."

"Sorry about that. I had no idea that dude would—"

"I know. You're blameless. It was just a misunderstanding when you drove off and left me alone to face that human Gatling gun."

He moved briefly through moonlight to disappear into shadow on the other side of the church.

"You got the key?"

"Questions first."

"Listen, I got no idea where Deandra is."

"I know where Deandra is. That's not what I want to know. Things have changed, Marcos. The stakes have gone up."

"I know the fam is worried sick about me. You tell 'em I'll lay low with Grifo in Burque till things quiet down up here."

"Marcos, shut up."

"I don't know how much Churro gave you to bring me the key, but I'll give you another twenty. How's that?"

"Deandra's dead."

"What the ...?" He stepped into the light and paused there, hands dangling at the ends of his long arms. "How,,, how do you know that? It's probably just gossip. People here gossip like–"

"I saw her body, Marcos, lying on the bank of the Rio Grande."

His head dropped as he slunk back into the shadows. She waited. Was he still there?

"It's important you tell me what you know about her whereabouts for the last few days. And who might have wanted her dead."

Silence. Finally a few muttered words.

"I'll take care of this."

"What are you talking about? Who do you think killed her? In your cousin's memory, speak up."

"That prick Angelo has been pushing his luck for a while."

"You knew about Angelito? You think he killed her?"

"Word gets around. He's gonna regret the day..."

"Why didn't you stop your cousin from working for him?"

He burst back into the moonlight.

"Now you're gonna try and blame me for everything that goes wrong with that family? I've heard this before. Gimme the key. I'm out of here."

He lurched toward her. She backed up, hid behind the arch of the courtyard gate.

"Give me specifics first. Who does Angelito work with? Who are his clients?"

"He knows some gnarly dudes."

"Give me names."

"This is a small town. Somebody just got killed. You think I'm gonna shoot off my mouth about who might've done it?"

"Tell me about the last time you saw her."

"Last Friday. We had a bonfire out by the river."

"By the boat launch, right?"

"She came for a little while, had a couple beers. Said she had to meet somebody. I kidded her about it. She got all bitch-faced and said she was gonna make more money than me. That's the last time I saw her."

"Was she with Candy Rivera?"

"Deandra didn't have her own wheels but I didn't see Candy. Now will you give me the key?"

"Did she say anything at all to suggest where she was going?"

"She said she had to move it cause it would take forty-five to get there. Around this place forty-five in any direction takes you outside town."

"Do you think she meant Chimayo?"

"Chimayo?"

"You've got a habit of repeating everything you don't want to answer."

"The *jeva* had her own contacts."

"Are you sure Angelito wasn't making appointments for her? Surely you don't want that dude to get away with pimping out your cousin."

"I told you. I'll take care of that *guëy*."

At that moment, tires rolled over the gravel in the parking lot at the entrance to the compound. Marcos burst into the central area of the courtyard, his wiry silhouette splashed with ivory light.

"Gimme the key, quick."

She heard steps, spun around, detected movement. Then shots pinged off the adobe facade of the church, ricocheted off paving stones. Marcos doubled over and slumped to the ground. She dashed through the courtyard to a gate by the corner of the church building and sprinted to the back of the church. At the other back corner she paused and peered around, listening. More steps, voices, car doors slamming, tires spitting up rocks. Followed by silence. She leaned into the mud-plastered wall, air puffs exploding one after another from her rounded lips.

Suddenly another figure barreled down the alleyway toward her. She leaped back. The figure curved toward the back of the property and disappeared into the darkness. Minoa ran after.

Author Bio

EA Mayes writes mysteries set in a gorgeous but weird New Mexico where cultures mingle and murder always follows. EA taught college literature and cultural studies. She's ghost-written books, bonded people out of jail and interpreted in court. Check out her mysteries *Rattlesnakes Strike Twice, Gavilan Mesa, Oñate's Blood* and *Death at Apache Kid*. Read her crime fiction newsletter at eamayes.substack.com and check out New Mexico curiosities found in the novels at eamayes.com.

www.ingramcontent.com/pod-product-compliance
Lightning Source LLC
LaVergne TN
LVHW100507110826
845146LV00002B/546
9798989000432